PRAISE FOR AM

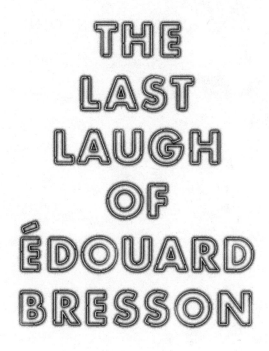

THE LAST LAUGH OF ÉDOUARD BRESSON

ALSO BY AMÉLIE ANTOINE

Interference

One Night in November

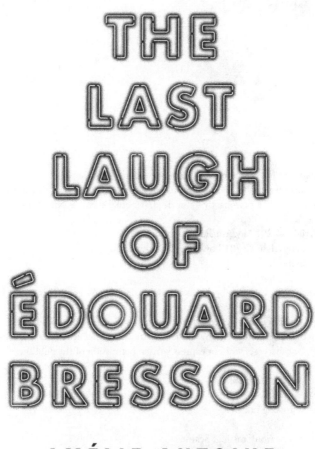

THE LAST LAUGH OF ÉDOUARD BRESSON

AMÉLIE ANTOINE

TRANSLATED BY MAREN BAUDET-LACKNER

amazoncrossing (●

Text copyright © 2017 by Amélie Antoine
Translation copyright © 2018 by Maren Baudet-Lackner
All rights reserved.

"The Dunce" ("Le Cancre") by Jacques Prévert copyright © 1949 Éditions Gallimard

Previously published as *Quand on n'a que l'humour* by Michel Lafon in France in 2017. Translated from French by Maren Baudet-Lackner. First published in English by AmazonCrossing in 2018.

Published by AmazonCrossing, Seattle

www.apub.com

Amazon, the Amazon logo, and AmazonCrossing are trademarks of Amazon.com, Inc., or its affiliates.

ISBN-13: 9781503904521
ISBN-10: 1503904520

Cover design by Rex Bonomelli

Printed in the United States of America

You think you're writing pure fiction, creating characters crafted by your imagination, and then, just as you're writing "The End," a strange feeling comes over you. And you experience the brutal realization that, without meaning to, you've drawn much of it from your own story.
To my mother. Naturally. To my mother, who did what she could, despite her wounds.
To my father, obviously, who is always there for me.
To Gaïa and Samuel, for whom I'm doing my best.
I hope it will be enough.

PART 1

1

March 31, 2017–8:30 p.m.

The dark bags under his eyes magically disappear as the skilled makeup artist silently tends to his face. She knows Édouard doesn't like small talk, that he requires absolute silence before he goes onstage. She busies herself with her task like a bee tending to a flower—foundation, iridescent powder, a hint of blush to hide the traces left behind by restless nights and hectic days. Édouard stays perfectly still. Staring unblinkingly at the mirror, he impassively observes his transformation. As if it were someone else, as if the reflection weren't his own but that of a total stranger.

To others, it looks like he's concentrating, going over his lines and sketches one last time. While in reality, behind his serene mask, he's falling apart. As he does every night. Everyone believes that stage fright has become an intangible memory over the years, a distant recollection that makes Édouard chuckle knowingly. That's how well he hides it. His stomach rebels, nausea ricocheting up his esophagus like a pinball. His pulse races; his hands are sweaty. *There's no way I can pull this off.*

"Dogs can smell fear, Édouard," his father used to groan every time the little boy cringed as the neighbors' German shepherd neared. He needed his father to hold his hand tight or put him on his shoulders, needed to be protected from the hairy monster heading straight for him, tongue out, unleashed. "He's a nice dog. There's nothing to be afraid of," their neighbor Bernard would say as he walked past. Lucien would brusquely withdraw his hand from the boy's. "Dogs can smell fear, so buck up, kid."

"All done," the makeup artist says softly, a satisfied look on her face as she studies Édouard's reflection. She's highlighted the comedian's thin lips with a touch of transparent gloss, a sticky film he resists the strong urge to lick off. He'll wait until she leaves, to avoid disappointing her.

"Thanks so much," he answers, because he's so polite, so humble. Because his fame hasn't gone to his head, as his producer, Jean-Michel, regularly marvels. He is what everyone thinks he is—he *has* to be. He has to match the perfect, upbeat, enviable image they have of him.

Dogs aren't the only ones who can smell fear—people can too. So Édouard smiles broadly at the young woman as she puts away her brushes, jars, and tubes, and she immediately understands that it's time to go. "Have a good night, miss," he says to her reflection. She can't help but blush with pride that he's called her "miss"—she hasn't celebrated her birthday since having children.

At last the door to his dressing room closes gently behind her. Everyone knows Édouard hates it when people slam doors, so they're careful, *very* careful. They like to pamper him, because they *like* him— despite his temper, he's a nice guy, after all. He's finally alone. He counts the blinding light bulbs that frame his face in the mirror. Fifteen dazzling spheres that burn into his retinas as his anxiety mounts. His smile slackens, then disappears completely since nobody is watching, studying, analyzing his every move.

His face becomes serious, determined. Today's the big day, the day everything changes. Their jaws will drop—he's sure of it. He savors the anticipation of surprising them once again and regrets that he'll have to settle for imagining their stunned faces: *No, Édouard Bresson wouldn't have taken it that far, would he?* Then again, the press *has* been calling him "the most unpredictable stand-up comic" for years now. He has to live up to his reputation, owes it to himself to set his sights higher and higher, aiming for the unbelievable, the unexpected. David Copperfield's greatest illusions will pale in comparison to the act he's about to pull off. The poor magician will be relegated to the B-list alongside people who think pulling a coin out of a naive spectator's ear is enough to enchant an entire audience.

He almost missed his train earlier this afternoon. His manager, Hervé, had told him it wasn't a good idea to leave Paris on the day of the show, especially this one. "This is your moment. You know that, right? You're at your peak. After tonight, there will be nothing left to conquer, you'll have done it all . . . Unless you want to go to the moon, of course!" he'd said, laughing at his own joke. Édouard joined him half-heartedly. The comedian decided to make the round-trip to Le Havre anyway. Taking the train has always made him anxious. Since he is invariably terrified of missing his train, he had to check the platform on the schedule board several times to make sure he hadn't made a mistake. He was particularly agitated for the trip back to the city. *Paris Saint-Lazare: Track 3.* He checked the train number on his ticket, then again on the overhead monitor. Several times. He made sure he really was on platform 3. Several times. And once aboard, he couldn't help but ask the first passenger he came across if it really was the one to Paris. Reassured at last, he sat down next to the window with his baseball cap and sunglasses still on. Strangely, the fame he once sought so desperately only increased his need for anonymity.

He arrived right on time for the rehearsal, which was a disaster, as usual. Édouard has never been able to make Hervé understand how difficult it is to perform to an empty venue. To become the Édouard everyone knows and loves, he's always needed an audience. Without one, it's all just hot air. Standing up on the stage in front of thousands of unoccupied seats and dizzyingly still bleachers simply makes him nauseous.

There was no way he'd pull it off this time; he'd gone too big, much too big. He never should have listened to his producer, never should have let himself get carried away by egomania. The show was sold out—the thousands of tickets had been snatched up in less than fifteen minutes the day they went on sale. He imagined his fans sitting in front of their computer screens, since that's how people bought tickets these days. Long gone were the days when people would stand in line starting at seven o'clock in the morning, in the cold or the rain, with a thermos of coffee, hardly moving until the box office opened at exactly ten o'clock— then the stampede would begin, everyone eager to get a seat, as a reward for those three hours of waiting. Now people just sat comfortably in front of their computers or smartphones, refreshing the page over and over again until they managed to get the coveted tickets. The show had been sold out for six months. An eternity. But deep down Édouard was still convinced that no one would show up. They'd forget the date, have other plans, or go to the wrong venue. And he'd find himself alone up there, alone with the silence, alone with his pounding heart.

And even if the audience he both hoped for and dreaded did turn out, he would screw everything up, he was sure of it. As sure as he had been from the beginning, listening to that little voice in his head telling him that his fleeting moment in the sun was all just a big joke. That someday people would finally see him for who he really was, realize that they had brought an empty puppet to life and filled him with their fantasies, that in reality, he was just *him*. Édouard Bresson, a nobody like anyone else. A guy who just wanted—needed—to make his loved ones laugh. The rest of the world was a bonus. They'd realize that he was an imposter who'd made it to the top by mistake, because how could anyone admire him that much anyway—he'd never done anything to deserve all that enthusiasm, all that love. *You'll see, Édouard—someday it'll all be over. One day they'll open their eyes and realize you're not really that funny, that you've already done it all, that you're all washed up, that there are plenty of others who are more entertaining than you. A new generation will take over, and suddenly you'll be a dinosaur, all but forgotten:* Édouard Bresson, doesn't ring a bell. Was he from Coluche's generation? *It'll all be over soon, and they'll talk about you in the past tense:* Remember that one guy—oh damn, I can't remember his name. Oh, I hate it when that happens; it's on the tip of my tongue . . .

Hervé bursts into the dressing room without bothering to knock, to make sure his protégé is ready.

"Could you mail this letter for me, please?" Édouard asks, looking preoccupied.

"Want me to pick up your dry cleaning too? I'm not your errand boy, you know!"

But the graying manager takes the cream envelope from Édouard anyway.

"It's important," says the star, an insistent look on his face.

"Too late for today," answers Hervé.

"Tomorrow will be fine. Thank you," whispers Édouard as his manager hurriedly leaves the room. He still has so many things to check on before the house lights go out.

As usual, Édouard goes into the bathroom to throw up everything left in his stomach. The two pieces of toast with jam and the cup of coffee from breakfast, the tasteless sandwich he distractedly gobbled down on the train, the Granny Smith that was entirely too shiny to be any good, and the espresso that rounded out his solitary lunch, then the five or six additional espressos from afternoon rehearsal. He has to keep up, handle the pressure—better coffee than something else. He quickly brushes his teeth, takes one last look at his reflection in the mirror, then turns out the lights in his dressing room. He breathes in as slowly as possible and suddenly thinks of his father, who, before slamming the door on his way to work at the refinery every evening, would offer up the very philosophical "When it's time, it's time."

2

Winter 1979

"When it's time, it's time," grumbles Lucien Bresson as he quickly slips into his khaki cargo jacket. Outside, the stars have begun to shine in the charcoal-black sky, signaling that Lucien's shift starts in half an hour. Édouard and his little brother, Jonathan, who is six years younger, are in their pajamas, ready to climb into their bunk bed at eight o'clock on the dot. The older of the two can't help but think what a shame it is that they have to go to sleep at the exact time their father leaves for work—when they could have finally made a little noise in the apartment. Enjoying the privileges of being the firstborn, Édouard gets the top bunk. He deliberately ignores Jonathan's constant pleas to trade, and is glad his mother does the same, explaining that it would be too dangerous for a four-year-old to climb up the rickety wooden ladder.

"Now that Dad's gone, can we play a round of Simon, Mom? Please?" asks Édouard, brandishing the electronic game with its four buttons: red, blue, green, and yellow.

His mother sighs. *If she says yes, everything'll be OK,* the boy thinks. These little *if* sentences have been popping into his head several times a day ever since he was old enough to put words together. He clings to these hopeful phrases with superstitious fervor, as if they have the power to determine the future. *If I make it to the crosswalk before the light turns red, everything'll be OK. If the building manager doesn't see me walk past her office, everything'll be OK. If Mom lets us play, everything'll be OK.*

"Just one round," Édouard insists as Jonathan claps excitedly in support. "We're never allowed to play with it when Dad's here . . ."

Their mother finally gives in, and the children jump up and down gleefully.

"You can play while I do the dishes, but after that it's straight to bed, OK?"

Without answering, Édouard turns on the "goddamn noise machine," as their father calls it, and its electronic sounds fill the living room, along with the squeals of the two young boys.

The racket doesn't bother Monique Bresson—quite the contrary, in fact. It makes her feel like there's a little life in the apartment for once. Because as soon as her husband comes back in through the door, he'll demand total silence. After working an eight-hour shift surrounded by the deafening din of pumps, furnaces, reactors, and all the refinery's other machines, after a long day spent inhaling the stifling smell of gas that works its way into his tiniest pores, Lucien can't stand any sound at all, much less the shouts and bangs of children playing. The boys have to whisper most of the time. On his good days, they can talk quietly. No laughing or crying allowed, no shooting marbles. The sound of a hard, round sphere hitting the baseboard brings them face-to-face with their glowering father, his eyebrows slanted away from his nose in a V-shape—"like a cartoon villain," as Édouard says.

He's just turned ten, and if he were asked to describe his father, he would say he's always angry. He's always grumbling about something, constantly yelling at his family. Because the night shift exhausts him the same way it exhausts hundreds of other workers, with its resulting odd mealtimes, insomnia, sudden fatigue, and irritability, making him feel like a robot who should be able to turn on and off with the flick of a switch. In addition to all that, Lucien is also a union representative at the refinery, a position that's left him unable to express himself in any tone other than the resentful, aggressive one he uses there. It's as if everyone is out to get him, as if every interaction is a fight. Lucien works, eats, sleeps, and rages. All the time, about everything. That's his life. But Édouard knows that's not what life is really about. There has to be something else; otherwise, what's the point? A life full of noise, laughter, unending tickles, glasses hitting the white-and-turquoise checkerboard tiles on the floor, the windows slamming from the breeze carrying away the terrible smell of stale smoke, cool air filling the apartment and sweeping the mail off the kitchen table, music on the tape deck, and Eddy Mitchell's voice echoing off the walls of the apartment that's a little too small for the four of them. That life has to exist somewhere.

Jonathan quickly tires of playing and starts rubbing his eyes. Édouard carefully tucks his brother into bed. "I'll go get Mom," he says.

Against the backdrop of the kitchen's orange-and-brown arabesque wallpaper, Monique is finishing the dinner dishes, gently humming "On the Road to Memphis" as her eldest watches silently, leaning motionless on the purring refrigerator. *If she doesn't notice I'm here, everything'll be OK,* he repeats in his head, soothed by his made-up beliefs.

His mother had wanted to name him Eddy, after her favorite singer, but her husband had said it wasn't even a real name. So Eddy became Édouard, even though Lucien had added that without the song "Les Chaussettes Noires," Mitchell's career would be in the toilet and that it was a hell of a waste to name his kid after a singer who would soon be all washed up. Monique held her ground, though, and now she can't help but smile when she turns on the bathroom radio and hears her weary-looking idol crooning on every station.

Six and a half years later, in the summer of 1975, after a wait that seemed endless and unbearable, she gave birth to a second son, and Lucien simply sighed when she suggested "Jo" for Joe Dassin, whose music she had loved since "Siffler sur la Colline" had come out. At the Gonfreville-l'Orcher town hall, the civil servant recording the birth looked up at the new father perplexedly and asked, "Jo? Jo what? Jo—nathan?" and Lucien decided that Jonathan was decidedly more suitable. Monique sighed when he told her that an extra two syllables was no reason to make a fuss.

Monique had so longed to have a second child that she took to calling Jonathan her "miracle baby," because he had come precisely when she had begun to lose hope and retreat into her solitary grief, since her husband had said that one child was better than none at all, and that one made less noise too.

It wasn't that she preferred Jonathan to Édouard, not at all. It was just that Jonathan was so precious, like a rare gift, since she'd struggled so much to conceive. And since he was so precious, it didn't take long for her to conclude that he was also more fragile, that he needed her protection much more than his older brother, who was independent and didn't need anyone's help.

As soon as Jonathan was walking and out of diapers, the two brothers often found themselves outside, obliged to find somewhere to play where they wouldn't be in their father's hair. Of course, Édouard was responsible for taking care of his little brother, for watching over him and bringing him everywhere he went. Jonathan playing with his cars, driving them into the wrought iron radiator in the living room, was enough to make their father shout exasperatedly, "Out! Get out! Go play somewhere else!" The Duralex glass of cheap wine would hit the kitchen table hard, sending the bloodred liquid sloshing onto the oil-cloth, and in the blink of an eye the brothers would find themselves standing on the third-floor landing of their apartment building—often in socks, waiting silently in the dark until their father opened the door and threw two pairs of shoes in their direction.

"Jonathan wants a good-night kiss," Édouard says softly as his mother turns off the hot water. She swivels around and dries her hands with a checkered kitchen towel, a smile on her lips.

"And what about you? Too big for a good-night kiss?"

Édouard shrugs, affecting indifference, but his mother knows it's an act. While Édouard climbs the ladder, she kisses her youngest, who's already half-asleep in the bottom bunk, his stuffed bunny smelling of her perfume snuggled into the crook of his arm. She sings the same lullaby she sings every night, and, as always, her voice cracks on the *i* of *"petit naviiire,"* but it doesn't matter at all to the little boy sucking his thumb through a sleepy smile. Then she places her elbows on the side of the top bunk and can't keep herself from tousling Édouard's hair, just to hear him whine, "Mo-om," in a put-on surly tone.

"Good night, my big boy," she whispers before leaving the room.

If the door closes without a squeak, everything'll be OK, Édouard convinces himself.

The hinges don't make a sound when his mother pulls the door shut, so Édouard turns toward the wall and closes his eyes, reassured. He can hear his mother's quiet steps moving down the carpet in the hallway, heading back to the living room to turn on the TV.

An indistinct murmur breaks the silence, and Édouard lets himself be lulled by the muffled sound of unfamiliar yet reassuring voices.

3

An indistinct murmur breaks the silence, and Édouard lets himself be lulled by the muffled sound of unfamiliar yet reassuring voices.

Audience members are starting to pour in. He imagines them looking at their tickets for seat numbers, finding the right aisle. *I told you we were row 27, seats J and K. Why don't you ask the usher there, the one in uniform. That's her job, isn't it?* He imagines the bleachers filling up. *See, these seats aren't so bad after all!* He imagines some people getting jostled, others doing the jostling, the impatient showgoers and the enthusiastic ones. *Wow, look at those two giant screens. Édouard Bresson always goes all out!* He imagines the skeptics, bored in their seats. *My wife's the fan. I gave her the tickets for Christmas; that's why we're here . . .* He imagines his exuberant fans, the diehards enthusiastically taking it all in. *Come here, let's take a selfie with the stage in the background. This is so awesome. I'm going to post to my timeline!*

He can't help but smile, and for a fraction of a second he forgets the anxiety that's slowly invading his body, flowing over him like molten rock. Édouard has to content himself with the clamor since he can't actually see the people who've come to watch his show tonight. Just a few years ago, he could still sneak into the crowd incognito, choose a random seat, and watch people come and go, listen to audience members as they took off their coats and carelessly sat down, unaware of the anxiety he was experiencing as he prepared to go onstage—for them. In the beginning it was easy. He could sit anywhere without people paying him any attention at all. His face was still unknown, or at least not instantly identifiable. But as his fame grew, he had to start wearing makeup and costumes. Glasses, a fake beard, a scarf wrapped around the lower half of his face, right up to his nose, a hat, even a wig! It was a game, of course, a way to trick the audience, but, above all else, it was how he reassured himself that people were in fact there to see him, that the seats were filling up quickly. He was probably also trying to persuade himself that he could still go unnoticed in the crowd. Unfortunately, as time went by, people got wind of his little ritual, and audience members started looking for him in the seats, carefully observing their neighbors to see if they might really be Édouard in disguise.

So he'd reluctantly given it up. Forced to find a new way to get a read on the room, he'd learned to listen to the audience from backstage, measuring their fervor from the growing din as showtime neared. The ambient buzz neutral at first, then mounting as people grew impatient and began shouting and whistling before finally chanting, "Édouard, Édouard" in rhythm. That's how he knew people were there, waiting for him, asking for him. That's how he knew they *loved* him.

The fear is so intense now that it's almost painful for him to swallow. The nausea is constant, though his stomach is empty. The hot flashes are so extreme that he could swear his skin is on fire, and the cold sweats that follow them make him check three times, ten times, twenty times that his clothes aren't dripping with sweat. Despite himself, he wishes he had his lucky piece of sea glass—a perfect equilateral triangle—that he has always flipped over and over in his hand before going onstage. He's never been without it before tonight.

Last night he dreamed yet again that he was onstage, alone in front of the audience, unable to pronounce a single word. The same nightmare that relentlessly torments him the night before every show, always just as terrible. He wants to speak but can't make a sound. The venue goes horribly, painfully silent. *They* are waiting, and he simply stands there, mouth ajar, helpless and mute. Then they start laughing, an unremitting laughter devoid of pity. The mocking howls fly past him as he focuses on their tonsils, their tongues, their teeth. The entire audience is doubled over with laughter, terribly entertained by the idiot onstage. The darkness is impenetrable, with a single spotlight shining on him, marking him as their target. Édouard can't make out a single face, only mouths and sharp, pearly teeth. They are wolves, and he is a poor defenseless sheep. They start bellowing, "Baa, baa, baa," and the shame he feels instantly takes him back to his terrible stutter and his childhood spent as the butt of everyone's jokes.

He can feel the stage crew scurrying around behind him, going through the final preparatory steps for the show, careful not to bother him in the last few moments before it starts. He instinctively pulls his MP3 player out of the back pocket of his jeans, unrolls the wires, and pops the earbuds in. The volume is turned all the way up when he hits play, his eyes closed. The guitar riffs make their way to his brain, and when the hoarse voice of Survivor's lead singer joins the instruments, the decibels finally manage to cut Édouard off from the outside world, allowing him to forget where he is and what's coming next. He needs this four-minute ritual, listening to "Eye of the Tiger," as if he were preparing for the biggest fight of all time, four minutes during which the awaiting stage becomes a ring, four minutes that pump him up and make him feel alive and invincible. Some people need a line of coke to feel that way— for Édouard, this song has done the job for over twenty-three years.

Less than ten feet away, his producer, Jean-Michel, silently observes Édouard. The thought of the thousands of people waiting for the stand-up comic on the other side of the thin, opaque curtain is almost enough to make *him* tremble. He notices Édouard's lopsided grin, the intense gleam of his eyes in the darkness. He knows Édouard inside and out, and would bet his life the man's plotting something. He's got the same mischievous air about him as a kid about to play a trick, the same palpable impatience. *Please tell me he's not planning another one of his crazy practical jokes,* thinks Jean-Michel, whose eyebrows furrow as he remembers the comedian's past exploits—which have not always been a big hit with the media. Hervé tried explaining that there's no such thing as bad press until he was blue in the face, but Jean-Michel remains convinced that when there's money on the table, it's better to aim to please.

When the song ends, Édouard distractedly hands his MP3 player to the assistant standing discreetly several steps behind him. He can hear that the audience is ready: thousands of hands are clapping rhythmically, so fervently that his heart speeds up to match the tempo. The sound of feet stomping forcefully in the bleachers is exhilarating. They are screaming, shouting, squawking the two syllables of his name. Yearning, demanding, begging for his presence.

Édouard knows that in a few seconds, his anxiety will evaporate. He knows that as soon as the spotlights are trained on him, he'll shed his fear like a boxer sheds his towel before climbing into the ring. It's always been like that—the stage is the only place he can beat his anxiety, the only place he really feels like he's the person he's supposed to be.

He was born for this.

Just a few feet away, the packed Stade de France is waiting for him. A restless horde of over fifty thousand people is starting to lose patience as the night grows darker.

This is where he belongs.

4

June 1980

"This is where he belongs!" shouts Ludovic, as pleased with himself as if he'd just invented electricity. "Oh wait, I mean, where he b-b-b-belongs!" He shrieks louder, sending the entire class into fits of cruel laughter.

Édouard instinctively hunches his head between his shoulders, trying to protect himself from the verbal assault. He's known for years that it's best to ignore insults and teasing, since he can't stop himself from being a target; he's painfully aware that he's unable to open his mouth without st-st-st-stumbling over his words. It started when his brother was born, a little less than five years ago. Jonathan's arrival—and the way he spent all his time in their mother's comforting arms—had somehow left Édouard permanently flustered. At first it seemed inconsequential, almost trivial. The woman behind the counter in the bakery thought it was cute. His second-grade teacher found his hesitation endearing. There was no need to worry; it would pass just as quickly as it had come. And it wasn't every word either. *G*'s, *b*'s and *d*'s were his biggest problems. G-g-g-good morning, b-b-b-bye, and of course D-d-d-dad. Édouard suddenly felt like the offending syllables were stuck in his throat, and the harder he tried to get them out, the farther back they fled, cutting off his windpipe. He would suffocate, struggling to breathe. "Look at him, he's like a fish flapping around desperately on the shore," his father would complain. Monique was kind and encouraging. She would often say the problematic words for him, trying to help. Édouard would at first feel relieved, but then immediately worry about whatever next syllable he knew would refuse to come out. Would his mother always have to speak for him? Would he need an interpreter by his side for the rest of his life, someone to filter his thoughts, like those attentive mothers who translate their babies' babbling? As for Lucien, he was convinced his son was simply doing it for the attention. "Come on, don't you think it's weird that he started this when his brother was born? I'm telling you, he's doing it on purpose. If we ignore it, it'll pass. He'll get tired of this nonsense."

But month after month, the situation continued to get worse, insidiously, without anyone ever noticing that the stutter had become a real problem, a terrifying handicap for Édouard. The boy was seething on the inside because of all the thoughts he couldn't turn into intelligible sounds. He was constantly struggling with the roiling lava of words eternally trapped behind his teeth. Jonathan was growing up, learning to talk, saying his first words, and everyone was thrilled with each new accomplishment. *How about that, the kid knows how to say* wine! *Definitely his father's son, eh, Lucien?* The more his brother learned to say, the less Édouard could communicate. He became more and more afraid of the inner demon he didn't know how to fight, much less conquer. He carefully avoided words beginning with the dangerous consonants and invented all sorts of strategies to ensure his stuttering was as unnoticeable as possible, even if that meant keeping quiet most of the time. His mother constantly told him to take a deep breath and slow down, but he wanted to scream with the unfairness of it all. She apologized for him to others: *He can't find his words; it's hard for him.* Édouard wanted to explode, to yell at the top of his lungs that *no*, he was not looking for his stupid words, that they were all there, perfectly lined up in his head, ready to be spoken one after the other. He wasn't looking for them; they just refused to come out.

Monique felt so sorry for him, she finally started finishing all his sentences. His father would sigh in annoyance and turn away in the middle of Édouard's laborious explanations. *You've got to learn that there's no place in this world for people who hesitate!*

School was also full of mocking faces. The children would bleat as he stepped outside for recess and "accidentally" jostle him. They even broke eggs over his head on his birthday. "Those brats must be as dumb as they look! Eggs are expensive," Lucien would grumble when he saw his eldest's gooey hair. The boys in his class would hide his gym bag before PE, just so they could tease, "Aw, poor Édouard can't find his b-b-b-bag!" and burst into laughter.

Reciting poems in class was his number one fear. Up front, next to Mr. Follin, Édouard could feel their eyes on him and almost hear the salvos of insults that would soon be hurled at him. He stood stock-still, like a lone tree in a raging storm.

"He says no with his head," he said, relieved that he had managed to make it through the first line. The teacher nodded approvingly.

"B-b-b-b—" Édouard stopped, exhausted, resigned, but no one tried to help him.

"Go on, you can do it," Mr. Follin said softly.

His eyes brimming with tears of rage and shame, Édouard continued, "B-b-b-b—"

He wanted to knock over the chairs, hit the children who were smiling with unkind eyes.

"If I hear a single noise from any of you, you will *all* be punished!" bellowed Mr. Follin. He was full of good intentions and had no idea that collective punishment would just result in the children taking their revenge on Édouard. *We missed recess because of you. All because you're a d-d-d-dummy.* Édouard took a deep breath and did his best to concentrate, avoiding eye contact with anyone.

"It's all right, you'll get it next time. Don't worry," the teacher tried to reassure him.

If I finish the poem, everything will be OK, the voice in his head whispered, urging him on.

"B-b-but no with his head," exclaimed Édouard, but there was no triumph in his voice, because he knew he'd only managed to recite two lines and there were still dozens of hated words to pronounce, and that after that, there would be hundreds, thousands more to struggle with in the future, all throughout his life.

The bell rang, and the children rushed out to recess like a flock of sparrows. The teacher kept Édouard back for a moment.

"Are you OK? You did pretty well, you know."

The boy shrugged. "I wish I were normal."

"Whatever for?" Mr. Follin asked, surprised.

Édouard shook his head wearily and explained, "To b-b-e like everyone else, to go unnoticed!"

The teacher with the graying mustache smiled. "Is that really your goal in life? To be invisible? Is that what you want?"

Édouard didn't answer. He was tired of trying to communicate. Reciting those two lines had wiped him out.

"Go on, go play, but think about what you really want, OK?"

This morning, however, Édouard is convinced that being different is terrible. He would give anything to be unnoticeable, to be invisible. He knew the end-of-year field trip to the circus visiting Le Havre was not a good idea—at least not for him.

"This is where he b-b-b-belongs!" Ludovic shouts proudly. And to make sure everyone's understood his joke, he adds, "In the circus, since he's a circus f-f-f-freak!" Ludovic, his number one nemesis since second grade, keeps repeating the hurtful phrase over and over again, making the others tear up from laughter.

The rest of the class repeats the "f-f-f-f" in chorus until Édouard's ears can no longer bear the sound of the derisive fricative. *Hit them— don't let them win!* yells his father in his head. *That said, it makes sense that they tease him. I mean, just look at him—he's like a retard when he gets stuck on a word!* Lucien hadn't even waited for the boys to fall asleep before sharing his opinion with his wife; no, he just shouted it right in front of Édouard one day when he was tired of listening to his son mumble unintelligibly. *"Ignore them. They'll get tired of it and move on,"* his mother always advises in a commiserating tone. But it's been four years and they don't seem to be losing interest. *For four years I've done everything possible to get them to accept me, to get them to like me, to avoid being alone at recess and eating at the teacher's table at lunch,* Édouard always wishes he could reply. But he keeps quiet every time, wanting to avoid a scene. He thinks if he says as little as possible, maybe the situation will seem less real, more bearable.

"A b-b-b-big f-f-f-fat f-f-f-freak!" Ludovic mocks again, thrilled that he thought to insert "big" and "fat" as additional words to stutter on.

Ludovic Spitzer is the worst of them all. The meanest and most vicious. Édouard knows exactly why the tall, broad-shouldered boy singled him out as soon as he noticed his stutter. He channeled everyone's teasing toward Édouard to keep them from noticing his own last name, which naturally lent itself to all sorts of easy jokes. *Spitzer, go drool somewhere else,* Édouard wishes he could say, but the hardened Ludovic has made that impossible. He's now the undisputed ringleader of the persecuting mob, and nobody dares defy his huge fists and homicidal glare. He would trample anyone to save himself. And the rest of the class has fallen into line behind him, each of them secretly relieved not to be the butt of Ludovic's jokes. It's best not to make Spitzer an enemy.

What's even worse is that his bully is the son of his father's best friend, Jean Spitzer. They've worked together forever at the refinery and are always on the front lines of every union fight, the first ones to call for a strike, saying that they shouldn't be manipulated by jerk bosses who spend their time living large while workers sweat blood to keep the refinery running—to keep France running, even. Jean regularly comes over to their apartment unannounced, to talk to Édouard's father. "We need to talk, Lucien. Something serious is going on, but we can't talk about it at the plant. The walls have ears, you know." The two men close the kitchen door. "Keep it down, boys, or you'll have to go outside." The discussions always start with a glass of red wine—and by the time they're done, neither can walk straight. Édouard likes Jean, who always has a kind word for him. "Don't worry, kid," he says. "When I was your age, I still wet the bed. I grew out of it eventually. And so will you!" Jean always ends their little talks, which he means to be comforting, with a series of hard smacks on the back that nearly topple Édouard, but he doesn't mind. He's just pleased that the father of the boy who tortures him takes the time to make him feel better. Happy that at least someone's father seems to like him.

Every evening after school, Édouard goes into his room and closes the door while Jonathan plays in the living room or takes his bath. Relentlessly, he practices his words, whispering in front of the mirror. Because he knows his father refuses to make his life easier, and that he'll send him to the bakery for bread as soon as the need arises. *G-g-g-good morning. I'd like a b-b-b-baguette, p-p-please.*

5

March 31, 2017–9:00 p.m.

"G-g-g-good morning, I'd like a b-b-b-baguette, p-p-please."

This simple intro is enough to get the Stade de France roaring. The audience already knows the whole sketch by heart. From the darkness, the showgoers whistle and cheer as if he were the Messiah, just because he's finally come onstage and uttered this short sentence, doing his best to stutter. The laughter is frank, sincere, happy, but for a second, Édouard hears the echo of his former classmates from nearly forty years ago. *This one's for you, you little shits,* mutters his inner voice.

He waits conspicuously for the applause to die down, for the silence to slowly return. He crosses his arms over his chest, taps his foot in exasperation, checks his watch, raises his eyebrows, and screws up his mouth in the iconic expression so many of his fans now imitate, then sighs loudly. Laughter fills the room, and somewhere up high and to the left, an invisible woman screams, "I love you, Édouard!" He impassively runs his fingers through his light-brown, exquisitely messy hair; smooths his thin, dandyish mustache with his index finger; and indifferently declares, "Of course you do." The audience laughs heartily, already familiar with the deadpan style Édouard has been cultivating since his very first show. They're instantly won over by the comedian's nonchalance and composure.

He's never been able to explain the spellbinding effect he has on people when he gets onstage, the way women stare at him, the way men eat up whatever he's saying. From the beginning, journalists spoke of his magnetic personality and indescribable charisma. People immediately praised his ability to mime just about any situation, to portray any emotion in seconds, to bring an entire gallery of idiosyncratic characters to life, like a chameleon. Others noted that his routines were universal, that everyone could immediately see part of their daily life in them, that everyone could identify with them. People also highlighted his gift for words, how easily he manipulated them, using them like razor-sharp arrows that always hit their target, delivering a healthy dose of cynicism and dark humor. Naturally, some observers remarked that his good looks and the way he seemed totally disinterested in the effect he had on women were also important components of his dazzling success. Then one day a *Télérama* critic started referring to the "Édouard effect," and the phrase quickly caught on with other journalists, who were thrilled to finally have a name for something that was beyond their usual vocabulary.

Followed by a huge spotlight, he starts pacing, slowly, his hands clasped behind his back, impatiently waiting for the laughter to quiet. Then he lifts his head and flatly asks, "Are you done now? Can I get started?" The audience members crack up once again. Regardless of what he says, Édouard knows they're ready. They've come prepared to laugh, and he knows that anything that comes out of his mouth will send them into fits. It's almost magical. Though he's never managed to figure out exactly why audiences are so drawn to him, why they find him so captivating, he has always been able to make the most of it. He's always known how to use his mysterious gift—despite being entirely convinced that it could disappear at any time, certain that it could all just be some inexplicable cosmic accident.

Finally, a fragile silence settles over the crowd. Édouard stops pacing and turns toward the audience, whose eyes are affixed on his lips. He carefully looks up and puts on a shy smile. The only faces he can see are the ones in the front rows, just below the stage. The rest of the stadium is a dark blur as his fans sit comfortably beneath the dusky sky. With an awkward, nasal laugh, he rubs his palms on his jeans, miming anxiety. He pretends to pull the same Breton-stripe sweater he's always wearing down until it settles just above his belt. He clears his throat, closes his eyes, takes a deep breath, then gently exhales through his mouth, as if to expel his stress. Laughter sounds here and there. Édouard starts meticulously biting his nails, swaying gracelessly, scratching his neck as if a swarm of mosquitoes has attacked him. He makes face after face, sighing repeatedly, exaggerating the puff of his cheeks, whining with fear, his eyes and mouth open wide, imitating Munch's *The Scream*. He goes through an entire gallery of faces filled with unspeakable terror—without a single word. Five minutes and seventeen seconds without speaking. Finally, he crosses one leg over the other and leans slightly forward, as if he's dying to go to the bathroom and can't hold it much longer, and a wave of laughter barrels through the stadium like a tsunami. Édouard is a virtuoso conductor directing the jaws of the fifty thousand people sitting in the audience.

As soon as he hears the first howls of delight, he stands up straight and returns to looking impassive. He conscientiously smooths his mustache as he waits about thirty seconds for the roar to die down again. He then flatly declares, with all the poise in the world, "You came here tonight so I could make you laugh. There's no point in lying about it—I know what you want from me. Well, it seems that's taken care of, so now we can relax a little. I think you've gotten your money's worth."

The wave of laughter washes over him again, even stronger this time. Édouard bathes in his fans' untainted elation.

"If you can't keep it down, I'm not going to be able to get a word in edgewise. That would be a shame—particularly given how much you spent to be here tonight." His voice remains stoic, aloof, even cold. It's what they've always loved about his act.

A third wave crashes over the monumental stage. Giggles lick at his toes, and Édouard is overwhelmed by a feeling of invincibility. He's the king of laughter; he has the power to bring all these people together and to make them happy for an entire evening. He can't see them, but he can hear them—their pure joy. It's Friday night, the night people let go of all the stress they've built up over the workweek.

"I guess it really doesn't take much. That'll teach me. I thought audiences were supposed to be demanding. What a joke . . ."

Édouard puts on a weary face, like a teacher at the end of his rope after spending years gesticulating at undisciplined students. He takes his cell phone out of his pocket and pretends to write a text message, reading as he goes: "I don't know why I work my ass off to write all these sketches for them. They laugh before I say anything funny."

His phone beeps, as if he's received a reply. The comedian quickly reads the message aloud: "Those are the recorded laughs. The ones we play in case you're not funny."

A fourth explosion of laughter goes off in the Stade de France, and this time the comedian is finally convinced the show will go off without a hitch—the audience is eating out of the palm of his hand.

"Great, maybe now I can get back to where I left off? . . . So, as I was saying," Édouard continues. He clears his throat and remains serious amid the ambient hilarity: "G-g-g-good morning. I'd like a b-b-b-baguette, p-p-p-please."

The skits follow, one after another at a breakneck pace. Édouard doesn't give his fans a second's rest, not even time to catch their breath between bursts of laughter. "When you leave here, you'll have abs of steel from laughing so hard. Guaranteed or your money back. For more details, see my producer!" With the crowd's support, the anxiety that had been suffocating him since dawn no longer has any effect on him. He has forgotten that he's in the Stade de France, forgotten that there aren't only fifty thousand people watching him, but millions, since the show is being broadcast live on TF1. He's forgotten that the tour DVD is being recorded tonight, that the tiniest little slipup would be unforgivable. Everything that kept him from sleeping and breathing normally now seems so distant. His fatigue evaporates, and the adrenaline in his system gives him wings. The comedian is exalted, on fire. He's giving it everything he's got tonight, like he does at every show: his heart, guts, energy, and soul. He feels like Prometheus, like he's stolen laughter from the gods to deliver it unto men. Nothing can stop him now.

6

Nothing can stop him now. A furious Lucien grabs both of his sons by the collar—much to the regret of Monique, who stifles a complaint about ruining their clothes—and drags them toward the front door.

"I'm sick and tired of hearing you two squabble about shards of glass! Get out of here! Move it!"

The box of hot chocolate falls to the ground in a cloud of brown powder as Édouard and Jonathan are lifted into the air and transported to the landing, where the door slams violently shut behind them.

"This is all your fault," says Édouard.

"I swear I didn't take anything of yours," pleads Jonathan. He frowns and sulkily crosses his arms over his chest.

Every other Sunday, Monique takes the brothers to their grandparents' house in Le Havre for lunch, along with their father if he's off work. In the early afternoon, while the adults are having coffee in the sunroom, the boys are allowed to go play at the beach, where Édouard can indulge in his passion: collecting little pieces of sea glass polished by the waves. Orange, bottle green, faded blue, opaque white. Jonathan always squats down and conscientiously helps his big brother fill the jar—despite the fact that he'd much rather play ball or fly a kite with him. At the end of the day, the jam jar full of multicolored shards finds its way back to the child-sized desk in the room the brothers share, and Édouard carefully places his favorite piece of sea glass—a nearly opaque pastel-green triangle worn smooth by the waves, which has special powers according to his little brother—on top of the lid. Every morning Édouard jumps out of the top bunk, gets dressed at the speed of light, then grabs his lucky charm and slips it into his pocket. But when he got up today, his cherished piece of sea glass was not in its usual place. Édouard immediately shook his brother awake to ask him what he'd done with it. Things quickly got out of hand: Édouard's patience was wearing thin with his little brother's silence, and a sleepy Jonathan was having a hard time figuring out what the early morning interrogation was all about. The conflict continued around the breakfast table as their mother made hot chocolate.

Which caused Lucien Bresson's blood to boil. He had just gotten home from the night shift, and the little shits were already screaming in his ears!

A compassionate Monique opens the apartment door behind the boys. She places a finger on her lips to let the children know not to make a sound, then quickly changes Jonathan out of his pajamas. She hands an empty yogurt tub to her youngest and two bananas to Édouard.

"Go eat those outside. Your father's exhausted. You do understand, right? Take your little brother to collect chestnuts. That'll keep you busy for a while."

"He can go on his own! I'm t-t-tired of always having to t-t-take him with me wherever I g-g-go!" exclaims Édouard, unable to whisper.

"It's your fault you're both out here in the hallway, you know. Jonathan didn't start this fight!" his mother replies firmly.

"But he stole my lucky ch-ch-charm!"

"That's not true!" yells Jonathan as he grabs one of the bananas. "I didn't take anything!"

"That's enough. I don't want to hear it. You can come back for lunch, but only once you've both calmed down. Do you understand?"

Édouard mumbles agreement while Jonathan scarfs down his banana and hands the limp peel to their mother.

"I'm counting on you to look out for him, Édouard!"

The boys reluctantly head down the building's stairs to the entryway with its floor-to-ceiling tiles. The building manager, Madame Rita, gives them a suspicious glance. Édouard keeps quiet. Once outside in the cool autumn morning, they hear one of the windows of the apartment being shoved open, then Lucien Bresson's bellowing voice echoing through the neighborhood: "You forgot your damn jar!"

The container explodes on contact with the sidewalk, barely a yard from Édouard's feet. With tears in his eyes, the boy runs over to pick up the few pieces miraculously left intact. Jonathan comes and apologetically hands over the Yoplait tub for the survivors.

"I promise, I really didn't take your lucky charm," he murmurs pleadingly.

"Just forget it, OK?"

The boys are still squatting on the sidewalk when Ludovic and his gang call over from the far side of the street. Édouard feels his whole body tense, but doesn't let anything show. His parents started sending him to a speech therapist three times a week the previous summer, and everyone has noticed that his stutter has improved. It hasn't disappeared, of course, but Édouard doesn't feel so handicapped in his day-to-day life anymore. He still gets stuck on words when he's scared or angry, or when he tries to talk too fast, but his first day of sixth grade wasn't as bad as he had imagined it would be.

He'd reluctantly attended the first speech therapy session, free of expectations, especially since his father had muttered that it was all a hell of a scam, that given the price, gold bars better come out of Édouard's mouth afterward. The young woman who'd welcomed him talked to him about voluntary stuttering. "You're going to repeat initial letters on purpose and learn to control them when they start getting away from you." Édouard felt like somebody was finally listening to him. He felt safe in the gentle warmth of her office, so he started practicing at home in his room. "My n-n-n-ame is Édouard and I st-st-stutter. D-d-do you have a p-p-problem with that?" His father had banged his fist into the table, as usual. "Is this what we're paying that tart for? To make the kid stutter even more than before he saw her?" Jonathan found the exercise hilarious and had fun copying. Lucien shook his head in annoyance. "She's going to mess up the second one too, at this rate!"

But Monique had refused to give in. "The school said she's the best in Normandy. The principal himself recommended her, so wait a while before you start spluttering that it won't work . . ."

In September, Édouard started middle school, and his heart jumped for joy when he realized his archenemy, Ludovic Spitzer, wasn't in the same class as him. Maybe he would be able to reinvent himself, become someone else, or at least no longer be the scapegoat for all his classmates. Maybe he'd even make friends. He wasn't exactly at ease when he had to go up to the board in front of everyone, of course, but the intense feelings of loneliness and shame that used to plague him were totally gone. He would start his first sentence with a voluntary stutter, and the whole class thought he was doing it on purpose, to annoy the teacher most likely.

Unfortunately, as Édouard's stutter improved, Ludovic had only become more aggressive—particularly since the eighth graders had noticed his last name from day one. They had a ball with it at recess:

"Loogie Ludo" was his new nickname. Outside of school, Ludovic enjoyed bullying Édouard even more than before, despite the latter's efforts to appear indifferent. And Jean's son could always find three or four buddies ready to laugh at his questionable jokes.

"Hey look, it's Édouard B-B-B-Bresson crawling around on the ground, guys!" The four boys come toward the brothers, who stand up immediately, as if caught red-handed.

"What exactly are you doing?"

"Nothing."

Édouard returns Ludovic's glare. He'd rather get slapped than look down.

"Perfect, because I've got a great plan all lined up. You can come along . . ."

"Where?" asks Édouard distrustfully.

"You know the abandoned house near the pharmacy? We're gonna go check it out. You can come if you're not too chicken!"

Ludovic proudly crosses his arms over his chest, and his posse bursts into laughter.

"Why would I be afraid?" Édouard retorts, sure of himself.

"I dunno, maybe because of all the stuff people say about the place? The last owner supposedly kidnapped kids and kept them in his bathroom before he cut their throats . . . Ever since then, no one who's gone into the house has ever come out alive . . ."

"Psh, only a dummy would believe those stories."

"Well, let's find out, B-B-Bresson! Are you coming?"

Édouard pauses, then nods. He knows he can't turn back without making a fool of himself in front of these jerks. Also, he wants to believe this might be his chance to finally gain Ludovic's respect, if not his goodwill. He's suddenly sure he'll prove himself to the bullies and that it will change everything.

"Come on, Jonathan. Let's go for a little walk."

When they reach the dilapidated house, Jonathan instinctively tightens his grip on his big brother's hand. He's only just turned five, and gathering chestnuts would have suited him much better than visiting a deserted old house.

"Do we really have to go in?" asks the kindergartner.

Édouard nods, sure of himself.

"What could happen? We're just going to look around, and then we'll come back out, OK?"

The six boys make sure no one is watching, then climb over the front gate and into the overgrown yard, where tall grass and dandelions compete for space. The windows on the second and third floors are gaping, with only a few pieces of broken glass still stuck in the frames, like sharp teeth ready to defend the property from intruders. Ivy is crawling all over the walls right up to the edge of the faded welcome mat sitting in front of the door.

"You first," urges Ludovic, who suddenly seems much less arrogant.

Édouard doesn't answer, but pushes down on the heavy oak door's handle, secretly hoping nothing will happen. His wish comes true—the door is locked. Édouard's about to turn back, faking disappointment, when Ludovic grabs him by the shoulder.

"We can go in through this window," he insists, pointing to an empty wooden frame on the ground floor.

One by one, the boys climb into the deserted building, where the drafts seem strangely icy compared with the temperature outside. Despite all the open windows, the walls smell of mold, like in a damp basement.

"Just a quick look around and we'll go," whispers Édouard in Jonathan's ear, as if the house demanded he lower his voice.

The children explore the first floor without a sound, but Ludovic doesn't seem particularly confident. The stairs to the second floor creak startlingly as the boys start up them to the bedrooms, making the kids all jump, almost imperceptibly.

"Come on, guys, buck up!" Ludovic jokes, his voice echoing off the walls.

The last bedroom is bigger than the other two, where they hadn't found much more than used syringes, along with cigarette butts that had been tamped out against the dirty walls, leaving black marks.

"We can go now," declares Édouard after glancing into the room, which seems as empty as the others.

"Wait, we haven't checked out what's behind that door over there," says Ludovic firmly. "The famous bathroom, I bet . . . It would be a shame to miss the main event, don't you think? You wanna do the honors?"

Édouard looks at the door on the other side of the room. It's covered in floral wallpaper that's coming unglued halfway down the wall, with dark-green splotches covering the surface.

"The floor doesn't seem very sound, Ludo."

Édouard doesn't know which of Ludovic's three henchmen has dared to open his mouth, but when he looks at the floor he notices one out of every three slats is missing and that the remaining pieces of wood are so rotten that in certain places the entire worm-eaten floor has collapsed onto the ground floor ten feet below.

"Looks fine to me," replies Ludovic unconvincingly. "So, Édouard, don't have the balls to check out the bathroom, huh? Afraid you'll find a ghost?"

"I told you I'm not afraid of anything," mutters the boy.

He wants to turn around and get out of this disgusting place, but something keeps him from leaving. Later he'll call it pride. Or stupidity.

He moves along the wall toward the bathroom, carefully placing one foot in front of the other. As he triumphantly opens the door to find nothing but an ancient bathtub, his attention is suddenly pulled away by a high-pitched scream. Édouard spins around just in time to hear the floor groan and see Jonathan disappear, as if swallowed by a giant cloud of dust that immediately burns their throats. Barely a second later there's nothing but a gaping hole left in the middle of the room. Ludovic and his posse flee without a second thought. Unable to move, Édouard hears them stampede down the stairs. For a second everything is muffled, like he's underwater, his brain trying in vain to understand what has happened. Then the cogs start turning again, and he too leaves the room, sliding along the walls. "Jonathan!" he yells on the stairs, hurrying through the dark to what looks like a dining room. His little brother is lying on the floor unconscious. The others are nowhere to be found. Édouard hears the gate creaking as the boys climb back over it as fast as they can. *What should I do, what should I do?* The terrified ten-year-old looks around desperately. He racks his brain for an idea, a solution. He searches in his pockets for something, anything, a magic wand to go back in time.

But all he finds is a piece of pastel-green sea glass, a perfect equilateral triangle. His lucky charm, forgotten there from last night.

With a lump in his throat, Édouard approaches his little brother. *Please tell me you're not dead.* He puts his ear next to Jonathan's nose. *Tell me you're still breathing.* Then he places the piece of glass in the palm of the kindergartner's hand. *That way nothing bad will happen to you. Hold on tight. I'll be right back—don't move. I'm going to get help.* A dense, heavy silence descends on the brothers. Then Édouard runs out of the house screaming, jumps over the rusted gate, sprints about a hundred yards to the pharmacy. He's out of breath. *If the pharmacist greets me by saying, "What brings you in today, son?" as always, everything'll be OK.* His chest burns, and he wants to cough and spit. When he walks into the pharmacy, the little bell over the door dings gleefully. The pharmacist looks up, adjusts his glasses on his nose, and asks with a startled expression, "What brings you in today, son? You look like you've just seen a ghost!"

7

"You look like you've just seen a ghost!" offers Hervé merrily as he watches Édouard, who's standing stock-still behind the black velvet curtain that closed in front of him only seconds ago. He knows how much the comedian hates being distracted during the show, how he insists on being left alone until it's all over, but Hervé figures his role as manager gives him special privileges.

"Just leave me alone for another fifteen minutes, OK?" Édouard sighs with his eyes closed. Hervé scurries off, mumbling indistinctly under his breath—most likely something about celebrities and their big heads.

Less than an inch of opaque fabric separates the comic from thousands of his excited fans. He's just run through an hour and a half of skits. His forehead is dripping with sweat, and he has to force himself to keep on his navy-blue sweater with white stripes. He pushes the sleeves up to his elbows. Magda bought this sweater for him years ago, as a good luck charm for his first important audition. Despite his nerves, he charmed their socks off that day, and he's never done a show without the wool sweater since, even though it's often too warm for him to wear comfortably onstage. The original got too pilly, too worn in the elbows, with a small hole from hot cigarette ash that once landed on the fabric. So Édouard keeps the precious relic in his closet, next to six identical replacements hastily purchased in a Saint James store. The Breton-stripe sweater has become his uniform over the years, his calling card, featured on all the billboards for his various shows.

The curtain sways gently, and Édouard immerses himself in the tumult the audience is causing as they yell, whistle, cheer, and applaud, clapping their hands together in unison, pleading for an encore. They're waiting for him. They won't leave until he makes a final appearance— they *demand* it. Édouard has prepared an all-new sketch for this final encore of his tour, which ends tonight. He spent hours imagining it, crafting the text, drafting and crossing out line after line in his Moleskine notebook. It's probably his most personal piece, since it's about the difficulties of fame—laced with a good dose of humor, of course. He shares anecdotes from his daily life over all the years he's been adored by audiences, the little nobody from Normandy who was the laughingstock of his elementary-school class, the boy whose success was nobody's bet.

Édouard counts to sixty. The seconds seem to stretch on forever, carried off by the cheerful shouts of the invisible audience. *Play hard to get, cultivate impatience, make them yearn for you.* Édouard savors the indescribable joy of feeling so completely loved. Then he pushes the curtain aside and returns to the stage, followed by the circle of white light that accompanies even his tiniest steps.

He casually strolls along the front edge of the enormous stage, his eyes scanning the crowd he can't actually see. He waits for them to quiet down, then jokes, "I guess the encore is included in the ticket price, huh?"

There's a smattering of laughter.

"Well, guess what: to wrap up this unique tour, I've prepared a little surprise . . ."

Enthusiastic shouts reach him from throughout the venue. His confidence bolstered, Édouard is about to continue when a man yells out, "Zita! Do Zita!" from somewhere in the bleachers.

The comedian smiles, ignoring the request. "A new sketch that nobody—not a single person—has ever seen before. I know, I know, you're thinking it might be awful, not funny at all."

From the darkness below Édouard, another fan shouts, "Yeah, Zita. We want Zita!" but he keeps going, unflappable. "I wanted to try this sketch out tonight, live, with no safety net. To see what you think of it and let you be the judges!"

Somewhere off to the right, several voices begin chanting, perfectly in sync: "Zi-ta, Zi-ta!" Soon the rest of the audience joins in, and thousands of people are begging him, *ordering* him.

Zita.

Édouard stops moving, his mouth still slightly open, as if he were searching for his next sentence.

Zita is the nutty character that first earned him his reputation and led to his success. Zita, the obsessive-compulsive building manager, loosely inspired by Madame Rita, the manager of his childhood apartment building. Zita has just one passion, cleaning, from washing and scrubbing to polishing and dusting. She always appears suddenly, sweeping the stage in the middle of Édouard's skits with her Portuguese accent and canary-yellow rubber gloves. Sometimes she takes it even further, heading out into the audience to brush unwanted particles off certain showgoers. But as soon as she hears the first few notes of a song by her beloved Enrico Macias, she undergoes a radical transformation, as if she were suddenly possessed by the demon of music—"moushica," as she says—artfully removing her gloves one finger at a time and then improvising an air guitar solo with her broom. People have always loved Zita. They fell for her at her first appearance. But Édouard has grown tired of her over the years, keeping her time onstage short since he still has to put her in—his fans expect to see her, demand to see her. He knows all this. But on this last night he wanted to skip Zita altogether. He's had enough of her following him everywhere like a Siamese twin. It's time to move on.

Hervé tried to persuade him. "You have to give the audience what they want, Édouard, and they're going to ask for Zita. You don't want to *disappoint* them, do you?"

But the comic persisted, sure of his decision. "I've written a new skit. They're going to love it, you'll see. I've had enough of jumping around to Enrico Macias like I'm possessed. It's important to keep things fresh, right?"

Hervé nodded skeptically. "Do what you think is best. You're the one onstage. After all, they're your fans."

More than fifty thousand people are now demanding Zita, stomping their feet in the stands, but Édouard perseveres, refusing to admit defeat. He raises his palms, slowly, requesting their silence, imploring them. The audience obediently quiets, hanging on their idol's every word. Édouard sighs, almost relieved not to lose control.

"Could you *please* stop interrupting me? It almost makes me want to disappear back behind the curtain! And where would that leave you all if I suddenly vanished? No Édouard, no Zita, nobody left to make you laugh!"

His voice is gentler than usual, and his lips curve into a tender smile, like the one parents sometimes have when watching their spirited children. The entire stadium wavers in an awkward silence as the audience decides how to react.

Then the "Zi-ta" chant picks up again. Édouard still feels confident, despite their insistence, and doesn't give in. "I don't think I've ever told you how hard it is to be an international star, have I?"

As the crowd wakes up fully, chanting the two syllables faster and faster, he forgets where he is, submerged in the growing roar, a tornado devastating everything in its path.

"I was in the grocery store the other day, when—" Édouard suddenly, irrevocably loses his train of thought. Nothing. His text has evaporated from the halls of his memory. Scrounge as he might for something, anything in the depths of his mind, he finds only emptiness—a heavy, brutal, inescapable emptiness. He has no idea what he's supposed to say, despite having spent dozens of hours writing and polishing each word of the skit until every sentence was perfect.

He can't remember any of it.

The "Zi-ta, Zi-ta" incantation works its way in, despite all his efforts to resist, and he instinctively clenches his fists, his face devoid of emotion. He can hear the voices but can only see the faces in the first rows, their mouths opening and closing around the beloved name.

He wavers, then finally gives in. It doesn't matter that he wanted to create a different kind of sketch, one in which he really put himself out there, one that walked the line between tears and laughter, between cynicism and total despair. He wanted to explain what fame is really like day to day. He thought he could share that with his audience, thought he could *count* on them. But his head is spinning, filling with the sound of the two repeated syllables. He feels like a caged animal, like the audience is throwing peanuts at him to get him to do a trick.

He throws in the towel and signals for the sound technician to start the music. When the first notes of "Les Filles de Mon Pays" echo through the Stade de France, the crowd goes wild, and Édouard could almost cry. *Give them what they want. The customer is always right.*

An assistant holds out a broom from behind the curtain, and Édouard hurries over to grab it before shouting to the delighted audience, "Moushica!" After three minutes of frenzied dancing, wielding the broom like an electric guitar, Édouard—or rather Zita—ends up on the floor, miming a complicated solo worthy of an incredible rock concert. The melody gently fades, and he stands up to announce flatly: "Well, that wash fun, but I have cleaning to do. Look at all thish dusht!"

The audience roars with laughter as he reels off lines they all know by heart. They eat them up—it's effortless. Édouard stands up straight with one hand by his side and the other on his stomach, preparing to thank everyone who came to see him tonight. He can't help but think that maybe it wasn't so painful to stay in the box he built for himself over the years after all, to give them what they wanted, to *be* what they wanted him to be.

He bends at the waist to express his gratitude, and the fans in the first few rows stand, clapping enthusiastically. Their faces are radiant, captivated. With a snap of his fingers, Édouard turns on the lights of the giant flying saucer they've occupied this evening. At last, he can see the thousands of unknown faces all around him, and as his eyes sweep over the stadium, he starts to feel dizzy, as if he has suddenly become the center of the solar system, with the world revolving around him. They're all standing now, and their joy crashes into Édouard like a tidal wave of such strength and intensity that for a moment he staggers under the weight of the acclaim and love gushing out of them like water through a broken dam. His throat tightens with emotion, and he can barely whisper, "Thank you." He repeats himself a bit louder even though he knows no one can hear him, that at best they'll read his lips on the giant screens set up on either side of the stage. The applause carries him to the highest heights, refusing to die down. He feels small and yet infinitely grateful for all these strangers vocalizing, each in his or her own way, for how much they love him—unconditionally.

Édouard brings his index finger to his lips, which are curled in an emotional smile. He shushes the audience, then raises his other arm toward the sky. Thousands of eyes follow, thousands of heads look up, thousands of ears await his next words. "I would like . . . I don't know if you're aware of this, but we have been lucky enough to spend our evening with a view of the heavens above. So I'll leave you with this request: I'd like you all to contemplate the sky now. Scour it for the stars we so rarely see over Paris. I hope you'll see lots of them tonight, because each one is a laugh that shot up into the galaxy tonight."

The spotlights turn off and the applause builds again. Before heading backstage, Édouard takes one last look at all the faces lifted toward the weakly sparkling stars. Finally, he allows himself to look at his brother, sitting in the front row in his wheelchair, which takes up as much room as two seats. As always, his smile and fervent applause are enough to make Édouard's heart explode in his chest.

His brother looks up at the jet-black sky, and Édouard whispers to him, "Thank you for being here."

8

December 1981

His brother looks up at the jet-black sky and Édouard whispers to him, "Thank you for being here." Jonathan doesn't answer. He's completely absorbed in the stars above, his brow furrowed in concentration.

"I can't find the Big Dipper."

Édouard leans out the window of their room and identifies the famous constellation for his little brother.

"See, it looks like a big pot with the handle there on the right."

Satisfied, Jonathan nods.

"Come on, let's close the window or Mom will get mad about letting the heat out," adds Édouard as he moves the wheelchair back a few inches, so he can reach the window handle more easily.

Jonathan has been home for a month now, after spending more than a year in a rehabilitation center on the coast, about two hours from Gonfreville-l'Orcher. Despite his monthly visits to the center, Édouard can't believe how much his little brother has changed. The little boy has become such a serious, thoughtful six-year-old. It's like he grew up all at once, leaving Édouard behind.

After the accident, Jonathan was medevaced to Le Havre—an unforget-table event for the entire neighborhood. Édouard became the brother of the boy who was taken away in a helicopter. *It was a Sunday, just before noon. I remember as if it were yesterday. I was mowing the lawn when I heard the roar of the blades* . . . Lucien and Monique Bresson reunited with Édouard in the ER, where the terrified eleven-year-old had been sitting on a chair, waiting for several hours, his knees tucked under his chin. Following an operation that seemed to last an eternity, the surgeon—a paunchy man squeezed into a white coat that was stretched taut at the waist—finally informed the family stiffly, per his duty: "Your son is now a paraplegic, paralyzed from vertebra T12 down. The MRI revealed bone marrow lesions. Unfortunately, he'll never be able to use his legs again." Faced with the parents' incomprehension, he added, "I'm sorry," in an almost annoyed, vaguely regretful tone. When they still failed to react, staring at him with vacant eyes, he said loudly, "He'll never be able to walk again, understand?" Then he disappeared down a hallway that smelled of bleach.

Monique turned to face her older son and asked urgently, "What happened?" Édouard opened his mouth, but despite his best efforts, the words wouldn't budge; they were frozen on the tip of his tongue.

Monique impatiently brushed her son's attempts to speak aside. "It's all your fault, anyway." She slumped into a plastic chair, devastated, then continued to talk without looking at him. "You were supposed to look out for him! We trusted you. You were supposed to take care of him, but you crippled him instead! Are you listening, Édouard? Because of you, he'll never be able to walk again! My baby will never walk again!" His mother's voice cracked, and the boy hunched down as far as he could, as if to shoulder the weight of her accusation, to carry the leaden burden he felt he deserved.

He desperately tried to speak—"S-s-s-s"—but his mother cut him off.

"You've done enough. I don't want to hear any more."

So Édouard never got to apologize. He locked his feelings inside, deep inside his heart, in his memory, buried under the thickest layer of guilt any child has ever had to bear.

Faced with his son's inability to speak, Lucien Bresson couldn't help but groan, "Great. Now we have two handicapped kids," he said, oblivious to his wife glowering at him.

Édouard felt so lonely in their bedroom, which was suddenly much too big, too empty. Every night and every morning when he climbed the ladder of their bunk bed, seeing the perfectly made bottom bunk turned his stomach. He wrote to his brother every weekend, hoping a nurse would read his letter to Jonathan, hoping it would brighten his day at the rehab center. For an entire year it was like he was holding his breath, not allowed to breathe without his brother by his side. He was afraid his mother would never show him the slightest sign of affection again. No matter what he did, the distance between them had grown so great it could never be bridged. He desperately wanted to cuddle against her chest and feel the warmth of her skin and the beat of her heart, but he stopped himself. He couldn't beg for scraps of her love, buried beneath so much anger and resentment. He wouldn't have survived it if she'd backed away, so to protect himself he resisted the urge to approach her. Monique desperately wanted to forgive him—she hated herself for having such bitter feelings for Édouard—but she gave up trying since her son seemed to deliberately keep her at arm's length.

"It's time for bed, boys!" Monique calls from the kitchen. With difficulty, Édouard helps his brother out of his wheelchair and into his bunk. He can't help but think that now Jonathan will never have the privilege of sleeping up top. The list of everything he's robbed his brother of doing is long. For the past year, he's kept a log of the things Jonathan will never be able to do because of that stupid accident: play soccer, stomp chestnuts open in the fall, swim in the waves, win a sack race at a friend's birthday party. Édouard has already filled four pages with his chicken scratch, without knowing exactly why he feels the need to list all the activities that are now out of Jonathan's reach.

"I'm sorry, you know."

"For what?" asks his little brother.

"For what happened, for not protecting you."

"You couldn't have known there would be a hole in the floor."

"Still . . . I never should have taken you in there."

Jonathan doesn't answer. Instead, he starts rummaging through the little backpack that's always hanging on his wheelchair. He takes something out and, with an almost shy smile, hands the mysterious object to his brother. Édouard immediately recognizes the triangle of sea glass.

"I gave it to you. Keep it . . ."

"I don't need it anymore now that I'm home."

Jonathan insists, and Édouard finally takes back his old lucky charm. He holds it in the palm of his hand but doesn't know what to do with it.

The next morning, Monique opens the shutters in their room with a loud "Everybody up! It's time for school!" and the boys groan as they drag themselves out of bed. They gulp down their hot chocolate and get dressed, then leave the apartment with their mother. They're running late, as usual. Since the elevator is out of order, Édouard carries Jonathan on his back, and Monique awkwardly hefts the wheelchair down the stairs. When they reach the elementary school where Monique has always worked as a lunch lady, serving about a hundred famished children, they part ways. Édouard continues toward the middle school. In front of the gate to the playground, a group of mothers without anything better to do are in the middle of an animated discussion, thrilled to trade gossip for a few minutes. As Monique and Jonathan near, their voices turn to whispers and their expressions become suspicious, cold, *disgusted* even.

"I mean, really, a child like that doesn't belong in school . . ."

Monique makes herself walk on, her back straight and head held high.

"I don't know why she even bothers. Can't she see he won't be able to do much with his life in a wheelchair anyway?"

Monique has gotten used to this kind of reaction since she started bringing Jonathan to school last month, accompanying him to his classroom, then helping him down the stairs to the playground at each recess, following his every move out of the corner of her eye in the cafeteria, ready to run over if her son should ever spill his tray.

"And you have to admit, he's not a very cheery sight for the other children. Mine's started asking questions—it's awkward!"

Monique is used to it, yes, but that doesn't mean she can block out the comments, that they don't sting. She wishes she could whip around and hurl a biting retort at the twits, but she holds back. She knows that the only reason the school tolerates Jonathan, the only reason his teacher does his best to help him, is because she works in the cafeteria, and the principal has always found her efficient and reliable. She keeps quiet, clenching the handles on Jonathan's chair a bit tighter and chattering loudly to him so that he won't hear any of the unkind things people are saying about him. Because there is no way her six-year-old boy is going to spend his days rotting away in their apartment; he has every right to see the world. And the world, at his age, is school. Period. Nobody will change her mind about that.

When he reaches the middle school, Édouard joins a group of classmates debating what the morning's math test will cover. He notices Ludovic at the other end of the courtyard, his back against the fence as he deliberately chews his Malabar gum, trying to look cool. When the former bully notices Édouard watching him, he hunches down, grabs his backpack from the ground by his feet, and hurries up the stairs to his homeroom. For over a year now, Ludovic has been doing everything possible to avoid Édouard, even crossing the street so he won't have to walk past him on the sidewalk. He would never stop to mockingly stutter "B-B-B-Bresson" in front of Édouard now. But somehow a part of Édouard almost wishes his enemy would attack him again, torture him, humiliate him in front of all the other middle schoolers hungry for fights and hazing. He wishes Ludovic would make him pay again and again for being dumb enough to follow him into that run-down house last year. He wishes his old enemy would make him pay for fighting with Jonathan over a stupid piece of sea glass, for provoking a point-less argument. He wishes he would make him pay for ripping off his brother's wings before he could even learn to fly.

To entertain Jonathan, Édouard puts on all sorts of shows, eager to hear his brother's treble laugh, which has become all too rare. He makes prank calls to toll-free numbers from the phone in the living room, with Jonathan glued to the receiver next to him, holding back giggles with the palm of his hand. Édouard throws himself into his act with passion. "Hello? Who's this? What do you mean I called you? You've got it all wrong, sir; you called me. I'm sorry, what? You must have, since my phone rang! Are you laughing at me? I bet you think it's funny to play pranks on people, huh? Don't you have anything else to do with your time?" Inevitably, the person on the other end of the line loses his patience, gets angry, and sometimes even hurls insults at the boy, delighting Jonathan, who finds it increasingly difficult to stifle his laughter.

Every night Édouard puts on a little production for his brother and parents, when his father's not at the refinery. "Ladies and gentlemen, please put your hands together for this global, interplanetary, interga-lactic event featuring the great, the extraordinary, the magnificent, the fantastic . . ." The introduction goes on for a few minutes, until Édouard has run down the list of synonyms he's meticulously memorized. Lucien sighs as Jonathan claps enthusiastically, unable to stop laughing. The more their father sighs, the harder his little brother laughs. Édouard dresses up, uses his mother's makeup. He gestures wildly, contorting his body into bizarre positions. He does a perfect impression of his father's constant yelling and grumbling. Monique pretends not to find it funny to keep Lucien from losing his temper. He imitates their Portuguese building manager, Madame Rita, who was obsessed with her broom: "But what is thish? Finger marksh on the glash! I can't bear it, can't shtand it!" Édouard dives into his character with glee, one of his mother's silk scarves wrapped around his head. His brother's giggling soothes his guilty conscience.

Later, when journalists ask him where he got his start, he'll answer that he's always loved making other people laugh, bringing them joy, helping them forget the daily grind for a minute. But the truth is that his vocation was born in the late fall of 1981, when he decided to do everything he could to make sure his little brother had the happiest childhood possible, when he decided to do his best to make him forget the weight of his unmoving legs, if only for a minute. It all started the day he decided, more or less consciously, to do whatever he could to feel useful—even fleetingly.

9

It all started the day he decided, more or less consciously, to do whatever he could to feel useful—even fleetingly. That day was the first day of an unbridled, though possibly futile, sprint to stay ahead of the growing, threatening cloud of guilt. Making others laugh made him feel like he had a place in the world, like he could become someone other than the boy who failed to protect his little brother.

Back in his dressing room, Édouard dolefully contemplates the dozens of bouquets, multicolored envelopes, and stuffed animals piled on a table in the corner. He gently closes the door, then leans his back against the thin plywood wall. The inescapable first crash has begun. Though the comedian is all too familiar with the intense feeling of emptiness that washes over him as soon as he leaves the stage, he's never been able to ward it off or even lessen it. It's like an elevator suddenly plunges all the way from the top floor down into the depths of the dark, hostile shaft. The first wave of loneliness always hits Édouard in his dressing room, as he's trying to catch his breath in the first minutes of peace after the show. The second—much worse—wave crashes into him in the middle of the night, when he's alone in his hotel room or apartment. He's always alone, whether or not someone else is there, whether or not he's given in to the advances of a woman more enterprising or seductive than the rest, whether or not his king-size bed holds another body. He is always irreparably alone. His whole life, the only thing that has gotten him out of bed every morning is his quest to fill the void, to forget the crushing feeling of isolation and of being lost, the very feeling that seizes him when he leaves the stage.

When he was a child, his maternal great-grandfather sometimes came to visit for a few days, sleeping on the old pull-out couch in the living room. The apartment turned into a campsite, with his things strewn all over the place, from the blood pressure medication on the kitchen table to the glass for his dentures on the bathroom sink. Inevitably, when the elderly man packed his things back into his battered gray suitcase, Édouard's throat tightened. *Why do you have to leave, Papy? Can't you stay a little longer?* As his dented Citroën Ami 8 pulled out of the parking place in the building lot, a terrible rush of emotion would knock the wind out of the boy. It was like sadness, but it would take him many more years to put his finger on the real name for the feeling that strangled his heart as the beige car drove out of sight—melancholy. A profound melancholy, like the one he still feels today whenever he's not actively engaged in making someone laugh.

He realizes now that he's sometimes—often, even—lost sight of what is truly important: his wife and his son. They grew apart little by little, and he hardly noticed because he was so sure that one more step wouldn't really change anything, that when he turned back they would still be there, patiently waiting for him, waving affectionately. *We're not going anywhere, Édouard. Of course we'll always be there for you.* Had he even ever told Magda how much he'd loved her, how he never really stopped loving her? How she had driven him to succeed, how he owed her everything for the unfailing support she had provided for so many years?

With his brother, he's maintained an affectionate but distant relationship, afraid that seeing Jonathan's wheelchair too often might finally send him off the deep end to be swallowed up by the hole in the worm-eaten floor that still features in his nightmares, still wakes him at dawn, heart racing, thirty-seven years after the fact.

And his parents, of course. He cut the cord as soon as he moved in with Magda, giving them a quick call from time to time, or at best meeting for a hurried lunch. *I've got work to do, sketches to write, shows to practice. I really have to go. I promise next time I'll stay longer . . .* Lucien would shake his head and pour more red wine into a glass limescale had rendered opaque. *Work? What a joke! Do they call acting like a clown in front of a bunch of idiots work now? I guess we've seen it all, dear . . .* Monique, sensing the tension between the two men, avoided saying anything at all.

His father had worked hard his whole life, putting all his energy into the refinery, without a day of vacation, without ever imagining he could do anything other than work, eat (that is, drink), and sleep. And then he kicked the bucket the day of his retirement party.

Édouard can still see the yellow helium balloons emblazoned with the Renault diamond logo that Lucien's best friend Jean had managed to get from his brother-in-law, a salesman at the Montivilliers dealership. The afternoon spent around Jean's barbecue was accompanied by plenty of alcohol, and his father's clearly tipsy colleagues ended up sucking helium out of the balloons and laughing hysterically as they compared their ridiculous cartoon voices. Lucien, delivering a perfect imitation of Donald Duck's nasal voice, launched into an incredibly sentimental tirade about how he'd never abandon his comrades, how they had to continue the f—

He was struck down by a heart attack before the word *fight* could cross his lips. Édouard watched him collapse haltingly, as if in slow motion, until he lay on the grass scorched by the summer sun. The yellow balloon he was holding escaped, in a hurry to reach the clouds, and Édouard hoped his father's soul had had enough time to grab onto the string, to reach heaven, or wherever, more quickly. He felt immensely sad, without knowing why his father's death affected him so. Then he suddenly realized it was now too late to hope Lucien would someday finally understand and respect him.

Monique joined her husband a few years later, most likely to put an end to the boredom of the colorless, solitary life that had suddenly been imposed on her. With one son she saw more on TV than in real life and another who had moved to Alsace—the end of the earth—to start his family, she felt she had become superfluous. She had accomplished her mission: none of her three men needed her anymore. So, with her idol Eddy Mitchell crooning "La Dernière Séance" in the background, she stoically let lymphoma eat away at her liver, spleen, and lungs until there was nothing left to save. Édouard would have liked to receive his mother's forgiveness before she passed, but she didn't offer it and he didn't dare ask. He would never know now if she stayed angry with him until the end. Once again, there was nothing but silence.

Yes, Édouard has often lost track of the important things in life, too busy running to stay ahead of grief and regret. And now, still motionless behind the door to his dressing room, he suddenly feels like his legs will take him no further. The reflection in the brightly lit, bulb-framed mirror doesn't lie. Wrinkles cut across his sweaty forehead, his lips are pinched, and the dark circles under his eyes are prominent, no longer camouflaged by the ridiculously expensive under-eye cream he buys. His light-auburn hair now features gray highlights, but his thin mustache, which melted Magda's heart on their first date, is still perfectly trimmed despite its own sprinkling of silver strands. Even the freckles that cover his prominent cheekbones and temples seem to have faded over the years, leaving his whole face looking worn and dull.

The passage of time is written all over his face. He is once again taken aback by the enormous discrepancy between the perfectly made-up reflection he inspects before the show and the pale, exhausted one he sees now, just a few hours later—as if a vampire has drained all his blood.

And yet the evening is far, very far, from over. He still has so much to do if he wants tonight to be his apotheosis. He barely has time to gulp down a glass of water mixed with a couple of effervescent energy tablets to help him get through the night's obligatory festivities. As he waits for them to stop fizzing, Édouard rummages unenthusiastically through the pile of floral gifts he's received. The bouquets will be distributed among the women on staff. What else could he do with them? The stuffed animals will be given to their kids. He'll only keep the notes, the letters that sometimes reek of perfume, the cards in which people invariably talk to him as if he were already their friend, because they feel like they already know him, from hearing his sketches and iconic lines over and over again. Édouard is everybody's best friend, but he has no friends at all. He would laugh about it if it didn't bring sobs up to the back of his throat. Everyone admires, adores, and idolizes him, the comedian tortured by loneliness. Sometimes he hates his famous face, detests his reflection in the mirror—whether perfect or washed out. He wishes that for one day, for just one single day, he could be anonymous, somebody normal who could walk down the street without being stared at, pointed at, and photographed like the Eiffel Tower. How many times a day is he stopped on the street by a fan who asks him to "say something funny," as if he were a vulgar joke machine, a robot only good for delivering hilarious one-liners. And after all, is he really anything more?

Hervé would say that's the price of success. That you pay for what you've done and deserve what you get. The price of survival seems entirely too high to Édouard sometimes.

It's 10:50 p.m. He's managed to wrangle five minutes of rest. Three energetic knocks on the door pull Édouard out of his thoughts.

10

Three energetic knocks on the door pull Édouard out of his thoughts. He turns off the television, and the panting Tour de France cyclists he has been disinterestedly watching disappear as the screen goes black.

He's home alone. His father is at work, and his mother is running errands with Jonathan. Édouard is taking advantage of the situation to laze around most of the day.

When he warily opens the door, he finds himself face-to-face with a shy young girl shuffling her weight from one foot to the other.

"Hello. I'm here about the ad . . . The posting you put up in the lobby. I thought maybe you'd found my scarf?"

She has an Italian accent, and her voice has a husky tone to it that instantly stirs something in Édouard's stomach.

"What makes you think I have a scarf here?"

"I found something. If you've lost something, come get it in apartment 207," she recites uncertainly from the flyer as her dark-brown curls rebel against a red-and-white polka-dot headband.

"Hmm, so let's say what I found is in fact a scarf. How do I know it's yours?" replies Édouard, thrilled to watch her cheeks flush and know his little game is making her uncomfortable.

"It's dark blue, with little mirrors around the edges . . . I live on the seventh floor," she nearly pleads.

Édouard is merciless. She's such easy prey—he can't let her go now.

"But maybe somebody else in the building has the same scarf too . . . It's entirely possible! And boy would I be embarrassed if that other person came and knocked on my door and I had to tell her I didn't have her scarf anymore, that I had been tricked by an imposter . . ."

The girl takes a step back. She's ready to run away from this weirdo.

"My scarf should smell like my perfume. I always wear the same one . . ."

Leaning against the doorframe, Édouard confidently crosses his arms across his chest.

"Really? Well, why didn't you say so before?"

He quickly dives toward the nape of her neck and takes a deep breath.

"Vanilla, right?"

She nods, unconsciously bringing her hand to her throat to protect herself from any future intrusions.

"I'm sorry, but now that I have all the information, I can tell you that I don't have your scarf. I've never seen it, in fact. Just another unsolved mystery, I guess!"

While Édouard is clearly pleased with his little show, the girl at the door is unimpressed. Her face conveys only disappointment.

"But what did you find, then? Another scarf?"

"No, not at all. I found a Pastis 51 baseball cap in front of the door to the dumpsters," he states, eyebrow cocked. "But I didn't want to dash your hopes right away, so I dragged out the conversation."

His neighbor shakes her head, and her dark curls move gracefully around her shoulders.

"Why didn't you just post that you found a hat? That would have been much simpler!"

Édouard sighs, as if frustrated to have to explain something so obvious. He leans in and whispers in a confidential tone, "If I had written that, anyone could have come knocking, pretending they had lost their hat. Can you imagine the long lines on the landing? People fighting, claiming it was theirs. No, thank you! I don't want to create unrest here. And Madame Rita wouldn't have liked it either."

The girl finally smiles shyly, and Édouard notices a little red lipstick mark on one of her incisors. He could tell her it's there, but he suddenly finds the detail so endearing that he keeps his mouth shut. Feeling much less bold, he takes his bravado down a notch and invites her in for a cup of coffee.

He's so sure she'll refuse given the way he's behaved that he doesn't budge when she agrees, still smiling. He finally moves aside to let her in and realizes his hands are clammy. He points vaguely toward the couch in the living room, then hurries to the kitchen to make two cups of coffee using Lucien's silver Moka pot.

"Milk or sugar?" he asks, peeking his head into the living room.

"Do you have any hot chocolate I could add?"

Édouard briefly considers how strange it is to want to mix hot chocolate and coffee, then decides maybe it's an Italian tradition he's never heard of before.

As he holds out her steaming beverage, he decides to get the conversation back on track.

"I'm Édouard."

"I know," she says, blowing on her blend of coffee and hot chocolate. "I'm Magda. I moved into the building last year. I see your little brother slaloming out front a lot."

Édouard often takes Jonathan out into the street, then sets up little red cones in a kind of obstacle course. The preteen obviously doesn't have a skateboard, but he can still give other boys his age a run for their money with his wheelchair.

The sky outside suddenly turns gray, and Édouard flicks on the floor lamp next to the turntable to keep the darkness from invading the living room. The first flashes of lightning cleave through the black clouds, then the rain starts pattering against the windows. Thunder breaks the silence that has taken over the room, where Édouard is vainly trying to come up with a joke for this girl who, paradoxically, intimidates him. Magda stands up and heads over to the French doors, where the raindrops pound violently against the glass. She's the first to speak.

"This is one of my favorite things in life," she murmurs, still looking out at the sky.

"Drinking coffee at a neighbor's?" asks Édouard, perplexed.

She shrugs.

"No, not that. Being inside when it suddenly starts pouring rain. It makes you feel like the luckiest person in the world, don't you think?"

"Kind of like when you're outside and it's a beautiful day, huh?"

Magda spins around to glare at Édouard, who is slouching on the couch.

"You know, you don't have to keep trying so hard to make me laugh. We could just . . . talk."

Later, when Édouard closes the door behind the young woman, he remembers her calm, raspy voice that makes him want to curl up under a blanket and listen to her talk about anything at all. He remembers her strange earrings—miniature Laughing Cow cheese triangles made of modeling clay that moved wildly at her slightest movement—which he had found fun if not incredibly tasteful. He remembers her pearly white eye shadow because there was more on her left eyelid than on the right. He remembers her lipstick, of course, and the very slight gap between her front teeth, the three moles perfectly aligned on her neck, and her sweet, heady perfume. He can't say what color her eyes were or if she was thin or fat, or what she was wearing. He just has fragments of Magda, despite the fact that when she was in his living room, he had no idea he was recording all these little details. But after she leaves, whenever he thinks of her while lying on his top bunk, his hands crossed under his head, all these little puzzle pieces instantly pop into his mind.

That night, after picking Jonathan up from school in their mother's Passat, Édouard takes his little brother to try out a long course he's made with dozens of carefully arranged traffic cones and a kind of trampoline he built with pallet wood their father brought back from the refinery. Despite the natural confidence he has at eighteen, he can't help but glance furtively up at the seventh-floor windows, imagining Magda watching them from her window, even hoping for it.

"Are you sure I can do it? I don't want to fall flat on my face or destroy my chair . . . ," Jonathan asks as he worriedly studies the elaborate course his big brother has laid out.

With a nod, Édouard reassures his younger brother, who quickly reaches top speed as he heads for the improvised trampoline. He lands perfectly and even adds a controlled sideways skid for show.

"Great job, buddy!" encourages the older boy. "See, I told you there was nothing to worry about! I knew you'd do great!"

11

"Great job, buddy! See, I told you there was nothing to worry about! I knew you'd do great!" The door to the dressing room opens and a radiant Jonathan wheels in, glowing with pride. Édouard moves aside to let his brother into his tiny dressing room.

"Can you believe they are still applauding for you out there? It's just crazy!" he exclaims as his older brother gulps down his fizzy energy drink.

Édouard bends over to hug his brother, then sits down on the only chair in the room.

"Another tour down . . ."

"That was quite a finale! I mean, when you told me about reserving the Stade de France last year, I thought maybe you'd lost touch with reality, but man, what a night!"

Édouard can't help but find Jonathan's generous enthusiasm endearing, even though his brother's unfailing support since the beginning of his career has never seemed like something he deserved, even though sometimes Édouard would rather Jonathan turn away from him once and for all, for any reason, valid or not.

"You shouldn't have come from Strasbourg. It's so far. I feel bad . . ."

"That's ridiculous! I hope you're kidding. No way I'd have missed your big night, not for anything in the world! I want to be able to say, 'I was there!' a few years from now when people talk about the day Édouard Bresson became a legend!"

"You always exaggerate," the comedian replies with a smile, suddenly excited at the thought of just how right his brother is.

"I think you're the one who doesn't get what's going on around you, how much people love and admire you! Hundreds of them are out there hoping just to shake your hand or glimpse a smile . . . You draw bigger crowds than the pope!"

Uncomfortable, as usual, with so much praise, Édouard changes the subject.

"How's Céline? And the girls? They didn't come with you?"

"No, Céline thought it was too far, and you know that the kids missing half a day of school is out of the question for her! The girls are good. We just celebrated Louisa's eighth birthday last week. That reminds me, she made a drawing to thank you for the present you sent."

Édouard takes the little envelope his brother holds out and opens it to find a drawing done in different colored markers of—he assumed—the four members of the family around a huge layered birthday cake. In the bottom right-hand corner, the little girl had carefully inscribed, *Thank you, Uncle Ed. Sincerely, Louisa*, each letter in a different color. Already eight years old. Which means he hasn't been to visit his brother in over three years. He's hardly noticed the time passing and suddenly wonders if the huge Duplo castle he sent is suitable for her age.

"Did she like my present? I don't know what she likes to play with these days," Édouard says apologetically.

"Don't worry, it was perfect. You have to come see us this summer. Or before, if you can find the time in your busy schedule."

Édouard nods and smiles weakly.

"Of course, yes, that's a great idea. I could come for a weekend. I would love to see the girls. They must have changed so much."

Jonathan eagerly pulls out his wallet to show his brother school photos of Louisa and Marion. On the glossy paper, the two little girls smile mischievously. Édouard runs his thumb over their radiant faces. He barely recognizes his brother's children, their faces thinned out, hair long, so grown up. They look just like their mother, with the same mouth and the same light-brown eyes.

"And Céline?"

"She's doing really well. She's been thinking about changing jobs for a while now. We'd like to open a bed and breakfast, leave our jobs to work together."

"That sounds nice," Édouard agrees.

"We've already found a property to renovate, with a few barns we could also turn into rooms. We just have to go for it!"

Édouard is impressed that Jonathan and Céline are still so crazy in love with each other after fifteen years of marriage, enough to want to be together 24/7. Impressed that they still have shared projects and dreams, that everyday life hasn't dulled their feelings for each other.

Deep down, Édouard has always felt that it was a miracle his brother met Céline. At the time, he seriously wondered if the young woman was sincere. He was so afraid that she would run off once she realized sharing her life with a paraplegic wouldn't be easy. But Céline stayed, and found a way to make every task seem simple and easily surmountable. One time, when Édouard was alone with her, he couldn't stop himself from saying that he hoped she wasn't planning on breaking his brother's heart, because Jonathan didn't need to get over heartbreak in addition to all the rest. Céline frowned, suddenly worried, and asked, "What's all the rest?" And Édouard finally understood from the perplexed expression on her face that she really didn't know what he was talking about, as if Jonathan's wheelchair was invisible to her. He realized Jonathan was incredibly lucky to have met a girl like that, even though it still seemed totally ridiculous to talk about his brother being lucky at all.

"So, you're happy, then?"

Édouard looks deep into his brother's eyes, worried his question was too direct, too indiscreet. *Are we allowed to ask people flat out where they are on the happiness scale?*

Jonathan laughs as he slides his wallet back inside his sport coat.

"Of course we're happy!"

Édouard nods in relief. He doubts things can really be so simple, but at least his brother isn't unhappy. His little life as an accountant with a wife and two kids is simple, even terrifyingly monotonous, but despite it all, he seems satisfied with it, or at least that's what he says. Édouard knows that with two working legs his brother probably would have had a radically different life. He would have been able to dream bigger, even if he couldn't make all his wishes come true. If only Édouard hadn't ruined everything. Maybe his brother doesn't feel like anything's missing because he hardly remembers the accident or the few years of his childhood when he could walk and run. Jonathan is like a child who was born blind, who has no idea how important colors and shapes can be. He can't imagine how it feels to run with the wind whipping at his face. And the worst part is that he supposedly doesn't even miss it.

"I have to go sign a few autographs, and then I'm taking the team out for dinner. Want to come?"

Jonathan shakes his head.

"Thanks, but I wouldn't feel comfortable. You know me . . . I'm just glad I got a few minutes alone with you—there are people who would kill for that!"

"Hey, they can go without me. They don't really need me, you know," answers Édouard.

"Are you kidding? You've just finished a tour you've been on since September. Your team has traveled all over France, Belgium, and Switzerland with you! You at least owe them this last night out! I'm staying with Céline's parents anyway, so I don't want to get back too late."

"OK, I won't push you, then . . . While I'm thinking of it, could I give you a package for Arthur?"

Édouard gets up to rummage through the backpack he takes with him everywhere, and pulls out a little cardboard box with Arthur's name scrawled across the top in black marker.

"Of course, but it's been years since your son's been to see us in Strasbourg, you know. Like father, like son, I guess," replies Jonathan, with a wink.

"I think he has plans to visit you soon."

"OK, but why don't you give it to him yourself? You haven't had another falling-out, have you?"

"No, no. It's just that I'm working on a surprise for him, like when he was little," explains Édouard.

"No problem, you don't have to explain yourself. I hope there's nothing that can go bad in there, though!"

Jonathan puts the box into a little bag on the back of his wheelchair, eager to see what his brother has planned to surprise his son this time.

Two more knocks on the door, and Hervé's head appears.

"We're waiting on you, Édouard!"

"Just one minute."

Jonathan rolls backward, preparing to leave. Édouard spontaneously places his hand on his brother's forearm for a moment.

"You know I'm sorry, right?"

Jonathan looks confused.

"Sorry for what?"

"For everything . . ."

"Knock it off! I can hear the sappy music playing already! I'm counting on you to come visit us in Alsace this summer, OK?"

Édouard nods, and his brother waves goodbye as he pushes through the doorway.

"Wait!"

The comedian jumps up, grabs a pale-pink potted orchid from the table covered in gifts, and hands it to Jonathan.

"Here, give this to Céline from me. There's not a woman in the world who doesn't like flowers."

12

"There's not a woman in the world who doesn't like flowers."

The green-apron-clad employee smiles at Édouard, who is trying to decide between a bouquet of roses and an aloe vera plant. Magda recently read—in one of those magazines containing more fashion spreads and perfume ads than real articles—that certain plants can improve air quality by absorbing potentially harmful particles. Édouard took the information at face value and let his wife fill their one-bedroom apartment in Le Havre with all sorts of greenery. It still feels strange to say "my wife," but he guesses he'll get used to it soon enough—after all, they've only been married a few months, since December 26, 1992. Magda chose the date. *You see, that way our families will only have to travel once, for Christmas and our wedding.* They'd been together for over five years, and it was clearly time to make their relationship official, as Monique was always telling them. They chose to have a small, intimate ceremony at the Gonfreville-l'Orcher town hall, then at the church in Harfleur. A few months later, when they announced to their parents that they were expecting their first bundle of joy, everybody assumed that's why they had gotten married, despite the fact that the baby was conceived on New Year's Eve, as Édouard always clarified, trying to avoid people's teasing: *Oh, now I see why you were in such a rush to tie the knot, with a bun in the oven* . . .

"Or even an orchid. They require a little TLC, but they're exquisite flowers! Here, I have mottled pale-pink ones. I'm sure your wife would love them."

Édouard pouts as he continues to pace the lush shop. He doesn't answer the florist, whose patience with her indecisive customer is wearing thin.

"I'll take the aloe vera."

"Whatever you think best," replies the woman from behind the counter, quickly wrapping the plant and affixing a ribbon to the package.

"They say it absorbs toxins in the air."

"If you say so . . ."

Édouard quickens his pace, in a hurry to get back to Magda at the maternity ward. He's only been away for a few hours to take a shower, grab some things for the next few days, and buy some basics they were missing, like preemie onesies and pajamas. Arthur made his way into the world a month and a half early, when nobody was expecting him. Édouard still hasn't put the wooden crib together—the box is under their bed. The doctors have been reassuring so far: despite Magda's anxiety, the delivery went well. She probably wouldn't recount the twelve hours of labor with a smile on her face, but the end result was a tiny baby full of life despite the slight blue tint to his skin. He instantly squealed with all the force his little lungs could muster to let them know they were now a family of three.

Édouard acted like none of it scared him, like he was ready to protect them both from anything and everything, but the truth is that he's not feeling quite so confident this morning. He can't help but wonder if he—the eternal adolescent who spends his time telling immature

jokes to anyone who will listen—is really ready for it all. He read in
Magda's eyes, as she doubled over with the pain of a contraction, that
she believed in him, trusted him, and that gave him the strength he
needed to be reassuring for her. *It's all going to be OK. You're doing great,
honey, just a little longer.*

When he reaches the maternity ward, he gets lost in the maze of
identical pastel-pink hallways. During his unsuccessful hunt for the
wing Magda is in, he comes across the neonatal unit, and his legs immediately slow. Without thinking, he places the suitcase and aloe vera
plant on the floor in the hallway and walks into the room to see his son.

His son.

For months, he wondered how he would feel when the baby finally
arrived, concerned he'd feel nothing except indifference for the tiny
human he would be responsible for. He never told Magda about it,
afraid that she would worry, or worse, that she would be horrified. *He's
your son. How can you imagine such things?*

After the birth, the midwives and nurses quickly took Arthur to be
weighed and intubated. They massaged him, warmed him up, and gave
him a thorough examination before putting him in a nice warm incubator. "He'll have to be in there for a while, but don't worry, he's healthy.
Your little boy is a fighter," affirmed one of the midwives as she finished
stitching up the young mother. Édouard and Magda smiled weakly and
held tightly to each other's hands. Then he left to go get clothes for his
wife and son, having only briefly seen Arthur. He was almost relieved
to leave him there in expert hands, since his were still trembling from
the fear that it would all go wrong.

Now, as he nears the plastic bassinet, he finds the monitors that
beep and blink, the tubes and sensors all over the baby, intimidating.
The wiry arms and legs as small as one of Édouard's fingers are startling,
as are the tiny, perfectly formed mouth, eyes rimmed with incredibly
long lashes, and the fragile chest gently rising and falling. *A miniature
baby,* he thinks as his throat tightens.

"You can touch him through the incubator, if you like," offers a nurse who comes to check on the monitors in the room.

Édouard nods and, after thoroughly washing his hands and forearms, settles in across from the baby, who is calmly moving his little limbs. Édouard brings his hand closer and delicately strokes his son's cheek with his index finger. He runs it over the baby's shoulder and down his arm, plays with his tiny fingers, which immediately grasp his thumb with unexpected strength. The baby keeps a ferocious grip on Édouard, who stays still, happy to contemplate the miniature fingernails, each smaller than a piece of confetti. He finally realizes how absurd his fears were. When the newborn's fingers hold on to him like a life raft, he feels the dam within him break, sending a torrent of love crashing over him.

When he finds his way back to Magda, Édouard, still shaky, hands her the aloe plant without a word, and his wife smiles tenderly—she knows exactly what her husband is feeling.

"So you went to see him too?"

Édouard sits on the side of the bed and quietly nods, then burrows his face in her curls, enjoying the comforting scent of vanilla.

"See, there was nothing to be afraid of," she adds as she hugs him close, and it occurs to Édouard that no one else has ever understood how he was feeling without a single word crossing his lips.

Two days later, when he calls Valéry Lestienne, his boss at the real estate agency where he's been working for the past five years, Édouard gets the lecture he was expecting.

"It's been over three days, you know! How am I supposed to handle everything by myself? I'm not omnipresent! I can't be at the office,

Amélie Antoine

handle presale agreements, and take people to visit apartments all at the same time!"

"I know, but Arthur arrived earlier than expected, and Magda needs me at the hospital. I just need until the end of the week . . ."

"Out of the question! Plenty of people with much better qualifications are taking care of your wife and kid at the hospital. So you get your ass back here. There are a dozen appointments with your name on them."

Édouard hangs up and represses the violent urge to throw the phone across the kitchen. Sometimes he wonders why he lets his boss talk to him like that, then remembers that, unfortunately, his salary doesn't fall from the sky.

Édouard's father was always so sure his son would come work at the refinery; it was simply a given. So when, at just seventeen, Édouard told him categorically that there was absolutely no way he'd ever set foot inside the plant, Lucien almost spit out the Beaujolais nouveau he was greedily sipping.

"Well, how about that—my son has delusions of grandeur. Can you even hear yourself? You're too good to work at the plant, huh?"

"I just want to do something else. That's all."

"Oh really? Like what? Do share."

"I haven't decided yet."

"Obviously. You'll end up like your father; you can count on it. And there are worse things in life, believe me . . ."

With a sour look on his face, Édouard went to his room and slammed the door, doing his best to upset Lucien and his delicate ears even more. Both father and son considered the subject closed.

After high school, Édouard decided to do a two-year degree program to become a real estate agent; he wanted to gain financial independence and leave his family's apartment, where bad memories had devoured the few moments of happiness they'd known—moments no one was sure had ever really happened anymore. Though he'd toyed with the idea of doing something totally different plenty of times, particularly while watching hilarious sketches during stand-up shows on TV, he had never seriously considered it. Since childhood he had been convinced that dreams always end up trampled and broken. Lucien was satisfied with his son's reasonable choice. *What's important is that you earn a living doing a real job.*

As soon as he was able—in other words, as soon as Valéry Lestienne finally hired him after exploiting him for two years as an apprentice—Édouard began looking for an apartment to rent in Le Havre, near the agency. Magda was finishing up a degree in art history, hoping to become a guide at the André Malraux Museum of Modern Art, since she had volunteered there every summer since high school. Édouard was eager to move in with her and at long last start a new life by her side.

He was nineteen years old, but when he announced that he was leaving the nest—hardly a nurturing environment—everyone was shocked. Monique had wiped away a few inopportune tears with a dish towel, and Lucien, reeking of alcohol, had yelled, "Good luck!" Jonathan had kept quiet, even as he watched his brother pack his things.

When Édouard had finished piling his clothes into a duffle bag, his little brother murmured, almost inaudibly, "So you're abandoning me?" Édouard, who knew that leaving quickly would make it as painless as possible—like ripping off a Band-Aid in one go—hesitated for a fraction of a second, then decided to pretend he hadn't heard Jonathan, despite the stabbing pain he felt in his heart.

The short, pleading sentence ricocheted off the inner walls of his skull, a nagging echo. *So you're abandoning me? So you're abandoning me? So you're abandoning me?* And Édouard immediately extrapolated: *So you crippled my legs and now you're abandoning me? I can't even stand because of you, and now you're abandoning me?*

Édouard knew those four little words would remain burned into his memory forever, just like that Sunday so many autumns ago when the floor had collapsed, and Jonathan had disappeared in a cloud of dust.

It had taken all his strength to leave. He'd envisioned Magda's smiling face, focusing on it like a beacon in the night in order to stand up with his bag over his shoulder and look enthusiastically at his brother. He had to hide all his sadness and regrets, to casually begin his goodbyes.

"Well, I guess I'm outta here! As soon as we're settled, I'll bring you over to see the apartment. It's tiny, but I can't afford anything else."

Jonathan forced a smile.

"And you know, I'll come by every weekend. It's not even a fifteen-minute drive!"

"Don't worry about me. I'm all grown up. And now I'll have tons of space without all of your crap!"

Édouard held his hand out for his brother to shake—they were much too old to hug—then hurried out of the apartment where he had grown up. Once he reached the darkness of the landing, he bit his fist, painfully remembering all the times he and his brother had found themselves out there in the pitch black, thrown out of their home by a father who couldn't stand the sound of a single laugh or shout.

Now, on a stiflingly hot Tuesday that has the entire city in a daze, Édouard cannot be with his wife and son at the hospital. Instead, he takes potential renters to visit apartments all day long. As usual, he acts like a clown for clients, pointing out dubious advantages of dilapidated properties. *What do you mean the walls are moldy? Not at all! It's obviously patterned wallpaper. Very in vogue, the hot new thing in Paris, you know.* They laugh, as usual. Édouard turns every visit into an act. It's the only thing he likes about his job: making clients laugh even when he doesn't manage to sell them on a place. *And the best part of the whole place, ladies and gentlemen: the owners are willing to leave you this incredible toilet seat made of authentic camel hair! Your bottoms will thank you.* The potential renters double over with laughter. Édouard could snap his fingers at the exact moment they'll start to crack up—people are incredibly predictable.

"You're a funny guy. You should be a comedian!" offers the man as he leaves the apartment he won't be renting.

"You know, you're not the first person to tell me that. I might just start believing it," Édouard replies with a smile as he locks the door behind them.

Later that night, he finally gets to see Magda, who's starting to get some color back in her cheeks. As he reverently observes Arthur's fingers grasping his pointer and refusing to let go, Édouard thinks about what his last client of the day said. It's true that it's easy for him to make people laugh. He's loved acting like a clown ever since his brother lit up at his jokes when they were younger. It's true that everyone says he has a gift for it—except his father, of course. Magda even used the word *talent* once when she was talking to her friends about him. Maybe they're right, maybe they see something in him that he's not even conscious of?

When he started work at the real estate agency, Édouard had bought a Moleskine notebook in a stationery shop downtown on his first day, to take notes during visits and jot down clients' information, but he's never written anything professional in it at all. The pages of the notebook are instead covered in Édouard's chicken scratch; they're filled with jokes, funny anecdotes to share with his brother and Magda, with whoever will listen. He puts every little idea down on paper, without knowing why he feels compelled to save it all.

When he watches the faces of people on TV who have decided to turn their talent into a career, who must have risked their boring everyday lives and reliable salaries for an opportunity to follow their passion, Édouard always feels a little jealous. Could he have a place onstage, doing sketches for thousands of people? Does he have the guts?

Arthur opens his eyes and looks deep into his father's. The moment seems to last a lifetime, as if the baby knows something Édouard doesn't. Strangely, Lucien Bresson's face pops up in the young man's head. His father, who has always represented everything negative to Édouard. The absurd life of shift work, a narrow idea of happiness comprising the neighborhood bar and union buddies. When Édouard thinks of his father, it makes him want to beg the powers that be to ensure Arthur never feels that way about him. He wants to inspire pride in him— what's the point of having children if they don't admire and respect you? Will he be worthy of his son if he sells apartments for the rest of his life? Will it be enough?

13

Will it be enough? Will less than fifteen minutes be enough time to sign autographs, to make sure no one leaves disappointed? His die-hard fans are still waiting outside—they know exactly which exit Édouard will use as he tries to slip out of the Stade de France. The comic gets goose bumps as he sees about a hundred people still lingering behind the security barricades.

Hervé grabs him by the shoulder before he can walk through the heavy metal door. "Not so fast! The journalist from TF1 wants to do a quick interview before the thrill wears off, while you're still all wound up!"

Édouard sighs, conscious that he's acting like a spoiled child.

"I thought they had everything they needed."

"Listen, when TF1 wants to put you in the spotlight, you suck it up! How many stand-up comedians do you think they've featured live during Friday night prime time? How many of them do you think have benefited from a two-hour behind-the-scenes special? Do you even realize how many people you're going to reach when they air the special tomorrow, during Saturday night prime time?"

"OK, fine," mutters Édouard as Hervé drags him back to the dressing room, where a makeup artist dabs at his forehead with a sponge covered in flesh-colored powder.

"It's mattifying," she explains hurriedly.

Staring off into space, Édouard suddenly thinks of his mother, sees her standing in front of the speckled mirror in the bathroom every morning, busy applying talcum powder to her nose and cheekbones. He only realized much later, when he began having his makeup done before a show or television interview, that she couldn't afford to buy real foundation.

"We had more than ten million viewers tonight! The numbers just came in," Hervé continues, unstoppable.

"That's great."

"'Great?' You've got to be kidding me! Ten million people on their couches watching your show live! No one has ever gotten numbers like that before! I don't think you realize how monumental this is!"

"Good thing I pay you to realize it for me, then, huh?"

Hervé closes his eyes and takes a deep breath. Édouard knows his manager too well—pushing him any further would not be a good idea. He puts his hand on the shoulder of the man who's always believed in him.

"I'm kidding, Hervé. It's just the pressure. I'll feel better tomorrow. Of course I realize how amazing this whole evening has been. Thank you."

His manager smiles slightly, then rushes out of the room to give his final instructions to the reporter waiting just a few yards away with a muscly cameraman.

When interviewed, Édouard often prefers to answer questions as one of his characters—particularly when he doesn't like the reporter sitting across from him. He couldn't care less if the critics think he's dodging questions. Tonight, as he greets the young woman with her auburn hair in an artfully mussed bun ready to roll out her list of ready-made questions, Édouard decides to be Zita. After all, his fans begged for her earlier by yelling and stomping, so why not give them what they want again? Especially since the reporter's face is repulsive to him, as if disdain were permanently etched on her features.

The comedian strikes an exaggeratedly feminine pose and twirls a strand of hair around his index finger, as Zita loves to do between chores, as he answers the first couple of questions. He can see the reporter is disconcerted, and that behind the camera Hervé is emphatically and repeatedly mouthing no, but he's used to doing what he likes rather than what people expect.

"I am sho pleashed that sho many peoplesh were able to watch me on the televishion tonight, but I musht shay I am un poco worried, because during the two-hour show they could have been doing houshwork—cleaning their windows, polishing their, how do you shay again, yes, their shilver."

Édouard puts on a serious face, despite the reporter's tangible irritation.

"Thank you, but I would really like for you to reveal more of yourself, Édouard. You've always cultivated a certain mystery, but our viewers would love to know more about who you really are—your family, your friends, your daily life. For example, was your son at the Stade de France tonight? He must be very proud of the amazing feat you pulled off this evening."

As she finishes the sentence, Édouard clams up, though his face remains impassive and he's still wearing Zita's sparkling smile. During his more-than-twenty-year career, he has almost never spoken a single word about his private life, has always preferred to let the media make up his life, imagine his story, put together his daily comings and goings from tiny clues they manage to scrounge up. It troubles him that people want to know things about him that have nothing to do with his onstage persona. So he uses his colorful characters to protect himself.

They allow him to be daring—a little too daring, as Jean-Michel would sigh. And tonight will not be any different.

The young woman holds out the microphone so intently that it almost seems like she expects Édouard to swallow it whole. Is Arthur proud of him? How could he even answer that? The seat he'd reserved for his son in the front row had sat empty, and Édouard had obstinately refused to look at the glaring hole during the show. His son hadn't even made the effort to give the free ticket to a friend, or to sell it for a profit. He hadn't called to tell his father if he would be coming or not. There had only been silence. The new norm between them for almost a year now.

The microphone bobs impatiently under his mustache, and Édouard slips back into character.

"Yesh, my shon Rodrigo ish very proud of me, even though he'd rather hish mother shpent lesh time on TV and more time cleaning the kitchen. He's shuch a lazy boy!"

The reporter smiles tensely, and the looks they exchange show the power struggle they're engaged in.

"I think we can stop here. I've got everything I need. I don't want to bother you any longer," says the woman, regretfully giving in. She signals to the cameraman that the interview is over.

"It was a pleasure," replies Édouard, lightness returning to his voice. "I'm glad to have met you."

Vanquished, she shakes his hand, and the comedian heads toward the exit where his fans must be growing impatient.

He signs tons of autographs on posters, notebooks, and T-shirts. People take pictures with him, cameras flashing in bursts, and he does his best to smile big every time. He says, "Thank you, thank you, thank you," repeating himself tirelessly. "You're the reason I'm here today, you made all of this possible, you know."

Then, in the middle of the dense crowd standing along the metal barricades, which are beginning to tilt dangerously, he sees Laurence. He gives her a discreet nod toward the taxi with the tinted windows waiting to take him to the restaurant, letting her know to meet him at the vehicle.

As she approaches the taxi where he's now standing, Édouard signals to the attentive security guard that it's OK.

"Hi, Laurence. I hoped you would be here tonight."

He gives her a quick hug, then steps back to look at her face. The last time he saw her was a little less than a year ago, during his last tour of France's major cities.

She came to the show in Toulouse, thrilled to see Édouard in the city where she's spent her whole life. Tonight he can't help but notice—like he does every time—that she's aged a little. The vertical lines between her eyebrows are deeper, her complexion less rosy, the oval outline of her face less defined than a few months ago. Édouard and Laurence are the same age, and every time he sees her it sets him thinking about the passage of time and his own aging, like looking at a reflection in a mirror.

Laurence is one of his first fans. She saw one of his very first shows at Le Point Virgule in 1995 during a vacation in Paris visiting a childhood friend. She came up to him afterward, filled with contagious enthusiasm. "I love your sense of humor. You're going to go far." And she's kept tabs on his career ever since, buying a ticket for at least one show every tour—two if she can afford it. After a few years, Édouard started to grow fond of her and offered to give her free seats, troubled that she had to spend more and more to see his shows. But she always refused, insisting on paying for her own tickets. Édouard has always been flattered by her admiration and faith in him, offered without any expectations.

"So what's next? A show on Mars?" Laurence asks kindly.

Over the years, through short conversations stolen at the back exits of his venues, Édouard has gotten to know her. She once came to a show very pregnant—*Twins, can you imagine? Goodbye sleep!* He has watched the girls grow up in photos, touched that Laurence can so easily share her private life with him, how she confides in him as if she's always known him, as if it were normal to tell him all about her world. As if he were a part of her *family* almost. Before long, he found himself looking for her in the rows of audience members, waiting for her, hoping to see her, like an old friend you can always count on. When the media had a field day with his divorce, Laurence didn't mention it to Édouard, choosing to respect his sense of privacy. She simply offered an encouraging "Good luck," accompanied by a more meaningful look than usual, and he understood what she meant. He was grateful she didn't stomp all over his new misfortune, like everyone else had. And yet Laurence had revealed to him just a few months earlier that her husband had left her: "One spring night he'd had enough of the twins fighting all the time, so he packed his bag and left, without warning, without so much as a goodbye, leaving me nothing but his dirty socks all over the house." But when it was Édouard's turn, she simply said, "Good luck," and that was enough.

They talk for ten minutes as Édouard deliberately ignores his impatient manager, waiting inside the taxi. Before he leaves, he whispers something into her ear with an enigmatic look on his face. She nods, and he pulls a brown envelope out of his black jean jacket and carefully hands it over. Just as she grabs it, Hervé opens the back window of the taxi and leans out, clearly annoyed.

"Whenever you're ready . . . Everyone else is already at the restaurant!"

The comic hugs his most loyal admirer again, discreetly whispering, "Thank you," then finally opens the door to the gray sedan and slides in next to his unhappy manager, apparently on the verge of starvation.

"We're beyond late, as usual . . ."

14

"We're beyond late, as usual . . ."

Djamila Meddour's impeccably manicured fingernails drum the armrest of her padded seat. She glances at her watch, irritated that the audition hasn't started yet.

Behind the curtain, Édouard is biting his nails, terrified despite Magda's excited exclamations of "You'll do great!" The young couple has left Arthur with Monique for the first time ever to make the round-trip to Paris, to the legendary Le Point Virgule, where many of the most famous comics got their start.

For this group audition, he's scheduled to go first and wonders if that's good or bad. Probably would have been better to go last so they'd remember him. He knows his sketch by heart, has painstakingly curated every last word, and has practiced dozens of times in front of the mirror and for Jonathan, his test subject, who yells, "Keep!" or sighs and says, "That's crap. Drop it!" confident in his assessment.

For over a year now, Édouard has been touring the few theater-cafés in Haute-Normandie that accept amateurs, testing out sketches approved first by Jonathan, then Magda, his heart overflowing with joy when audiences burst into laughter and applause. But often enough, he wants to give up, discouragement suddenly washing over him. *I can't do this. No one even smiled tonight.* There are times when all he wants to do is walk off the stage in the middle of his set and go hide in his car and forget about the impassive spectators and their cold glances, forget about them continuing their conversations while he desperately tries to attract their attention with his jokes. His self-confidence depends entirely on the sparse audience's reactions, despite the unfailing support of his wife and brother, who constantly remind him that he has an undeniable gift for making any situation hilarious.

"You're up," says an employee of Le Point Virgule. "Don't keep her waiting."

Édouard has less than ten minutes to win over the woman in front of him and make his mark. Ten minutes that could decide the rest of his life, even though Magda keeps telling him that even if he doesn't make the cut, it won't be the end of the world, that there's no monopoly on humor.

He walks onstage, smiles shyly to his audience of one sitting impatiently in the front row. So this is her, the artistic director who could launch his career.

Édouard shuffles from one foot to the other, wrings his hands, bites his lower lip. Djamila Meddour looks like she might lose her temper—he knows she's thinking he's just another clown who won't be able to get a word out, too overwhelmed by the stress of the audition. *What a waste of time!* She raises her eyebrows at the frightened Édouard, and her eyes seem to silently scream, *What are you waiting for? Do you think you're the only one auditioning?*

The young guy gives her a ridiculously apologetic look. He has yet to open his mouth. He looks up, as if trying to remember his lines, then sighs heavily.

This little number lasts nearly five minutes—half the time Édouard has to convince the woman to give him a chance. Djamila isn't sure exactly when her annoyance turns into amusement, doesn't know when she realizes that the young man standing before her isn't actually terrified, that he's putting on a show. Something shifts imperceptibly in the air between them, and she suddenly finds herself laughing at Édouard's caricatured anxiety.

Then he speaks. Just one sentence.

"N-n-n-no one has ever found me funny, but I'm going to prove them wrong in five minutes."

Ballsy. Djamila wonders what has made this kid so presumptuous. She barely notices Édouard's voluntary stuttering, and signals him to continue.

"I don't know if you're anything like me, but whenever I go grocery shopping, I somehow always manage to pick the line that's not moving. Every. Single. Time. Then I turn to tell the person who's just gotten in line behind me to get out of Dodge. Go, flee now or you'll still be waiting here in half an hour!"

Édouard is transformed. He's so intense it's like he's *living* his routine. He plays his character, tired of waiting, as well as the elderly woman who shamelessly cuts in front of him. "Um, she's literally stepping on my feet, climbing over me as if I weren't here!" He plays the jaded cashier with her slow, monotone voice: "Sorry, I'm going on break. You'll have to wait until my coworker finishes her cigarette." In just a few minutes, he displays an entire gallery of remarkably authentic characters—and it's all spot-on. The most hysterical situations seem to be straight out of everyday life, situations that everyone instantly recognizes and identifies with.

The contrast between this cast of characters and the excessively introverted guy from the beginning is so pronounced that Djamila wonders if he might actually suffer from schizophrenia. It seems like the most plausible explanation for his ability to transform so quickly and convincingly.

When Édouard stops talking and seems once again to be alone onstage, the feared artistic director studies him carefully. The young man takes a deep breath and anxiously awaits the verdict.

The silence lengthens and thickens around them.

Finally, Djamila uncrosses her legs and sits up straight in her seat. "Not bad. Would you be up for open stage night on Sundays?"

Édouard nods, stunned.

"We'll see if you can make the audience laugh."

"Th-thank you. I won't let you down."

Djamila brushes her ebony bangs out of her eyes and lets out a mocking laugh. "I'm not the one you have to worry about disappointing."

She waves him off the stage. Nine more to go. Édouard hurries backstage, impatient to share the good news with Magda.

The following weeks are exhausting. Édouard works at the real estate agency Tuesday through Saturday, then makes the round-trip to Paris every Sunday to be part of Le Point Virgule's emerging-talent show, *Le Trempoint*. Magda encourages him, and, though he feels bad about being less available for his wife and son than he would like, he tells himself it's temporary and that this is hardly the time to give up.

The day Djamila summons him to her office after one of his shows, he's sure it's all about to end. *If her door is open when I get there, everything'll be OK,* he thinks to reassure himself. But the bright-red door is closed, and Édouard can feel the hope draining from his body as he gently raps on it and enters without waiting for an answer. He noticed earlier that the audience was more reserved, less interested. Maybe Alphonse, the crooked real estate agent character he's been working on, isn't up to par yet, or maybe he just didn't do as well as previous weekends. Or maybe . . .

"Do you have enough material to last an hour?"

"Excuse me?"

"Do you have enough material to last an hour?" repeats Djamila in her usual exasperated tone.

"Yes, I think so," offers Édouard hesitantly.

"You think so, or you're sure?"

"I'm sure," he replies more firmly.

"I have a hole to fill in September. Three nights a week, Thursday through Saturday, seven o'clock. If you do well, we'll slot you in at eight in October and November."

She doesn't even wait for an answer—it's an offer no one would turn down. Édouard stifles his urge to thank her, already familiar with Djamila's disdain for anything that smacks of weepy sentimentalism. He simply turns and leaves, his heart racing.

He's been shuffling through the same four or five tried-and-true sketches for over a year. Now he has two months to come up with enough material to last an hour onstage.

He spends the summer working hard, his evenings devoted to writing new skits in his leather notebook, then feverishly scratching them out and starting over. Magda walks on eggshells, unsure how to soothe his anxiety. His fear of failure is constant now that he's been offered the chance of a lifetime. She's gotten used to his habit of jumping up and grabbing his notebook right in the middle of a conversation, a family meal, or a walk along the levee. Nothing surprises her anymore. She doesn't even ask about all the new ideas that pop into his head—she knows he'll tell her that she'll see them when the time is right.

Arthur celebrates his second birthday, and as he happily babbles and claps at the sight of the dancing flames, then sputters all over the cake when blowing out his candles, Édouard thinks about how he might actually make his son proud. If all goes well, in a few years Arthur will be able to brag to his school friends that his father's job is to make people laugh. That's why he's doing all this, after all: to see the wonder in his son's eyes and know that he's worth something.

September finally arrives, and Édouard's first full-length shows are a success. Night after night, week after week, he wonders why people keep coming to Le Point Virgule to see *him*.

Djamila puts him on the schedule through the end of the year, and one night, as he turns off his bedside lamp, Magda suggests that it may be time for him to quit his day job, that he's going to burn himself out by continuing to juggle everything on his plate. "Worst-case scenario we cut back a bit and count mostly on my salary . . ."

Édouard smiles in the darkness of their room, then jokes, "Given that Arthur won't eat anything other than potatoes anyway, it's not like he'll be making a huge sacrifice."

Magda laughs. "Aren't you going to write that one down?"

That night he struggles to fall asleep. Doubt takes over again, hovering above him like a threatening shadow. *What if it's all just a dream, a flight of fancy?* Could there be somebody up there entertaining themselves by making him believe he's on the right track so it will hurt even more when he hits a dead end? When you climb too high, it's easy to fall. Why should he be allowed to dream, why should he have the chance to reach for the sky when his twenty-year-old brother still falls asleep night after night under the empty top bunk, without having the right to yearn for anything at all?

Édouard tosses in his bed all night, throwing off the tangled covers, unable to find the sleep he desperately needs. One burning, destructive question echoes in his ear.

Does he really deserve all this?

15

Does he really deserve all this? Jean-Michel brushes off his protégé's question with a wave of his hand and an excessively loud chuckle. "Come on, Édouard, you can't seriously still be wondering that? I mean, why ask yourself such twisted questions? Can't you just enjoy it, take advantage of it? Even if you didn't deserve it, what would that change? Do you think the guy who suddenly finds himself homeless after working like a dog for forty years deserves what he gets? No! Life isn't about merit. Come on, have some champagne—you need it!"

His producer slips a flute filled to the brim into his hand. The whole team is waiting for him to toast. In just thirty minutes it will be April 1. Maybe he'll realize at the stroke of midnight that the entire evening has been one big practical joke.

The thirty or so people seated around the table in the restaurant they've bought out for the after-party raise their glasses in a joyous din, and the sound engineer, Francis, shouts enthusiastically, "Speech! Speech! Speech!" The others hurriedly put down their glasses to clap in unison, impatient for a final word from the man they've been working for since September, the man they've followed around Europe for more than two hundred shows, almost every night for seven months. An exhausting record for Édouard, and for them as well.

The comedian hasn't prepared anything. He's been entirely focused on the final show at the Stade de France, his ultimate challenge before a well-deserved rest.

"G-g-g-good evening, my friends," he begins mischievously, and the small, tastefully decorated, vaulted room goes quiet. Seated at the head of the table, he places his glass next to his plate before continuing. "I'll keep this short, because I think you've heard enough of my jokes by now. And I really just have one thing to say tonight: Thank you. Thank you for sticking with me through this crazy, draining tour, through to the amazing show we pulled off tonight. Thank you for working tirelessly, passionately, and furiously to make sure every show was on par with the audience's expectations. Thank you for putting up with my whims, moments of doubt, and fits of anxiety and anger. I never would have been able to do all this without you. So thank you, from the bottom of my heart."

His team, gathered around the table, smiles warmly as Édouard's words evoke a different memory for each of them. For Mickaël, the lighting director, the word *whim* is particularly meaningful. He still remembers how demanding the comic was during the tour, going so far as to provide him with Pantone color references for the spotlights, because they had to be just right—as if his life depended on it. For Cynthia, the stage manager, it's *fits of anger* that sets her thinking: she can still hear Édouard shouting whenever she didn't instantly understand exactly what he had in mind. As for Hervé, he won't be forgetting the comic's moments of doubt anytime soon—he often felt more like Édouard's therapist than his manager, constantly trying to convince him that this tour would be a success and that he would, as always, be good enough. Everyone knows what a perfectionist Édouard is, how important all the details are, and they all appreciate the acknowledgement and thanks he's provided tonight.

Édouard picks up his overly full glass again, tipping a few drops onto the impeccably ironed tablecloth.

"Careful, buddy, that's Ruinart champagne!" warns Francis teasingly.

The entire team applauds, then stands to clink their glasses together. The hum of conversation and laughter returns, and Édouard takes advantage of the warm clamor to leave the table, heading for the spacious restroom, where dimmed lighting and subtle classical music perfect the cozy atmosphere.

He gets out his cell phone and opens his contacts. Arthur is first, in alphabetical order. He hesitates for several seconds, then taps his son's name and brings the phone to his ear. He counts the rings, instinctively holding his breath.

After seven unbearable, uninterrupted peals, Arthur's voice mail picks up. His son pronounces a single word—his first name—followed by the annoying generic recording, ". . . is currently unavailable. Please leave a message after the—"

Édouard hangs up before the robot can finish the sentence. He takes aim at the urinal and relieves his bladder, looking at his face without seeing it in the large mirror that takes up most of the wall. A powerful wave of exhaustion barrels into him as he mournfully dries his hands amid the deafening roar of the dryer.

He tries again—because you never know. He dials the same number, hoping with every fiber of his being to hear Arthur's voice on the other end of the line. In vain. He stares at his phone, and a message pops up. He hurries to open it—maybe it's a text from his son. He'd take even a few short words. *Congratulations on tonight. You were amazing! I hope you're out celebrating with friends.* The text is from Yoann, and the comic smiles sadly as he thinks of his former partner from Hospital Clowns, the only person from that part of his life he's kept in touch with over the years. Yoann conjures up feelings of melancholy, and nostalgia for a time when Édouard sauntered around the hallways of the Gustave Roussy hospital dressed as a clown with a huge, quilted nightcap that hung to the floor—he was constantly tripping over it, much to the children's delight. Édouard's throat tightens as he thinks about how to answer Yoann, how to thank him, but all the possibilities seem too impersonal, so he puts it off. *I hope you're out celebrating with friends.* His team is with him, just a few yards away, but not his family. Not Arthur.

It's impossible for Édouard not to wonder if his son is deliberately ignoring his calls or if he's just busy. Is there any chance Arthur watched the show on TF1, or is he crazy to even hope that? He could be with his girlfriend, at the movies, studying for his tests, or asleep. Maybe he can't hear his phone, or he's gone out and forgotten it at home.

Whatever the reason, he hasn't bothered to call his father on the most extraordinary night of his life—at least in other people's opinion. If anyone asked Édouard that question and he actually agreed to answer, he wouldn't hesitate. The most extraordinary night of his life was not spent at the Stade de France, but at the Le Havre hospital, the night his son was born, nearly twenty-four years ago. The dizzying anticipation of the unknown, awaiting an unimaginable happiness, the overwhelming feeling of being so insignificant compared to the life waiting to begin within Magda's taut belly. He hasn't forgotten a single detail of the confusing emotions that coursed through him that night.

Arthur would think such a confession was hilarious—he probably wouldn't believe it for a second. Of course, Édouard *has* experienced intense, almost primitive emotions onstage, but nothing comparable to the night his son came into the world. But then he lost his way, because you never realize how happy you are until you've looked back at that happiness, until you've trampled it by looking for something else, something better, higher, farther away—always a little farther away, because nothing ever seems good enough. Of course, he felt exhilarated when he finally found himself up onstage for the first time. Of course, in that moment, he forgot about how complete he had felt the first time he met Arthur.

But tonight, after this incredible evening, he knows what has counted most for him in life, even if he wasn't smart enough to realize it when there was still time, even though he never managed to tell Magda and Arthur, even though he—the celebrated syllable trainer and sentence conductor—could never find the right words.

In fact, if his son had answered his phone tonight, what would Édouard have said? Would he simply have made unbearable small talk? *Yes, the audience was huge. It went really well. Did you see me on TV?* Would he have been able to slip something real between the platitudes, said that he meant well, that he regretted that their fight had gotten so out of hand, that the last thing he ever wanted was to have a falling-out with his son?

Having grown up with a father who didn't believe in him, Édouard was convinced that what his child needed was the opposite. He had to encourage him, push him beyond his limits. So when, at barely five years old, Arthur had fun making his stuffed animals talk like puppets, Édouard began constantly urging him: "You have a gift, don't waste it. You're so good! Keep practicing." Throughout his son's childhood, he enthusiastically focused on his talents as a ventriloquist at every possible occasion, confident that his praise would take the boy wherever he wanted to go. "He's just a kid having fun. Let him be," Magda would say and then sigh. Arthur took theater classes twice a week for years. He did incredibly well in school, but Édouard would insist as he signed his report cards, "That's nice, but who cares about good grades! You're so much better than that, Arthur!"

The boy fell in line without argument, simply happy his father was interested in him when he was around. He would do anything to attract his father's attention, though the comedian was too often absent, away on tour.

So Édouard almost fell off his chair when his eighteen-year-old son told him he was giving up acting, that the stage wasn't for him, that he didn't want that life.

"What will you do after you graduate, then?"

"Go to college, Dad."

"College? But what for? What will you study?"

"I haven't decided yet. Maybe medicine."

"Are you kidding? My son can't become a doctor! Doctors lead depressing lives, Arthur! You'd be with sick people all day! Or worse, people who are *afraid* of getting sick!"

"Stop it, Dad." Arthur sighed, weary of trying to have a serious conversation with his father, who made everything a joke. "Law school is tempting too . . ."

"Oh, Arthur, please, please tell me you're joking! Anybody can become a doctor or a lawyer. The ability to make people laugh is a priceless gift—one not everyone has. You are talented. Please don't waste it!"

Though Édouard saw the parallel between this scene and the one with his own father at almost the same age, he failed to understand that his attitude had the same end result as Lucien's years of belittling him. He sincerely thought he was doing the right thing by his son. The discussion never became a full-blown fight, but after that, Arthur became increasingly distant, and his father did nothing to heal their rift. He was sure his son would soon realize how silly he was being. Édouard just *knew* Arthur was destined to follow in his footsteps, and couldn't understand his reaction. Keeping a gift like that from the world was criminal. You couldn't just casually turn your back on it and choose an ordinary job. For Édouard, talent was a higher calling, so much more than desire. It was a gift, something that *transcended* you, not something you chose or could ignore. His son would have to realize that eventually—there was no other way!

When Arthur started a pre-law program, Édouard continued to insist it was a fleeting whim. And now his son's about to receive a specialized master's degree in obscure legal theory and take the bar exam. The distance between them has continued to widen with every disappointment and misunderstanding, with every resentment and resignation.

Arthur hasn't made a puppet speak in a very long time.

Before putting his phone back in his pocket and returning to the table, Édouard checks one last time that the ringer's on. He would hate to miss a call, even though he doubts he'll get to hear the voice he yearns for tonight.

16

He would hate to miss a call, even though he doubts he'll get to hear the voice he yearns for tonight. So, after the show, Édouard leaves the others, who are determined to continue the festivities in a hip bar the next street over. Instead, he returns to the calm of his hotel room near the Saint-Lazare train station. Eleven o'clock. Will Magda be asleep, or will she call him? He doesn't want to risk waking Arthur with the strident ringing of the phone, so he can only wait, fingers crossed in the hope his wife will call.

He's been on at the Olympia Thursday through Sunday for nearly four months now, sold out every night. Every week nearly eight thousand people come to see his latest show, *Dreams for Sale.* He arrives home in Le Havre late Monday morning, exhausted, then leaves again early Thursday. He spends the first part of the week writing, wearing earplugs to dull ambient noise, then practices his sketches for the three nights of shows ahead. Arthur and Magda spend the weekends together without him, and the five-year-old boy refuses to believe his classmates when they tell him their dads live at home seven days a week. "No way," he exclaims, outraged by such nonsense.

Things have all happened so fast for Édouard. He spent last year at La Cigale, with a thousand people in the audience every night, on the heels of his triumphant first eighteen months at Le Point Virgule. The venues keep getting larger and larger as Édouard becomes increasingly "bankable"—as they say in the biz. He's become a prized guest on TV programs and radio shows, where Zita, the compulsive cleaner, and Alphonse, the real estate agent, are big hits. All the biggest comedy festivals want him, and his name is always at the top of the bill when he accepts. His viewership and popularity are both soaring.

In February he'll be starting a four-month tour through France. He's ready to put on a hundred shows, willing to put his family life on hold even though it breaks his heart that he won't see Magda or his son for the duration. But he can't slow down, not now. "When?" his wife asks often, saddened by Arthur's constant questions about when his father will be home. She wants to tell Édouard things are getting off track, that this isn't how she imagined their life would be, even though she's always encouraged and supported her husband. Her heart aches when her son exclaims, "Tonight we're having dinner with Daddy," as he turns on the television and finds the channel where his father's acting like a clown. She wants to cry when, night after night, their son kisses the giant poster of Édouard above his bed and lovingly whispers, "Good night." And yet she doesn't know what to do. She doesn't want to halt her husband's ascent—it's his dream, his passion, and she's the one who pushed him to realize his talent, knowing that he would always yearn for bigger things.

Édouard has suggested they move to Paris, but she knows that wouldn't resolve the problem caused by months-long tours. And she would have to rebuild her whole life in the unwelcoming capital, where everything is foreign to her. There are plenty of museums, of course, and she would almost certainly find work as a guide, but does she have the strength, the desire to be a stranger in a huge new city? Would she really be less alone, far from her family, with only Édouard to count on?

"Success is starting to go to his head," people sometimes say backstage, when the comedian scolds an ineffective or inattentive employee. He's always been a perfectionist, and anxiety takes hold of him before every show, which partially explains his moods, but still, something has changed. The media laud him constantly—the critics are unanimous in their praise. He fights the pull of superficiality and endless champagne fountains, but he can tell that little by little he's becoming intoxicated with his continued success. It seems like nothing can stop his relentless climb. He's not even surprised anymore by the sheer number of posters advertising his shows as he walks through the streets of Paris. It's easy to get used to, and then normalize, little by little, even the most unbelievable things. His face is in the Métro, on buses, on newspaper stands and billboards, in magazines, on TV. He's everywhere now.

That Monday, when Édouard gets home from Paris around noon and Magda comes home for lunch to see him, their reunion is timid, almost awkward. He gives her a quick kiss, then collapses onto the couch, exhausted as usual.

"I'm making spaghetti. Sound good?" asks Magda.

"Perfect. How was your weekend?"

"Good. And you?"

"Great. Last night I think I really surpassed myself. At the end, the audience gave me a standing ovation! Can you imagine? Parisians on their feet for me!"

Magda puts the pot on to boil, then turns to smile at Édouard. "You deserve it, you know that."

He doesn't answer.

Their conversation of bits and pieces staggers on, never quite coming together as anything memorable. Each of them is hoping to find the right thing to say, but they're like two musicians playing in different keys.

"What did you do with Arthur?"

"Nothing special. Grocery shopping, then his music class on Saturday afternoon. He loves playing the tambourine. We should get him one. Sunday, I took him to the park since it was nice out."

"That sounds fun," replies Édouard, unable to think of anything else to say.

He makes a mental note to find a music store in Paris and bring the instrument home to his son the following week. That'll make him happy. Despite himself, he feels torn between regret for not being there for sweet little family moments and the impression that his wife and son are stuck in an unenviable rut that reminds him of his father and the life Édouard couldn't wait to put behind him.

When they're finished eating lunch, before heading back to work, Magda perches herself on her husband's lap and pulls Édouard's head to her chest to stroke his hair. He lovingly wraps his arms around her waist. The only sound is of sparse chirping from the sparrows outside the window.

"Will you make two round-trips for Christmas?"

Édouard has shows on both December 24 and 25. He wasn't given a choice when they scheduled it and hasn't dared ask to spend the holidays with his family. Magda doesn't understand why he pushes himself like this—it's not like he has a boss to silently obey. "Later, I'll be able to do what I want, but right now, I can't follow my every whim," he had said with a sigh. She had simply shrugged, resigned, holding back from telling him that if he really wanted to be with them for Christmas, nobody could stop him, and that his career would hardly come to a halt over two missed shows.

"Yes. I'll come home right after my show on Thursday night. That way I'll be here in the morning when Arthur wakes up to open his presents! Then I'll head out again after lunch."

Magda nods gently, lips tight.

Édouard continues. "It's only a matter of time, honey. Soon we'll be the masters of our own fate, and we'll do whatever we want!"

The following week, when Édouard returns home and goes to pick up his son from school, he can't wait for Arthur to unwrap the present he found while traipsing through the streets of Paris's ninth arrondissement in freezing December temperatures. At home, the little boy hurriedly rips off the royal-blue paper and shouts joyfully as he examines the tambourine, which is bigger than his head.

"Look, Mom, it's the same as the one in music class!"

Arthur jumps around the apartment to the beat of his new instrument, merrily tapping away. An hour later, his enthusiasm is still running high, and he's singing at the top of his lungs to accompany his drumming.

Édouard is at his desk. He's been desperately trying to come up with a new sketch for the past few days. He can feel it at the tips of his fingers, but it keeps slipping away, and it's starting to wear on him. If only he could tune everything out, concentrate in absolute quiet, he's sure he would be able to assemble the scattered pieces of ideas he's collected, that it would all make sense.

"Arthur, can you make a little less noise? I think we've had enough tambourining for one evening." The boy is too caught up in his game to hear his father. He continues to jump and shake his new toy.

Suddenly the only thing Édouard can focus on is the unbearable racket ringing in his ears, keeping him from working, from thinking. So when Arthur next walks past him, he turns around and furiously grabs the boy's arm. Arthur looks at him, confusion in his eyes, then whimpers in pain.

"Quiet!" Édouard explodes.

17

"Quiet!"

The animated conversations suddenly stop, like candle flames snuffed out. As confused eyes turn toward him, Édouard realizes he's just shouted. He laughs nervously and takes a showy sip of Saint-Émilion.

"Ignore me—sorry! I'm just so tired," he explains nonchalantly.

Jean-Michel and Hervé exchange worried glances, but conversations pick up where they left off, and the din once again fills the restaurant.

Édouard looks down, pretending to concentrate on the grilled dorado stuffed with colorful vegetables lying on his plate. Its viscous eye suddenly makes him nauseous. He's never understood why the fancier the restaurant, the more likely it is to serve dishes that are disgusting to look at. He digs through the fish's hollowed-out body, extracts a forkful of julienned carrots and zucchini, and unenthusiastically brings it to his mouth.

"If everything goes well, the DVD of tonight's show will be out at the end of June. We're hoping to sell two million copies to make up for the Stade de France deficit."

Édouard nods as he chews, barely listening to Jean-Michel's overly serious words; the man only ever thinks about one thing:

money. Profits, shortfalls—it's all he ever talks about. Fair enough since he's the one who's handed out the big bucks since the beginning, the one who still chooses to bet on Édouard's unfailing success. He's been repeating the same thing for seven months: "Do you know how much the Stade de France is going to cost us? Do you know how hard we're going to have to work to make sure we're in the black afterward?" But Édouard doesn't care about money. As long as his staff is paid and his fans are satisfied—anything else can be fixed. Édouard's job is to make the thousands of people in the audience dream a little. That's it.

His producer's drawling voice continues to fill his left ear, but the comedian can't focus on the swirling words. To his right, Hervé is talking with Cynthia, the stage manager, who punctuates each of Hervé's sentences with an attentive "mm-hmm." Once Édouard has noticed the *mm-hmm*s, they suddenly become omnipresent, irritating, like a drumbeat to which everyone is unconsciously marching. At the other end of the table, Francis is apparently telling the lighting assistants a hilarious story, sending them into fits of high-pitched, almost aggressive laughter. The staccato sniggering layers over the disagreeable *mm-hmm*s, and Édouard can feel the ball of anxiety in his stomach stirring slowly but surely after a few hours of relief. The motionless dorado looks at him mockingly, its multicolored vegetable guts spilling out of its slashed abdomen. The silver knives and forks ding against the china, grate against the slate knife rests like nails on a chalkboard, clink against peoples' teeth. The countless wineglasses and champagne flutes knock into each other every time someone takes a drink. The wine bottles bang down onto the table—Édouard can almost feel the surface vibrate each time. All this noise works its way into his ears and overwhelms his brain. His heart beats faster to the crescendo of shouts and laughs assailing him from all directions. The explosive sounds fill his stomach, alongside the few pieces of vegetables he's managed to swallow since the beginning of the meal. The ball of anxiety grows, pushing against his diaphragm, but he knows that vomiting won't appease the voracious demon for long. His anxiety cannot be tamed. Like the tide, it simply washes out for a while, leaving behind a froth of shame and despair. It's just a calm between two attacks, as Édouard has come to understand all too well, since this companion is constant; it's with him when he wakes, in his bed at night, during the day, at the grocery store, at the movie theater, in the street, at the mailbox—anywhere, anytime. It's always waiting, crouched inside him, hiding in the deepest part of his being, to the point that he can sometimes forget it's there. Then, a few hours or days later, it rears up victoriously again.

The noise is unbearable, ubiquitous, suffocating. He hears mouths chewing, soggy swallows, exclamations, discreet coughs, virus-ridden sniffling, even hands smoothing rebellious strands of hair. It's all painfully perceptible, intolerably intrusive. Sweat begins to bead at his temples as the oxygen leaves the room. He feels stifled and harassed by the clamor coming from the happy thirty-odd diners.

He has to get up. *Make an excuse, anything will do.* He carefully pushes the chair back in to avoid attracting too much attention. *Leave.* He has to get out of this room that's suffocating him as surely as if someone had put a rope around his neck. *Home, quick. Flee. Escape.*

"Are you OK, Édouard? You don't look so well . . ."

Hervé studies him worriedly.

"No, it's nothing. It's just the blowback from the show. I'm going home, I'm wiped."

His manager nods. "Do you want me to take you?"

"No, enjoy your dinner. You deserve it! I'll take a taxi."

"You sure?"

Édouard gathers all his strength to summon a convincing smile for Hervé. "Of course, I'll be fine! You're always worrying about me!"

The comedian waves goodbye to the table, in a hurry to get out into the fresh air and the nocturnal quiet. He tries not to cringe when the entire team applauds him one last time, but he would swear his eardrums are about to rupture.

Once outside, he takes out his phone to reserve a taxi. Ten minutes to wait, alone, to gather his wits in hopes the anxiety loosens its grip. Édouard takes off his Breton-stripe sweater, leaving only a T-shirt covering his torso. It's a relief to feel the cold air filter under the cotton fabric.

Heels click-clack on the pavement, and he turns to see Tiphaine, his press agent, walking swiftly toward him, her purse under her arm.

"I was afraid you'd be gone," she purrs upon reaching him.

"What are you doing here?"

"I thought it'd be a shame for you to spend the rest of the night alone at home . . ."

"Not tonight, sorry. Go back and enjoy your night with the others, OK?"

"But we could enjoy each other, couldn't we?"

The young woman gets closer. He can almost feel her warm breath on his neck. A cold sweat breaks out along his spine as anxiety once again bares its teeth, ready to devour him, ready to make him disappear. Édouard swallows hard, and Tiphaine imagines that it's her long legs and plump lips that are affecting the comic. She boldly slips her left hand under his T-shirt and moves it higher until Édouard stops her, firmly removing her fingers.

"Not tonight. I'm sorry," he mutters again.

"But I thought that we . . ."

"I'm absolutely exhausted. You get that, don't you? I need to rest. Alone," Édouard clarifies.

He's been sleeping with Tiphaine off and on for over two years, on nights when his loneliness is too heavy to bear, or when he feels inexplicably light and carefree. The young brunette is undeniably endearing, but Édouard doubts her side of things is any more exclusive than his. Monique Bresson would have said Tiphaine was a good person if she'd ever met her, but Édouard has never wanted a companion, just somebody to fleetingly fill the void when it becomes too vast.

"I'll see you around, then."

She admits defeat and kisses Édouard goodbye on the cheek, then heads back into the restaurant. He'd bet a limb she's already thinking about her next prey, to ensure she doesn't end the night with her appetite unsated.

As he waits for the taxi, Édouard's thoughts turn to Magda. Things could have been so different. He could have—should have—behaved differently. It took him more than fifteen years to realize it, though, and now he's not sure that "better late than never" holds true, because the pain of this realization is so intense that it's like it was yesterday.

From the depths of his memory, a bitter remark makes its way to the surface. A remark that sealed their fate as a couple, as a family.

"You're here so rarely that I don't even miss you anymore."

18

"You're here so rarely that I don't even miss you anymore."

Though the words are spoken softly, sadly, they feel like a massive slap in the face to Édouard. He tries to recover from the blow, sitting at the table, head in his hands, jaw clenched tight. Magda is smoking at the window she's left slightly ajar. She leans out every time she exhales a puff of smoke.

"What do you want me to say, Édouard? Would you rather I lie, that I continue to pretend everything's great until resentment has eaten away at me for so long that I finally come to hate you?"

Édouard rubs his temples, unable to look at his wife. He can't say exactly what he's feeling right now. It's all still so confusing. He feels like a grand piano has been dropped on his head from the tenth floor of an apartment building, and he's just been jackhammered through the concrete. He doesn't know if he'll recover. He's not sure he *wants* to.

"Could you say something, please? I didn't imagine this would be a one-way conversation."

Magda finishes her menthol cigarette, runs the butt under the faucet for a second, then flicks it out the window.

Édouard finally looks up, still in a daze.

"I don't know what I could possibly add. You've said it all, haven't you? You've told your sad story, and now all that's left is for me to bow out, right? What do you want from me? Do you want me to beg, to tell you things will be different?"

"No, I've heard that too many times to believe it anymore. Nothing will ever change for the better, Édouard. Not for Arthur and me. You haven't seen your son in three months—can you imagine what it's like for him to grow up, to forge his personality with half—no wait, a quarter of a father? Do you realize that you're nothing but a face on TV and a voice on the radio anymore, or at best someone he talks to on the phone, when you actually manage to find five minutes to call?"

"For fuck's sake, Magda, I do my best! What do you want me to do? Quit? Leave it all behind and take some stupid job so that I can be here to push the grocery cart and clean the windows with you?"

Magda lets out a sad laugh, then pulls the kitchen door shut so that the rising volume won't wake her sweet little six-year-old who has school in the morning.

"I've never asked you to do that, Édouard, and you know it. I was the first to support you, to push you, and to reassure you when you doubted yourself. I dare you to say otherwise! But this just isn't livable anymore. I can't bear it. You're never here—you're always in Paris or on tour. You never stop. You keep saying you're going to slow down, but then you just schedule more and more shows, interviews, and TV appearances. You say that you'd have to be crazy to turn down opportunities like that, but in the meantime your son is growing up and you're not there for him. I'm wilting, the life slowly being sucked out of me from living like a single mother, because that's what I am, Édouard—a single mother!"

Her shaking hands light a second cigarette, and she inhales deeply to calm her nerves. Her husband remains silent as her storm of emotions rages.

"There is no other solution, OK? I didn't marry the invisible man. I'm barely thirty years old—I'm allowed to have a life. I *deserve* a life! Same goes for Arthur. I can't stand watching him wait for you anymore, hoping you'll actually show up for once, only to be let down again! You weren't here for his birthday this summer because of some stupid festival that was more important to you. You weren't here for his first day of first grade, or when he broke his arm climbing that tree, or when he hid his first tooth under his pillow and whispered to me that he was going to ask the tooth fairy to bring his daddy home instead of giving him money! Christ, Édouard, I'll stop there, but the list goes on and on. And the worst of it is that we had this same conversation last spring. Nothing has changed. Nothing! Because your career is your life. Because, no matter what you say, it's all that matters to you."

Édouard clenches his fists, his throat tight. He wants to say something, but can't think of anything that could possibly appease Magda. Nothing.

"I thought we would be different from everyone else, but nobody's ever really different in the end. Believe me, it'll be better for all of us. You won't have to shuttle back and forth between here and Paris. Because really, even when you're home, you just lock yourself in your office writing sketches. You're absent even when you're here—you realize that, don't you? In the end, it won't change much. It will just put an end to the cycle of hope and disappointment."

Two trails of tears make their way down Magda's cheeks until she abruptly wipes them away. Édouard wants to get up, to take her in his arms and remind her of all the good times, of all the little things that meant they were supposed to be together forever. He wants to remind her of the times they played hide-and-seek with Arthur, pretending not to see him despite the fact that his toes always stuck out of his hiding places. Of the times he took them on surprise outings, when he would blindfold them both, and Arthur would gleefully cry, "Where are we going, Daddy?" The mornings when he would get up first and put one of his father's old records on in the living room and then wake Magda by whispering, "Come dance with me," in her ear. She would get up with a tired smile, and they would gently sway to the sound of Jacques Brel. Magda would place her head on his shoulder and let Édouard lead, let him rock her as he softly sang in her ear, *"Quand on n'a que l'amour . . ."* And then Arthur would join them, standing on his father's feet, his arms wrapped tightly around Édouard's knees. "Dance, Daddy, keep dancing!" The three of them would awkwardly spin around the room until the song ended, until Magda would slowly let go, smile at them both and ask, "How about some breakfast?"

Édouard wants her to remember all of that. How those moments are more important than all the rest. He wants to make all kinds of promises until she gives in, until she agrees to give it another try. But even he is tired of making promises he knows he can't keep.

"I thought you would be my anchor through it all," he murmurs defeatedly.

Magda softens and studies the face of her first love, the man she still cares for so much despite everything that's come between them.

"I know. But I'm not sure that I should have to be the one to keep you from drifting. I haven't succeeded, anyway. And I'm tired of being 'the wife of.' I want to be me, free of your shadow."

In his heart, Édouard knows this is it—this is the end. He knows he can't fight anymore. It snuck up on them without them noticing, and now they simply have to accept it, as gracefully as possible, even though he knows that afterward the pain will be insurmountable, that he'll have to drown it, beat it back, and muzzle it to keep it quiet.

"I'll leave in the morning, unless you'd rather I go to a hotel tonight."

"Don't be ridiculous. We're not going to become strangers. Stay, spend some time with Arthur . . ."

"No, I have work. A ton of things to do in Paris."

Magda bites her lip as she closes the kitchen window. Édouard prefers to let her believe that he is—as always—completely predictable and disappointing. Nothing urgent is waiting for him in the capital. He just wants to leave this home that is no longer his—which hasn't been his for a long time really, though it's only tonight that he's realized how cold and inhospitable the place has become to him—as fast as possible. Yet he feels like he's doomed to sink without his wife. Because she's one of the only people who ever loved him for him and not for what he's become. Because with her he could be himself, he could be discouraged, depressed, fall apart. He could reveal his weaknesses without worrying about her trampling them—in fact, quite the contrary. The only thing he's never talked to her about, because he's never been able to get the words out, is Jonathan's accident, his responsibility and feelings of guilt. It's the one thing he's kept hidden inside, behind layers of protective jokes and puns. Though he's been tempted to share the weight of it all with her, he's never been able to work up the courage. He was too afraid that if he revealed his secret, Magda would never look at him the same way again, that he would become the boy who almost killed his brother in her eyes too. Would it have changed anything between them if she knew about this colossal flaw, the one that has guided his steps since childhood?

"Well, we did the best we could." Magda sighs before turning out the neon light above the sink, which had lit the entire room. She opens the door and heads toward their bedroom. Her bare feet are silent on the tile floor.

Édouard is still sitting in the kitchen, in the quiet darkness, as if turned to stone.

He spends New Year's Eve 1999 at a party where everything is excessive. The guests are all stars or spouses of stars—or their mistresses. The Veuve Clicquot flows, and the buffet includes lines of coke for every course. The heated pool is full of bikini-clad women drinking fluorescent cocktails. The absurd world of fame and fortune has opened its doors to him now that he's free to take advantage of everything Paris has to offer. The world might end tonight, but at least he won't die alone. The past several months have been difficult, with a separation that's left a gaping hole in his heart, so tonight Édouard is letting it all go to his head. It's nice to hear nothing but accolades, comforting to have beautiful women at his feet, reassuring that people he doesn't even know are so full of unconditional praise for him. Money and fame mean nothing is impossible. Alcohol helps him forget, and tonight the goal is to just go with the flow. To take advantage of it all.

At the same time, in Le Havre, Magda and Arthur are comfortably ensconced in their living room couch, wrapped up in a giant fleece blanket with a big bowl of popcorn on their laps. The boy is mesmerized by *Toy Story*, his favorite movie since he can remember, the only one he can watch over and over without ever getting tired of it.

When Buzz Lightyear shouts, "To infinity and beyond!" for the millionth time, an inebriated Édouard passes out in the bathroom of the five-star Parisian hotel that's hosting the millennial celebration. In the lobby, the countdown has started without him. A few seconds later, he begins the year 2000 facedown in his own vomit.

Magda kisses her son lovingly and whispers, "Happy New Year" in his ear, even though she knows Arthur's been asleep for a while now.

After the divorce, Édouard begins working even more, putting on shows almost every night and increasing his TV appearances. He stops going back to Le Havre, refusing to let nostalgia or melancholy get the best of him for even a minute. No time to anguish—his fans and the media love him, and the biggest producers are looking to woo him, rolling out the red carpet.

Arthur takes the train to Paris to see his father, according to their custody agreement: half of school vacations. Not every other week or weekend—that would be too complicated for Édouard.

On a whim, the comic purchased a huge loft a few steps from Gare de Lyon—given his nightly earnings, he could easily afford to. The only criterion he had for choosing the place was that it be close to the RER A train line so he can take his son to Disneyland Paris as often as he wants to go. He even bought two annual passes—he has to make up for the divorce somehow. He put up a huge Woody poster in Arthur's new room, despite the pain it caused him to sink thumbtacks into the freshly painted wall. He bought all the *Toy Story* toys, from Mr. Potato Head to Bo Peep and the G.I. Joes, and placed them carefully along the top of the beige dresser he spent three long hours putting together.

The first time Arthur sets foot in his father's apartment, he jumps for joy. "I wish I could stay here all the time, Dad. It's so cool!" Édouard smiles, but can't help thinking about how ungrateful children are. Good thing Magda isn't there to hear her son's exclamation.

The comedian's lifestyle becomes increasingly frantic. He never rests because he is deathly afraid that if he does, it will all stop. The more people admire and compliment him, the harder he works. Being one of the best isn't good enough—he has to be number one. Because if he's number one, then he must be worth something. If he's the best, maybe someday anxiety will stop ripping him to shreds before every single show, or at any time of night or day, insinuating that it's all just a charade, a flash in the pan that will soon be stomped out—maybe even tomorrow, who knows—leaving him with nothing. Nothing but his son, who marvels at his gifts, who never criticizes him, who's happy to take only what his father can give. So he couldn't care less that people in the business are starting to say he's full of himself or has a big head:

being the best will be his revenge, but also irrefutable proof that his life has *meaning*.

August is the only time Édouard ever takes a real break, refusing all contracts, parties, and interviews. Arthur spends the whole month with him in the capital, and Édouard has promised himself to focus exclusively on his son during the last four weeks of summer vacation. He tries to cram an entire year's worth of parenting into a single month.

For Arthur's birthday, Édouard always organizes a treasure hunt. Over the years, it becomes increasingly difficult as the boy grows up into a smart young man. In the beginning, the treasure hunts take place inside the apartment. Arthur has to find clues that lead him to his gift. The following year, the game includes the rest of the apartment building, thanks to the kindly participation of Édouard's neighbors, thrilled to have a chance to chat with such a big star. A few years later the hunt swells to the scope of the neighborhood. Édouard organizes everything meticulously, and the thrilled Arthur is always impatient to brag to his friends about Édouard's amazing riddles when school starts up again.

For four weeks, the comedian spends without restraint, humors his son's every whim, takes him on unbelievable experiences, like bungee jumping, flying in a helicopter over the city, or enjoying ride after ride at the Fête des Loges fair in Saint-Germain-en-Laye. And of course, days are spent trekking all over Disneyland Paris hunting for Buzz Lightyear, Arthur shouting excitedly at the idea of the famous astronaut giving him a hug.

Because if there is one thing that is more important to Édouard than anything else, it's not disappointing his son. If there's one person he hopes to make it all up to, it's Arthur.

19

If there's one person he hopes to make it all up to, it's Arthur. But can he? Maybe it's too late. Maybe Édouard is destined to always turn to his loved ones only when it's too late. Jonathan and his enormous cloud of dust, Magda and her menthol cigarettes, Arthur and his voice mail, which he keeps getting tonight, as usual.

He knows his son won't answer. There's no point harassing him—especially since Édouard wouldn't want him to see that he already called several times.

The comic pulls a gray wool beanie down over his ears and puts his Breton-stripe sweater back on to free up his hands.

The taxi he called finally makes its way up the side street, then stops in front of him. He quickly climbs into the back. Without so much as a glance at the man behind the wheel, he reels off his address in a monotone, eager to finally get home.

The driver—about thirty years old, in a dark tracksuit—puts the address into his GPS, typing incredibly fast. He turns toward Édouard and explains, "It'll take at least half an hour."

The comedian murmurs a vague uh-huh as he buckles his seat belt. The sedan starts up, and he lets himself be soothed by the gentle movement.

The poorly shaven driver studies his fare in the rearview mirror, his brow furrowed as he tries to place him.

"Hey . . ."

Édouard turns to meet his gaze in the mirror, waiting calmly for the driver to finish his sentence.

"I might be totally off base, but are you Édouard Bresson?"

The comedian shakes his head. "No, sorry."

"That's so weird, because you really look like him."

"I know. People say that a lot. Sometimes people even stop me in the street to ask for a picture!"

"I believe it. Are you sure you're not taking me for a ride? I mean, even your voice sounds like his."

"Absolutely sure! But one of these days I'm going to have to try my hand as an impersonator. I wonder what kind of money I could make doing that."

The driver keeps looking at Édouard, who stops himself from asking the driver to focus on the road.

"I'm sorry to stare, it's just that I really can't believe you're not Édouard Bresson. I mean, I don't doubt you or anything. What reason would you have to lie?"

The comedian smiles weakly, hoping the man will give up and move on. *If he moves on now, everything'll be OK. Let's talk about the weather or turn on the radio, to whatever station. But stop talking about Édouard Bresson.* After all, was it really dishonest to tell the driver he was mistaken? What does the tortured man on the verge of a panic attack in the back seat of this taxi have in common with the famous stand-up comedian everyone loves and envies? Does the cheerful face plastered on posters have anything at all to do with his own weary features and dull, waxy complexion? Can anyone actually say *who* Édouard Bresson really is? Does he even *have* an identity anymore? When did other people's admiration and wonder stop carrying him through life and instead become so stifling, so heavy with responsibilities and obligations? When did it all go wrong? It happened progressively, imperceptibly, along with life's other sorrows, disappointments, and regrets—Édouard never saw it coming. And now, in this taxi, he wishes he could be anybody other than Édouard Bresson, that victorious bastard with his ultra-bright smile, his valiant doppelganger whose life is a constant explosion of happiness in the eyes of the world.

He pulls his beanie down a little lower, ignoring the way the wool makes his skin itch. He wishes he could disappear into it, like a rabbit in a top hat. He wishes he could disappear and be left alone, wishes he could get away from that goddamn Édouard Bresson, who only really exists in people's imaginations, who's no more alive than the posters faded by the rain and covered by newer, more important, more profitable ads.

The driver finally gives up and turns his doubtful eyes to the ring road flashing past in an orange glow. Édouard lets his thoughts drift. He stops fighting the bitterness that dries his throat and tightens his chest.

When the taxi parks in front of his building, the comic pays the driver without a word. He climbs out of the car and starts walking quickly toward the front door, then hears the driver's window creak down.

"Excuse me, sir?"

The weary Édouard turns to face the obstinate young man.

"I know you're not him, but would you sign an autograph for me anyway? Just in case? My mother loves you, I mean Bresson, and I was thinking that even if you *are* just a look-alike, she'd still be thrilled to have an autograph. I really don't want to be a bother, but one little signature wouldn't take too long, would it?"

The two men size each other up, both perfectly aware of what the other knows, neither of them fooled. Édouard finally relents and bends over to sign a page in a graph-paper notepad.

"This won't be worth anything, you know."

The driver nods. He doesn't know how to reply. He studies the scribbles on the page—an illegible signature with the date—as Édouard stands up. Before turning around, the comedian thinks for a second, then leans close to the insistent young man again.

"If I were you, I'd keep that piece of paper safe and sound. You never know. Maybe it'll be worth something someday. Life is full of surprises!"

The driver looks confused and wonders if the man striding rapidly away is messing with him. *An Édouard Bresson autograph isn't exactly a winning lottery ticket,* he thinks, as he puts the taxi in drive.

When he reaches the door to his loft, Édouard rummages through his bag to find his keys—the very same keys that inspired a hilarious number on all the objects people constantly misplace. The comedian suggested that the foolproof solution for finding a lost object is to aggressively accuse the first person to cross your path. "You took my keys, remember? I gave them to you so you could get the mail. Come on, think harder, remember where you put them!" The accused will feel obliged to look for the missing object as you go about your business. Often enough—recently, even—strangers have come up to him outside his building to exclaim with a smile, "Thanks to you, when I don't know where I've put my wallet, I always accuse my husband so he'll find it for me!"

It's not even close to being one of Édouard's best sketches, but it's part of his legend, recorded in collective memory, like Coluche's famous

Schmilblick sketch. Because the audience has the last word in the end, regardless of the artist's opinion.

A few minutes later, his fingers wrap around his keys. Édouard struggles in the dark with the lock for a moment, since the hall light has gone out.

Once inside, he can still feel the anvil on his rib cage, so he forces a deep breath through his mouth in hopes of lifting the weight, if only for an instant.

20

Once inside, he can still feel the anvil on his rib cage, so he forces a deep breath through his mouth in hopes of lifting the weight, if only for an instant.

In just twenty minutes, he'll be standing on the stage a few yards away. He scans the orchestra-level seating as it fills with people and their merry din, chooses a half-empty row, and heads toward a couple in their late twenties. He makes sure his brown wig is perfectly in place, then adjusts his sunglasses and sits down in the empty seat right next to the woman, who is busy typing on her phone.

He's putting on his latest show, *39+2 Years Old*, at Bercy tonight. The house is sold out, and thirteen thousand people are there to see him, but he still hasn't outgrown his need to spend a few minutes incognito among the crowd, pretending to be the anonymous showgoer he sometimes dreams of being. Discreetly observing as people look for their seats and have banal discussions before the show is somehow soothing for him. It eases his nerves before he makes his big appearance amid all the applause. There is something incredibly stimulating about rubbing elbows with fans who don't recognize him. And, of course, Édouard loves playing with fire—the risk of getting caught is exhilarating.

The young woman with the blond ponytail asks her companion what time the show is supposed to start, and Édouard can't stop himself from diving into their conversation.

"It's after nine! He should already be onstage by now. The ticket says nine p.m.!" he exclaims in irritation, lips pursed.

The blonde turns toward him, surprised to suddenly find herself in a conversation with a stranger.

"Thank you. It'll start soon, then, I'm sure," she replies hesitantly.

"I sure hope so, given the price of the tickets! A little respect for the audience would be nice, don't you think?" Édouard continues in a strident tone. He really enjoys having a little fun when he's incognito.

"True, but it's to be expected of a star. They always make you wait, let anticipation build! It's part of the show," his neighbor contends cheerfully.

"Part of the show, huh? You're awfully forgiving. I bet he's in his dressing room downing glass after glass of ridiculously expensive champagne!"

"You're not going to ruin tonight for me. I love Édouard Bresson so much I won't say a single bad thing about him! My husband and I have seen all his shows, right, Gabriel?"

The baby-faced man with dark hair looks up from the program and nods with a smile. "Chloé is right. We have all his DVDs at home, and before each new show we watch all the old ones to get up to speed!"

Édouard throws up his hands in defeat. "Wow, I see you're real fans. What exactly is it about him that you love so much?" he asks, unable to stop himself.

The impeccably made-up woman looks pensive. "Hmm . . . I guess I really like his deadpan style, the way he never smiles and is always so blasé. I've always found it bold, and so funny. Oh, and his characters are dead-on, seriously!"

Her husband leans closer to Édouard. "Yes, Zita is amazing, don't you think? It's just unbelievable that he managed to dream up that crazy old bat! Sometimes I wonder if the guy isn't a little nuts to come up with such off-the-wall sketches."

Chloé agrees. "I'd definitely like to know what he's like in real life. I find it hard to imagine him as normal!"

"I'm pretty convinced that all artists belong in the loony bin," answers Édouard in a conspiratorial tone.

He hears an annoyed voice behind him and feels a hand on his shoulder. "Excuse me, I think you're sitting in my seat. I've double-checked my ticket, and this is the right row. What's your seat number?"

Édouard jumps up. "I'm sorry, my mistake. Bresson is late as usual, so I have plenty of time to find my seat. We pay enough for the tickets, you'd think the guy could be prompt, but that's life, I guess. The world's going to hell in a handbasket!"

Édouard waves fondly to the young couple, sidles to the end of the row, and disappears. It's past time for him to get backstage.

"Tonight, my friends, I'm going to talk to you about a difficult topic, about something taboo, a topic that will surely ruffle some feathers here: turning forty. I know, you're wondering how I can put on a show about being forty when I'm still so young at thirty-nine plus two. It just takes a little i-ma-gi-na-tion. Sir, yes, that gentleman over there with the sparsely furnished noggin, I see you already starting to wilt and shrivel and harden—it's easy to imagine what it's like to be well over forty, like you. Good on you for shaving that dome—gotta get out in front of the gossip!"

The bald man sitting in the fourth row bursts into laughter and shakes his head.

The moment Édouard walked out onto the stage, the anvil miraculously lifted, like always. He can finally breathe easy. The practiced words flow off his tongue. He's already won over the audience—he can feel them in the palm of his hand. It's an indescribable feeling, as if they're linked in perfect symbiosis.

"Forty can hit you at any time. No, really, it can. Sometimes it hits you smack in the face when you're only thirty—the world is unfair."

The audience bursts into loud laughter, as if they had been waiting to let it out. Édouard stops short in the middle of the stage, facing them, an outraged expression on his face.

"Why are you laughing? There's nothing funny about it. This is tragic. Do I need to spell it out for you? Don't tell me I should have paid assistants to hold up signs telling you when to laugh!"

The chuckles continue, unwavering.

"Do you mind? . . . Forty, as I was saying, can descend upon you at any time, like a hair in your food. Well, for those of us who still have hair, right, sir?"

He's chosen his mark for the night: the smooth-scalped man in the fourth row. Édouard can see in his eyes that the man has accepted his role as scapegoat for the night and is a voluntary participant. People love it when the comedian unrelentingly teases the same person from the beginning of the show to the end.

"Let me give you an example: Imagine one of your friends is at a concert and calls you from there so you can hear one of your favorite songs live. We've all had that happen, right? We've all stood alone in our living rooms listening to a singer garble something that sounds a little like a melody we love. Well, when you're on the right side of forty, your friend calls you around eleven o'clock or midnight and you pick up. But when you've gone to the dark side, what happens then?"

Édouard draws the silence out for a few seconds, his eyebrows raised as if expecting an answer.

"That's exactly it. Nothing. Nothing at all. Nothing happens, because you're fast asleep. It's a school night—that's right, things are getting real. We're too old for nonsense like that now. Plus, what do you really think of your buddy being at a concert on a weeknight? How irresponsible, how immature!"

Audience members begin to clap.

"Would you like a few more examples to see where you stand? Here's a reliable test: herbal tea. Oh yes, that's right. Those of you who love 'a nice warm cup of herbal tea' can raise your hands. Go on, don't be shy, I know you're out there. Maybe you, sir? I'm sure that there are even people here tonight hoping I won't finish too late because they have to get up early tomorrow!"

Édouard feels himself warming up. It's like being home.

"Then there are those who take their pillows with them when they stay overnight somewhere, or worse—their slippers! Sir, you're laughing, don't deny it, I saw you. I suppose you take your slippers with you everywhere you go, right? Show us your feet . . . Phew, there's still a sliver of hope—you have on sandals tonight. That said, we could have a whole other discussion about sandals . . ."

The bald man squirms contentedly in his seat, pleased to be the focus of so much of Édouard's attention. The comic continues, unshakable. He does sketch after sketch for two hours, barely leaving the audience time to swallow between bursts of laughter. There can be no respite, no downtime until it's over.

All of a sudden, he notices a woman around fifty sitting in the second row, absorbed by the bluish screen of her cell phone. He stands still and stares at the woman until she realizes his disappointed expression is directed at her.

"You there. Yes, you. Did you think I wouldn't notice you're sending text messages? No biggie. Come here a second, will you?"

Édouard snaps his fingers, and a spotlight shines on the woman, who laughs in embarrassment.

"Come here, I said. I don't bite. Come up to the stage. Let her through, people—there, there you go. What's your name? Régine? Well, Régine, how does it feel to be standing here in front of thirteen thousand people?"

Régine shrugs, intimidated.

"So, who are you texting? Show me. Who's François? Your husband? Does he really have anything that important to say?"

Édouard reads the message out loud.

"*'Do you know what time it'll be over, so I can come get you?'* Oh, isn't he romantic!"

Régine agrees, feeling increasingly uncomfortable.

"Listen, how about I call him and let him know myself. That would be easiest, right?"

The woman giggles nervously, not sure what to do. Édouard touches the screen and holds the phone up to his ear as the audience laughs wildly. He places his index finger on his lips and concentrates on the call.

"Shh, it's ringing. Hello? Hello, yes, François? Hi, this is Édouard! I just wanted to let you know you can head out now. I'm almost done. That way Régine won't have to wait too long outside for you, especially since the streets around Bercy don't have the best reputation! OK, great. I'll let her know. Goodbye, François."

The comedian looks satisfied as he hangs up, then turns to Régine.

"It's all set. He'll wait for you at the end of Rue de Pommard. You can go back to your seat now," he adds as he helps her down the steps from the stage.

"OK, everyone, I don't want to make François wait too long, so I'll let you go, especially since . . . especially since I'm totally beat. It's late and I don't live next door, and to be honest, I want to go to bed. I have work tomorrow!"

The comic waves to the crowd and bows elaborately to the thousands of laughing people. His forehead drips with sweat as he smiles.

The audience stands in unison, and a powerful hurricane of applause whirls around Édouard, again and again.

21

The audience stands in unison, and a powerful hurricane of applause whirls around Édouard, again and again.

Tonight's show was flawless, he thinks, as he turns off the TV. He's always watched or listened to his shows when he gets home, taking precise mental notes on when the jokes worked and when they didn't, when his words triggered the audience's laughter or when a pun fell flat. Édouard has always been a hard worker, a perfectionist, despite what his father thought. He's always studied and analyzed his gestures, intonations, and facial expressions to figure out exactly what started a wave of laughter.

With the television off, the apartment is dark and silent. Édouard has a terrible time with the silence after spending an evening onstage. After every show he vacillates between the desire to stay with other people, to make sure the noise doesn't die down too quickly and that loneliness doesn't sneak up on him too suddenly, and the urge to go straight home to free himself of the obligation to be funny and playful, to suffer through and overcome the excruciating postshow free fall that always leaves him depressed.

He gets up from the beige leather couch to find the box of Atarax he left on the counter earlier. He's been home for hours and feels like a caged lion. He mechanically pulls out the pills and pops a third from its aluminum bubble, then swallows it dry. By the time he's taken the third pill, things always start to get *a little* better, just enough for him to fall into a restless sleep filled with ghosts and shadows. Tonight, or rather this morning, he has no intention of going to bed, but he hopes nonetheless that the anxiety medication will help him relax.

Everyone else must be fast asleep given the time of night. Arthur in his studio apartment in Rouen, lying peacefully next to his girlfriend. What's her name again? Édouard searches the far corners of his memory, annoyed that it always gets stuck on the tip of his tongue. He's never met the girl, of course, but he knows from Magda that they've been together since last year. It ends in *a*, he thinks, but about three-quarters of women's names end in that letter these days: Naïma, Maïna, Leïla— something like that.

At his in-laws' apartment, Jonathan is probably huddled on a worn fold-out couch, his lifeless legs resting on the mattress. Édouard has always wondered what it's like to feel nothing from the waist down. But he's obviously never dared to ask his brother. Jonathan seemed happy tonight, but Édouard can't repress his doubts—it would take a lot to convince him that, in the end, his brother has a pretty good life, maybe better than his own in a way.

As for Magda, she must be asleep in her husband's arms. Christian, the man who replaced Édouard so easily just a few months after their separation. Do they sleep holding each other, Magda's head on his hairy chest as it gently rises and falls? Or do they spend the night on their own sides of the bed, turned away from each other? He remembers the time when he wanted to go back to her, to leave Paris and return to Le Havre, the time when he was ready to beg her to forgive him, ready to forget his career for her and Arthur. It was one of those nights when the solitude was terrifying and the feeling of missing them overwhelming, both probably amplified by fatigue and a little too much alcohol. He almost got in his car to go to them in the middle of the night, hoping to start over. But he was too drunk to drive and fell asleep on his couch instead after looking nostalgically through a photo album, reliving those few fleeting years of happiness. And a few days later, Magda told him she was moving in with another man, a man she'd met just a month earlier. Édouard kept quiet and magnanimously admitted he'd lost, convinced that it was the best outcome for everyone.

For Magda, who deserved someone who shared her dreams, someone who could protect her and take care of her. For Arthur, who might find a replacement father in Christian, one with fewer flaws than the original. And even for himself—it was so much easier to surrender, to wash his hands of it all and convince himself that the arrival of his replacement would keep him from failing a second time.

The world has stopped to rest, but he can't stop pacing in circles around his overly spacious loft, despite his exhaustion—the exhaustion he's pushed through for so many years. He's tired of feeling guilty all the time because the wound from his childhood has never totally healed, despite his brother's love and kindness. Shattered to have accomplished so much, to have reached the highest heights, only to realize that everyone who really matters to him is still down below, so far away that he can hardly make out their faces in the fog. Wounded to remember how he dreamed of making his son proud, while in the end, all he managed to do was to place a little more distance between them with every passing day. Troubled to realize that if a genie suddenly appeared and offered him a single wish, he would ask to be normal and anonymous again. He used to dream of being the brightest star, but now all he wants is to be transparent, invisible, far from the spotlight and cameras.

He wants to be forgotten.

It all seems like such a waste that he starts to feel dizzy. The pills have made his muscles relax, but his mind refuses to give in, refuses to let go.

Édouard heads back to the couch to sit down, suddenly feeling weak and slow from the Atarax as it dissolves into his bloodstream. He opens the wooden chest he uses as a coffee table and takes out a bottle of Talisker. He pours himself a glass, filled to the brim, and breathes in the delicate peaty scent, his eyes closed.

"Cheers!" he says aloud before taking a long sip that sets his throat on fire.

Today is April 1. April Fools' Day. The day Édouard has always gone to great lengths to come up with the most original and unexpected practical jokes. Being the funniest person in any room has always been his role, the role he assigned himself to assuage his raging guilt.

As a child, he would trick Jonathan ten, even twenty, times in a single day, right up until bedtime, until April 2 if possible. He would tape funny signs to the back of his brother's wheelchair, to their father's back—even if that meant getting a firm smack when Lucien Bresson grew tired of seeing Édouard dancing around him like a clown for no apparent reason. He taped them to Madame Rita's back as well when she was busy cleaning the windows in the entryway to the building. All to hear his little brother's soothing laugh.

Later he continued his April Fools' tradition with Magda and Arthur, coming up with increasingly complicated tricks, designed to impress year after year. He couldn't bear the thought of disappointing them, of one of them saying that the previous year had been better. Fill the soap bottle with oil. Cover the toilet seat in plastic wrap. Make candy apples with onions. TP the car in the middle of the night. Pretend to be dead—though Magda and Arthur didn't find that one particularly funny. Bigger, better, more. Every year.

He knows what he's planning to do today may be seen as a tasteless joke, but what matters most is catching them by surprise, staying unpredictable. And he feels there's something truly magical about doing it today. Maybe no one will believe it, maybe when people wake up, they'll say it's another practical joke, that it can't be real. Maybe they'll continue to doubt for years, convinced he duped them all, as usual. They'll say that it has to be a huge, amazingly well-orchestrated trick—Édouard Bresson's last laugh before heading off to a deserted island to take it easy and enjoy cocktails beneath the coconut trees, after spending years making other people laugh nearly seven days a week.

The comedian finishes his whiskey and notices his tongue feels heavy, almost cumbersome.

If they hadn't had that ridiculous fight that fall Sunday morning, if the abandoned house hadn't been there, would he be in this luxurious apartment today? Would he have been so demanding of himself, would he have been able to love himself a little, just enough to believe he deserved to be happy?

Questions ricochet around the inside of his skull in slow motion, because of the pills and alcohol. He would love to remove all these thoughts from his head, once and for all. He needs them to stop hovering like vultures. He wants his mind to be empty, wants to enjoy the soothing, downy, comforting void.

He stands up slowly, holding on to the edge of the couch to keep from stumbling. He nears the glass doors to the balcony, eager to breathe in the fresh air.

The street below is still deserted. The lights are all off in the building across from him, not a single orange-tinted rectangle offering up a view of silhouettes going about their business. He leans on the railing, head in hands.

He suddenly imagines himself stepping over the freezing railing, visualizes the gymnastics necessary to make it to the other side, his feet perched precariously on the narrow concrete ledge. He can feel the superhuman effort required and his strength fading. *If the streetlights go out before I've counted to ten, everything'll be OK.*

The first rays of the rising sun appear on the horizon, just behind the Eiffel Tower in the distance. His fingers grasp the metal bar, his heart beats a little faster, a little deeper. The harsh glow of the streetlamps below suddenly disappears—it must be after seven o'clock. Paris is stirring. Édouard looks up at the sky, and he feels more peaceful than he has ever felt before.

The world is about to start turning again, but he is finally going to stop, to rest. He's going to vanish when people least expect it. He's going to disappear right under their noses.

PART 2

PART 2

left bEhind

April 1, 2017

Well, that was one hell of a surprise, huh? I'm sure it was the last thing you were expecting. Of course, I'm in the same boat. Who would have thought that when the sun rose this morning the great, the tremendous, the extraordinary Édouard Bresson would no longer be of this world? That France's favorite comedian for almost ten years now—with an official survey to prove it, thank you very much—would have chosen to end it for once and for all. *See ya, I'm outta here. Enjoy your memories of me, your posters and DVDs. Oh, and don't forget, my backstage interview is on TF1 tonight. Funny, right?*

To be honest, I'm having a hard time excluding the possibility that it might all be a big, bad joke. Just like you. Especially on April 1. I'm sure the bastard chose the date on purpose. To make us wonder, to make us laugh about his fake death before discovering that maybe it actually was *for real*, as the kids say. To make us think maybe the master has pulled off his greatest prank ever. You know he'd be perfectly capable of doing something like that.

I mean, my father was never very good about respecting limits. The line between laughter and tears is often so fine it's intangible. Like when you were little and people tickled you: you laughed, and kept laughing, until the tickling suddenly became uncomfortable, then unbearable, bringing tears of pain—not joy—to your eyes. My father never understood that strange second when laughter turns to tears. For him, life was one big joke; everything was good for a laugh. I remember an April Fools' Day when he pretended to have died in his sleep. I can still see his gaping mouth, his fixed, almost glassy eyes. I can see myself shaking him over and over again, harder and harder. "Stop, Daddy, it's not funny anymore. Wake up!"

My mother laughed sarcastically, then sighed in exasperation before finally starting to worry, fearing that maybe it wasn't just a stupid April Fools' Day prank, that maybe he really was lying there dead in the bed, maybe she needed to do something instead of standing there like an idiot, waiting for him to stand up and yell, "I really got you this time!" So she shook him with me, even slapped him. "Édouard, if you're faking it, I swear I'm going to kill you!" Then she tried to listen for his heartbeat, her ear glued to his chest, but my screaming kept her from hearing anything else. In a panic, she ran to the phone. "Hello, yes, I think my husband has had a heart attack. He's on the bed, unconsc—"

"Oh boy, I really got you. You should see your faces!" exclaimed my father as he jumped up, beaming with pride, so satisfied with himself he couldn't see he'd gone too far.

"The day you really die, no one will believe it, Édouard," my mother muttered dejectedly, her voice trembling—not with sadness but with anger.

My father just laughed. "Hey, that's not a bad idea! That would be one hell of a prank!"

Now it seems Édouard Bresson threw himself off his balcony last night. My father supposedly jumped from his ninth-floor Parisian apartment, slamming his skull into the gray asphalt below. I wonder if it was my father or the comedian who decided it was time to bow out.

He must have taken his final dive just as I was enjoying my umpteenth beer comfortably seated in an armchair at David's parents' house—they were out of town. The party had been going strong all night and then into the early morning, but nobody seemed tired, probably because we were letting off steam from taking practice tests all week. The sun was just starting to rise in Rouen, and I was watching Manel dance with two of her friends, moving her hips to an electro beat like only she knew how. I reveled in her carefree expression; her big dark-brown eyes; her insolent, provocative pose; her ebony hair tied up in a tight ballerina bun because she knows how much I love to watch the strands cascade over her shoulders when she pulls out the bobby pins one by one. I was having a good time. We planned to laze around the next day to recover from the late night.

And then some guy just had to check his Facebook page. After a few seconds of looking at the screen in disbelief, he passed his phone around. When the screen came near, David passed it to me without a word, his face pale. His Adam's apple traveled unusually high up his throat as he swallowed. I remember exactly what I said as I took the iPhone with the cracked screen from him. "Come on, hand it over! What's with the sad face? Has Johnny Hallyday finally kicked the bucket?"

And then I read it: *Édouard Bresson found dead. Sources say the comedian committed suicide by jumping off his balcony.* When I looked up again, I realized someone had turned off the music. Everyone was feverishly tapping their touch screens and exclaiming, "I can't believe it!" They seemed shaken, as if something had happened to someone they loved. Manel had stopped dancing. She had her hand over her mouth, in shock, on the edge of tears.

I, on the other hand, couldn't help but think about that April Fools' Day when I was barely five and my father lay on the bed like a dead fish washed up on a beach. I scrolled through the newsfeed on the phone I still had in my hand, reading a few posts here and there, all of them totally absurd. I smiled—he'd pulled it off, the big prank he'd been dreaming of for so long, the one no one else had ever attempted. I guess the Stade de France was just the first part of this unbelievably morbid practical joke. What a nutjob.

"It's a prank, guys. Don't get all teary-eyed—it's not real. Everyone knows the guy's crazy. I'm sure it's just a practical joke. He always goes overboard. He doesn't know when to stop."

I stood up to turn the music back on. The others watched me, confused. They were probably wondering why I seemed so sure of myself, why I thought I had any more authority than they did to talk about someone I didn't know. Manel came over and hugged me.

"No crying," I said. "He's faking it."

"But he's your father . . . ," she insisted quietly.

I looked at her reproachfully and she frowned, annoyed with my indifference. It just wasn't the right time to shout from the rooftops that the famous Édouard Bresson was my father.

I put my hands on her hips, pulling her close, wanting to feel her warm breath on my neck. "Come on, let's dance." No way my father was going to ruin my night with his bullshit.

Of course, I didn't get to ignore it for long. My phone started vibrating incessantly in my jeans pocket. Mom. I was tempted to turn it off—my father had already tried to call three times earlier in the evening, and I was fed up. Having your parents on your back all the time when you're twenty-three is a real downer. But Manel stopped dancing and looked at me expectantly.

"Answer it. It might be important."

I picked up, to please her; I knew she would make my life miserable if I didn't. And I really didn't want her to share my secret.

My mother was crying on the other end of the line, and I couldn't make out much of what she was mumbling.

"Calm down, Mom. I don't understand." Though I knew exactly what she was trying to say behind all that sniffling. "I know, Mom, it's just that I don't believe it for a second. I mean, come on, how many times did he pull one over on us?"

I went into David's parents' room to be alone and sat down on the impeccably ironed gray flannel duvet cover. My mother finally took a deep breath and managed to put together a full sentence.

"He's really dead. His manager, Hervé, identified his body. I spoke to Hervé on the phone. He was crying, totally in shock."

At that moment, I admit she made me wonder. I could hear her as she kept talking, but it was like she was far away, her words all mixed up—I'd stopped listening. I hung up after a few minutes, distraught. I felt like someone had just tried to sober me up by dumping a bucket of ice-cold water on my head.

Hoping to put my mind to rest, I checked Facebook again, then Twitter. Articles were popping up everywhere. Posts from devastated fans were spreading like wildfire. Grieving tributes and temporary profile pictures styled with navy-blue-and-white Breton stripes in memory of the Saint James sweaters he always wore onstage were trending. In my head, I was already thinking of him in the past tense. I felt like I was in free fall, the world turned upside down in seconds.

A few hours later, back in the studio apartment Manel and I share, I put on my running shoes.

"Where are you going, Arthur?"

"To get some fresh air."

"Do you really think this is the time? We need to go to Paris. You need to handle funeral arrangements and who knows what else . . ."

"My father has never needed me. There will be a ton of people vying for the opportunity to take care of all of that. Unless he suddenly reappears between now and then, of course."

"We should still go. I'm sure your mom is already there."

"One hour won't make any difference, so I'm going for a run. I don't think my father will hold it against me."

I left before Manel could chide me anymore. My sleep-deprived legs had a hard time keeping pace, and when I finally hit my stride, I suddenly realized that I was going to have to explain a few things about Édouard to Manel. About our relationship, or rather the lack thereof. She is one of the only people who knows I'm his son, but I haven't ever taken the time to explain why I go to such great lengths to keep it a secret.

I've never told her about elementary school, when the kids all refused to believe that Édouard was my dad because he never did drop-off or pick-up. "No one's ever seen your dad—he must be invisible!" And they all chuckled and knowingly nudged one another, encouraging further harassment, calling me a liar. When they saw my stepfather Christian drop me off one morning, that was it. "Your dad doesn't look anything like Édouard Bresson! You've been making it up this whole time!" I tried in vain to explain that he was my mother's second husband, to show them pictures of Édouard and me together, but they refused to believe me. I even tried fighting the kids with the biggest mouths behind the chestnut trees on the playground, but the teasing continued. I asked my father to come and show them all, several times, but he didn't understand how important it was. "I don't have time to make a round-trip from Paris to Le Havre just to pick you up from school! Use your head!"

I've never told Manel about how I was everybody's favorite target in middle school just because I couldn't recite hilarious jokes on command. "If Édouard Bresson is your dad, you should be able to make us laugh, right? C'mon, what are you waiting for?" As if humor were hereditary, as if I were just a miniature version of Édouard. And since I wasn't funny, since I refused to even try to be funny, I was rewarded with four difficult years of biting remarks that all conveyed the same message: it was no wonder my father had left given how incredibly boring and serious I was.

And I've never told Manel about my first relationship with a girl, in high school. The kind of girl guys dream about, who decided she wanted me, though no one could figure out what she saw in me, with my messy hair and braces. But it soon became obvious—she only ever wanted to talk about one thing: Édouard. She wanted to know everything about him and was constantly saying how amazing it must be to have a famous father. I minimized it all, convinced myself that, given how much she seemed to enjoy sticking her tongue down my throat, she must like me too. And, of course, I was in love with her. Pure and simple. Happy that she'd chosen me. Right up until the day she invited me home, led me by the hand to her room, and gleefully showed me the dozens of posters plastered to her walls. Posters of *him*. Posters she kissed one by one before going to bed at night. She wasn't even embarrassed to tell me. She seemed totally oblivious to the idea that it might hurt me—or gross me out.

I've never told any of this to anyone, actually. But I guess I'll have to now. Sooner or later, Manel will want actual answers to her questions.

While I was out on my run, the media interviewed my father's "entourage" and quickly unearthed all sorts of people desperate to share their opinions of Édouard Bresson's suicide. All the usual platitudes had their moment: "I could tell he'd been exhausted recently," said his manager. "We never saw it coming. It's just awful!" reflected his producer. Djamila Meddour, the artistic director who had launched his career, also played along: "The first time I auditioned Édouard, I knew right away that there was something broken in him, a flaw that he was desperately trying to hide, but that was precisely what interested me. I already knew from experience that the comedians who have suffered the most have the most to share with the audience."

Right.

That's the exact moment when I started thinking maybe something really had happened, maybe it wasn't a hallucination or a monumental mistake by the media. Either Édouard committed suicide, or he's taking us all for a ride. It's hard not to instinctively assume the latter is more plausible, hard not to believe that he's hiding somewhere, pleased with himself, planning to make a spectacular reappearance in a few days. He'll turn up tomorrow or the next day, hand a tissue to a sobbing fan, appear on a TV show, and shout, "Ta-da!" leaving the host mesmerized. And he's obviously convinced that we'll all be amazed, that we'll vigorously applaud his original idea. He must think his performance will go down in history.

"You have to go big," he used to say when I was a kid.

Well, I guess this is as big as it gets.

unraVel

April 3, 2017

Just as I'm starting to resent the fact that he didn't even take the time to explain himself or his actions to anyone (further proof that it must all be one big prank), I get a letter from him in the mail. I immediately recognize his thin, meticulous handwriting, his letters slanted to the right as if bowing in the wind.

For a second, I think that I was right after all, that it *is* a practical joke, since he's writing to me several days after his "death." I can already see him, hiding who knows where, chuckling over his great prank. When I notice the April 1 postmark, the joy of being right intensifies. Then I consider plausible explanations. Édouard could have mailed it the night before, or could have given it to someone else to send. The rush of adrenaline I got from thinking I had a scoop dissipates as quickly as it came on.

I climb the stairs to our studio apartment and put the letter on the coffee table, which has been covered in law textbooks and notes for weeks. I deliberately take my time. I heat water for tea, listening to the purr of the electric kettle, watching the steam billow out of its aluminum spout. There's no reason to hurry. I put away the dishes drying on the rack and wipe down the counter.

Once everything is perfectly clean, I sit down on the couch and pick up the letter again. I finally notice that Édouard wrote *Arthur Pazzoli* on the brown envelope. I can't help but let out a contemptuous laugh that echoes around the quiet apartment. I wonder if it was hard for him to write that last name.

I still remember his reaction when he found out how I "betrayed" him when I left for college in Rouen. It seemed like such an obvious solution to me—cut all ties, become anonymous, stop being "Édouard Bresson's son." So I took my mother's maiden name, Pazzoli. On official documents I had to make do with a hyphenated version, including my father's name, but any chance I got I simply erased the unwanted surname. It's true, if I had kept my father's name, I could have simply claimed I'm not related to Édouard at all. But after all that suffering, I needed to make a clean break. When people asked my name, I needed to be able to say Arthur Pazzoli. And when I wrote that name on my mailbox in Rouen, a wave of relief washed over me. I finally felt like I was me—just me.

A few months later, my father sent me a birthday gift that was returned to sender because he had written *Arthur Bresson* on the package. He called me. "Did you move? I don't understand why the package was returned. Very weird . . ." That's when I told him I had taken my mom's name. I bumbled through an explanation and was met with a long silence on the other end of the line.

"I didn't know people could just up and change their names like that . . . ," he replied in a daze.

I tried to downplay it: "It's not official yet. It's kind of a long process. I have to put together a file and prove I have a legitimate reason to change it."

Édouard listened, then quietly repeated, "A legitimate reason" to himself. I tied myself in knots, explaining more than I had planned about how I had to prove that my current name had a negative effect on my life. Things got out of hand, and Édouard swung violently from mute incomprehension to rage. He finally hung up on me after shouting into the receiver that I was basically disowning him. I never called him back, nor did he call me. The silence between us lasted for months.

Now part of me is curious to open the envelope, while the other part is sure nothing it says will have any impact on me. What could he have to say to me? Something reassuring to let me know it's just a joke, that I shouldn't worry, and that he's counting on me to keep his secret? I sigh in advance, but curiosity wins out and I carefully slide a knife under the flap of the envelope, so as not to rip the letter. It's not that I think it's precious or anything, I'm just a conscientious person.

The envelope contains a piece of graph paper covered in my father's handwriting, as well as a second, smaller envelope.

Despite my desire to remain totally indifferent, I start reading, more eagerly than I'd like.

> *Arthur,*
>
> *I have no idea how you'll feel when you read these lines. Maybe you'll even refuse to open the letter—fair enough.*
>
> *I let us drift apart for far too long to hope that it's not too late. I know it's silly to write that now, but what else could I write? I'm willing to guess the average suicide letter is pretty sentimental and overwrought.*
>
> *I'll do my best, nonetheless, to avoid anything too weepy. You know I'm much better at making people laugh than at tugging at their heartstrings.*
>
> *You must think I'm a terrible person to have turned my back on you like I did, and you're probably right. I must be a coward to prefer ending it all to finding a better way forward. But I'm so high on my pedestal that I don't*

see any other way down. No one would let me go back to a quiet little life. It's too late for that.

I wish we'd had a different relationship. I wish I had been a better father than my own. Maybe we're all doomed to repeat our parents' mistakes, generation after generation. Maybe trying to do the opposite is the best way to end up with the same failed result.

I'd like to tell you that if I could do it all over again, I would do it differently. That I would be a better husband and a better father. But we both know that's a load of bull. If I could do it over again, I'd do it exactly the same, because I'd get lost again, because I never really felt like I chose any of it, even if you're convinced I did. Hey, I almost wrote, "I didn't choose the stage, it chose me," but I stopped myself in time. I guess sentimentality is starting to eat away at my mind—I'll have to keep this short.

I'll get to the point. I know that, whatever I write, it will never be enough. You think you know everything about me, just like I thought I knew everything about you, simply because you're my son.

The truth, Arthur, is that you don't know much about me. I'm a stranger to you, and that is one of the greatest regrets of my life. Words can't explain it all, especially since I'm convinced that the only way you can really know a person is by gathering pieces here and there. Fragments, held in the memories of other people, come together like puzzle pieces to form the most complete picture of a person.

I wasn't as present in your life as I should have been. I missed a lot of important father-son events. Writing it doesn't undo anything, but please know that I did my best, despite my failures, flaws, and harshness. I did the best I could. Growing up, we believe our parents are all-powerful and all-knowing. The reality is that they're just regular people, as lost as we are, trying not to mess up.

I think the only moments of happiness you probably remember with me are the treasure hunts I organized for your birthday every year, when you came to Paris for the summer. I remember how excited you got, how hard you worked to solve the riddles, how happy you were to figure them out and find each new clue. I can still see your smile—I hold on to it, even though the image has faded over the years in the depths of my memory.

I won't be there to follow you through this last treasure hunt, and really, it's better that way. I know your birthday isn't for another few months. I'm sorry I couldn't wait any longer.

You'll find the first clue in the second envelope.

Love,

Édouard

When I finish reading my father's words, I repress the urge to crumple the paper into a ball. I feel like I've been slapped hard across the face. It's a goddamn goodbye letter. He can't have written all this if he's going to suddenly show up again in a few days, can he? Édouard is eccentric, but hardly a sadist, so what other conclusion can I draw? That he faked his suicide to disappear, to go live his life somewhere else under a fake identity, in a country where no one has ever heard of him? Is that really his grand idea? To leave me here and organize a stupid treasure hunt as if I were a kid again, as a consolation prize? What am I supposed to get out of it? Will this sordid game lead me to him? I don't understand any of it.

I mechanically open the second envelope, which is pastel blue. Inside, I find two tickets for Disneyland Paris. Pluto and Daisy Duck smile at me so brightly it almost feels like they're mocking me. On one of the tickets my father has written in black ink, *In memory of Buzz Lightyear.* It's like he thinks I'm still ten years old.

Jesus, and this is only the beginning. I put the tickets back in the envelope, then place the envelope in the coffee table drawer, annoyed by the absurdity of it all. He must have read too many shitty mysteries. A treasure hunt at Disneyland Paris. Fuck him.

remEmber

Two days later, Manel and I are waiting in line at Disneyland Paris, alongside hundreds of other people decked out in Mickey ears. It looks like the entire country has taken the day off. As it turns out, my decision to forget about my father's stupid game wasn't exactly set in stone.

Manel convinced me to make the trip out to the theme park. "We have to go to Paris for the funeral anyway. Why don't we just get there a day early?" She kept bringing it up until I finally gave in, even whining that her parents had never taken her, and that she'd been dying to go since she was a kid. When she told me I was incredibly lucky to have had a father who took me there several times a year, I thought smoke might come out of my ears.

Sure, it's true that I went to Disneyland Paris so many times that I got sick of it. But I don't have a single memory of my father picking me up at school or teaching me to ride a bike, no memories at all of him in my daily life. Obviously, since he wasn't there—he wasn't interested in being there for me. If he'd been able to get rid of me for good, I'm sure he would have.

Manel says I must be exaggerating, but that's only proof that she never met Édouard Bresson. My stepfather, Christian, has done so much more for me. He helped me move into my apartment in Rouen two years ago, for example. The extraordinary Édouard Bresson had other, more important things to do that weekend—as usual. I didn't ask for his help, and it never occurred to him to offer.

All he ever did was push me to follow in his footsteps, to play the clown and act ridiculous to make him laugh. He never understood that the only reason I ever went along with it was so he would pay attention to me. I attended years of theater classes so he'd like me better, in hopes that maybe he'd even show up and clap for me at the end-of-the-year play. All because I naively imagined that if I tried to be like him—without having a quarter of his talent or passion—it might bring us together. He never stopped to wonder if I enjoyed any of it, because it was obvious to him that I had been born for the stage. The day he finally realized that I wasn't good enough, and that I wanted to do something else with my life, he turned his back on me.

As if I'd ruined everything by daring to open my mouth and say what *I* had in mind for my future. And the only time I ever asked him for anything after that, he gleefully told me off.

It was just under a year ago, a few months after our argument about me taking Mom's name. I was helping to organize a university-wide charity event to benefit Lawyers Without Borders. We were having a hard time getting things off the ground, finding sponsors and acts likely to attract students, outside of a few campus bands. We finally managed to convince a singer who had been a finalist on *The Voice* the previous year, who agreed to perform a few songs to open the event. The posters and flyers were ready, and we had launched a campaign on social media when the selfish diva pulled out, just two weeks before the event. We were all devastated, of course. Until Manel came up with the bright idea of asking Édouard for help. I refused at first, but she insisted. "It'll give you a reason to make up with your dad. You haven't talked since he found out about your name. You have nothing to lose." And on and on. In the end, I gave in and picked up my phone. I explained to Édouard how dire the situation was, how important the fund-raising event was, then asked if he'd make a short appearance onstage. Just one sketch, his choice. I told him he'd be saving us from a massive failure.

I guess the opportunity to pay me back for changing my name was too tempting to resist. He let me tell my whole sad story, let me keep talking for ten minutes, then said he found it strange that I was suddenly no longer ashamed of his name, that I had suddenly realized he could be useful. I let him rail for a while, telling myself I deserved it. And then he asked, "So if I do this for you, are you still going to pretend you're not my son? Or are you willing to blow your cover?" I hesitated—too long for his taste. He barked that I could figure it out on my own, and hung up. After that, neither one of us felt like making the first move to reconcile. That was the last time I heard his voice.

As we wait to ride "it's a small world," the couple ahead of us is huddled over their camera. The woman, in a navy wool poncho, complains loudly as her husband clicks through the photos on the little screen. "They're all blurry!" she says with a groan. Her husband nods, just as discouraged as she is. That's all Manel needs to come to their rescue. She takes the camera, deftly adjusts the settings, then hands it back to them, proud to have been helpful. That's just the kind of person she is. She feels compelled to get involved in other people's lives. Sometimes it's awkward, but it's also the reason we're together today.

We met two years ago on the bus. She was sitting next to me, reading the newspaper over my shoulder. I had been stuck on my crossword puzzle for no more than ten seconds when she ecstatically exclaimed, "Maine Coon!" When I turned to look at her, she answered my confused look with "American cat, nine letters: Maine Coon!"

"I would have figured it out myself with more time," I replied sourly.

Suddenly uncomfortable, she blushed, and her ears turned red. "I'm sorry, I didn't mean, I didn't think . . ." I found her sincerity so touching that I moved my paper closer, to make it easier for her to read, sharing my crossword puzzle as a gesture of apology. She finished the whole thing in just a few minutes, and it took a superhuman effort for me not to pout.

As the morning wears on, it starts to rain—a light mist that slowly soaks everything in its path. Thrilled to finally be having the Disney experience, Manel leads me from ride to ride. I follow like a robot. I haven't been here since the last summer I spent with my father, the summer I turned fourteen. After that, I decided I was too old to spend the whole month of August with him. I wanted to go to camp with my friends. Plus, I was too big for my father to drag me to Disneyland anymore. He'd taken me too many times for it to be fun anymore. I didn't have to insist too much before he gave in and agreed to see me for just one week at the end of August.

But now, nearly ten years later, here I am again amid the colorful rides, brick paths, and inviting shops. It's strangely like flipping through a photo album that's been hidden away for years. The familiar scent of cotton candy, the parade music. I can picture us sitting on the curb in the hot sun. "This is the best spot for watching the floats and the characters, Arthur. You'll see. This year all the *Toy Story* characters will be in the parade!" I wonder if I'm imagining my father's enthusiasm, given how uncharacteristic it would have been.

"Look! He's over there!"

Manel's voice pulls me out of my memories. She points at something across the way.

"It's Buzz Lightyear!"

I stay where I am, in line for Space Mountain. Unshakable, she pulls me by the hand.

"Come on! We have to go see him!"

"But we've been waiting for half an hour already. We can't leave now."

She's already left, without waiting for me. I reluctantly follow.

"Hurry up! I'll take a picture of you with him!"

Manel's offer is full of the spontaneity she brings to everything in life, and her words echo my father's whenever we saw a character from *Toy Story*, which was my favorite movie back then—actually, it's probably still my favorite animated movie, even though I haven't seen it in a long time. He bought me full Woody and Buzz costumes, and I spent entire weeks dressed up, refusing to wear normal clothes. And my father let me—that sort of thing wasn't a big deal to him. He had no qualms about walking down the street with a cowboy or going grocery shopping with an astronaut who loudly spouted, "To infinity and beyond!" every three minutes.

Standing next to Buzz Lightyear with a tense look on my face, I do my best to ignore the line of children waiting their turn, eager to meet the giant character with his rigid plastic smile. Manel gives me a thumbs-up to let me know she's gotten the shot, and I hurry over to her, a little ashamed to find myself amid all these kids who barely reach my hips.

"Did you ask him?"

"Ask him what?"

"If he had anything for you! Your father wrote, *In memory of Buzz Lightyear* on the ticket—it must be a clue!"

"You're crazy! There's no way I'm asking that. Sorry to disappoint. Anyway, a different guy plays him every day, so how—?"

Manel wheels around, leaving me talking to thin air. She heads over to the astronaut, deliberately ignoring the parents and children angrily complaining, "Hey, wait your turn!"

"Excuse me?" she shouts on her tiptoes, making sure her voice penetrates the thick plastic helmet.

Buzz takes a step back in surprise. He places his hands on his hips and puffs up his chest.

"You're going to think this is a weird question, but do you have anything for my boyfriend?"

She points at me, and Buzz looks in my general direction, then gestures that he doesn't see who she's talking about. I imagine the poor guy sweating bullets inside his hard, airtight costume. He must be so confused.

"Let it go, Manel. Come on, let's get out of here."

As usual, she refuses to admit defeat. Buzz stomps heavily over to a group of delighted children, but she catches up with him and taps him vigorously on the shoulder.

"Wait, please! Are you sure? His name is Arthur. Arthur Bresson. Does that ring a bell?"

I instinctively clench my jaw when I hear Manel use that name. It's stupid, but it's like a Pavlovian reflex—it brings up so many unpleasant memories and feelings that I can't help but tense up.

Buzz stops in his tracks, then turns toward me. He crosses his arms over his chest. It's hard to know what he's thinking given his inert exterior, but maybe it's something along the lines of *Bresson? Like Édouard Bresson?* as he strains to see a resemblance.

The astronaut takes several giant steps over to me. He doesn't say a word, which is for the best, since a high-pitched, muffled human voice wouldn't go well with the costume. His arched eyebrows make me feel like he's staring me down, disdainfully thinking, *Am I really supposed to believe you are related to him?*

I'm starting to wonder why I agreed to come to this stupid place when he suddenly opens his arms wide and wraps them firmly around me. Shit, this guy is going to squeeze me to death, and nobody will notice a goddamn thing. I try to speak, but my mouth is squashed against his plastic biceps.

And then I realize. He's giving me a *hug*. He's waiting for my arms to wrap around his waist in return. As I mechanically complete the gesture of affection, a wave of emotion washes over me, though I can't adequately describe what I'm feeling. I almost want to cry—probably because he's hurting me by holding me so tight. I wait, and he finally lets go.

His giant arms struggle to reach under his costume at his waist. He pulls out a small, colorful package with *ARTHUR* written across the top in black marker. Even in all caps, I recognize my father's handwriting.

Buzz drops the box into my hands and does a little bow, making the group of children gathered around me and Manel burst into laughter. Then he goes back to posing for photos.

"You see? I was right to insist," Manel says softly as she rests her head on my shoulder.

"I guess you were."

"It's unbelievable. Can you imagine everything your dad must have done to organize this?" she asks admiringly.

I remain impassive. My father is capable of orchestrating much more impressive things. I know this is only the beginning. All he had to do for this one was bribe the guy who manages the characters to tell all the guys who play Buzz Lightyear to hug me and hand over the box. Nothing complicated about that.

We sit down on a bench to open the package. Manel seems more excited about the treasure hunt than I am. I rip open the brown paper wrapping to find a sample-size box of Honey Pops. I open the plastic bag and pour the tiny yellow balls into my hand. Manel eagerly grabs a few to snack on. I find a key taped to the bottom of the box.

Wordlessly, we sit side by side eating the dry cereal. I remember standing immobile in the cereal aisle as a child, taking forever to make a decision. I inspected each and every box, weighing the various free gifts inside, trying to find one with both a cereal that I liked and a cool toy to play with. My mother hated waiting for me to make up my mind. She always ended up choosing for me. "Grocery shopping is a chore, Arthur, so it'd be nice if you could make things a little easier for me." My father, however, let me have all the time I needed—he so rarely took me shopping that it was all fun and games to him. He would compare all the boxes with me, or leave me there while he filled up the cart, then come back when he had finished.

"Do you want to go back to Space Mountain?" asks Manel after wiping the sticky crumbs off her hands.

"No, I think I'd rather go back."

"Back to the hotel? Already?"

"No, not to the hotel. To my father's place. This is the key to his apartment."

When we reach my father's quiet little street, sheltered from the hubbub and honking of the adjacent boulevard, the first thing we notice is the mountains of bouquets piled on either side of the door to his building. There are so many that they spill out over the sidewalk, right up to the curb. It rained earlier this week, and the plastic wrappers are covered in tiny drops of condensation. Some of the flowers are already brown. Wilted. Dead.

Manel watches me grab armfuls of bouquets and place them in the nearest dumpster. It's quickly so full that the lid won't close properly, but at least the street is clean—nothing left but a few dirty white petals from a bouquet of roses that fell apart when I picked it up.

Since Manel hates the cramped elevators found in Parisian apartment buildings, we climb the stairs to the ninth floor. Our feet are silent on the thick carpet running up the middle of the steps. I automatically start counting the brass bars attached across the bottom of each one to hold down the carpet, just like when I was a kid. I remember that no matter how hard I concentrated, I never got the same number. My father convinced me that it was because the staircase transformed every night, varying the number of steps. So ridiculous.

The key turns easily in the lock. I push open the heavy reinforced door but can't bring myself to step inside. Strangely, I feel like a burglar. The apartment is bathed in soft light, swathed in a deathly silence.

I finally decide to go in, leaving Manel to quietly close the door behind us. I walk through the whole loft, running my fingers along the walls, furniture, and objects as if trying to make it all more real. The place is spotless, everything in its place, just like I remember it. The cleaning lady must have come recently—maybe even the morning of March 31. *I want it to be perfect today! Spick-and-span! I have big plans tonight!* I can totally imagine my father saying, his lips curled upward in the mischievous smile of a kid about to pull off a practical joke.

In the living room, nothing has changed. The off-white walls with a few touches of gray, the giant frame and its well-known picture of the Eiffel Tower taken from below, the beige leather couch with symmetrically placed charcoal pillows, the carefully arranged knickknacks on the marble mantel above the fake fireplace. The perfect show apartment—as impersonal as it gets. It's hard to imagine anyone actually lives here. That anyone could have ever lived here.

The only object that reveals someone has been here recently is an empty whiskey glass on the coffee table. My father apparently neglected to use a coaster to protect the wooden chest he uses as a table from his last drink. It's probably the only sign that points to the chaos inside, because Édouard never placed glasses directly on that chest, which I seem to remember he inherited from his grandparents. I got told off enough times for it as a kid that I'll never forget that particular obsession.

I take a whiff of the whiskey left in the bottom of the glass, breathing in the scent I so closely associate with my father. He would have a glass of Talisker every night before dinner. I never knew if he did it all the time, or only when I was staying with him. Either way, when he kissed me good night, his breath always had a spicy, slightly sweet scent to it.

The bed in his room is still made. No clothes lying around, no dirty socks thrown in the corner, no Breton-stripe sweater placed over the teal velvet armchair that perfectly complements the ash-gray walls. Nothing. My father could be on vacation, on tour. He could have moved—or thrown himself off the balcony.

I yank open the sliding door to his closet to find a row of button-down shirts on hangers. They sway gently, like fabric ghosts silently mocking me. *Did he really think his father would be waiting in here for him, hidden in a closet, his hand over his mouth to stifle a laugh?* I'm suddenly ashamed, but still feel disappointed. Despite all reason, my hands part the shirts. No one.

I grab Manel's hand and whisper, "We'll take my room." I don't know why I'm keeping my voice down, as if we're in a sacred, solemn place, whose silence we mustn't disturb.

I open the door to the room I spent so many vacations in, a room I haven't visited in years. The hinges creak gently, then everything is as I remember it. The twin bed in the corner, the Woody and Buzz Lightyear stuffed toys propped comfortably against the wall as if put there by a child just moments ago. The Disney posters hung on the wall with thumbtacks even though my father cringed at the idea of the holes they would leave behind. I still don't understand why it mattered, since he apparently never redecorated my childhood bedroom. It's almost like one of those mausoleums you see in movies where a child has died, and the parents can't bear to change anything, refusing year after year to turn it into an office or guest room.

"The bed's small, but I wouldn't feel right sleeping in my father's . . . Is that OK?" I'm still murmuring, as if I'm afraid of getting caught in a place that's off-limits.

Maybe on some level I'm still worried—or hoping—a key might turn in the front door and my father will burst through, shouting cheerily, "I really got you this time, didn't I!"

Manel agrees and drops her backpack onto what still seems to be *my* bed.

"Should we get something to eat?" she asks loudly, aiming to break the awkward spell that's settling over the loft.

"We can go look in the kitchen, but my father wasn't really into cooking."

I'm right again. There's nothing in the fridge but a carton of eggs and a tub of sour cream. It's a shame his cleaning lady doesn't do grocery shopping too. Manel suggests making pasta and starts rummaging through cabinets for a pot. I open the pantry, rifle through bags and boxes, and pull out some spaghetti. An orange cereal box catches my eye—Honey Pops, of course.

I grab the box. The bag inside is still three-quarters full, so I empty it into a mixing bowl like I did when I was little to get the toy. A rolled-up piece of paper falls into the glass bowl. I quickly unroll it.

A name and a phone number: *Yoann, 06 45 78 65 32*. Nothing else.

"Do you know him?" Manel asks curiously from behind me.

"No. Never heard of him."

I run through my memory, searching for some mention of the name, maybe by my father, but I turn up empty.

Refuse

Using a tired cliché, the media announced that it would be a "very private affair."

Very private, my ass. When Manel and I join my mother outside Saint-Ambroise Church, I wonder if all of Paris has turned out to mourn their favorite clown. I can't possibly count the faces as they stand in reverential silence, tears rimming their eyes or running down their faces as if they've just lost a family member. Their palpable grief highlights my inability to feel anything. These strangers are sobbing and suffering while I stand by emotionless. Everyone thinks I'm in shock, that I'll cry later, when I finally *realize* what has happened, as my mother said to Manel last night when they thought I couldn't hear them. Manel told her she thought the fact that I was starting to talk about Édouard in the past tense was a step in the right direction, but that I still needed time. Of course I don't talk about him in the present anymore—he wouldn't deserve it even if . . . I don't feel like I'm in shock. Not at all. To be perfectly honest, I think I just don't give a shit. My father is gone. Maybe that's sad, but it's not like he was around before, so what's changed? Plus, I'd look like a real idiot if I were hysterical and then it turns out he's not dead and he makes his big comeback in the middle of the funeral.

I discreetly tug at Manel's hand to keep us toward the back. We let my mother and stepfather get several yards ahead of us before starting toward the church again. I know neither Manel nor my mother approve of my insistence on maintaining my anonymity, but they're not the ones who would have to deal with the cameras and mics if people found out I'm Édouard Bresson's son. There's no way I'm serving myself up on a platter to the media so they—and then everyone else—can start and end every conversation with a single topic: Édouard, Édouard, Édouard. *What was he like? You must be devastated. Did he leave you a letter? Did you notice he wasn't doing well?* I can handle a lot, but not that, not after spending so many years trying to forget about him.

The entire country seems to be in mourning, and I feel completely out of sync, awkward in my too-tight dress shoes and suit I bought especially for the occasion. "There will be cameras everywhere, Arthur. Please make an effort." My father never wore a suit, not even when he married my mom, according to the yellowed photographs, but I keep quiet and do what I'm told to avoid starting unnecessary fights, fights that could so easily get blown out of proportion. Plus, my goal is to go unnoticed—I don't want to stand out from the rest of Édouard's elegant entourage. But his fans, at least, have got it right: they're almost all wearing Breton-stripe sweaters in tribute. It's so easy nowadays to share ideas like that. They circulate at the speed of light on social networks. The whole crowd seems to be dressed alike, forming a wave of blue-and-white stripes that saddens my mother. I can tell from the way her shoulders slump almost imperceptibly, as if the weight of these strangers' devotion to her ex-husband were too much to bear, as if it were material proof of what a waste his death was.

I'm sure Saint James must be making a killing thanks to him—it's one hell of a marketing opportunity they did nothing to deserve. Now that I think of it, it's surprising they never asked Édouard to be a spokesperson for the brand.

My face is impassive. I've put on the most neutral expression possible, both restrained and solemn. The paparazzi are everywhere, huge telephoto lenses competing tirelessly for the best shots. They all want to get the most moving, heartbreaking picture, the one that will make people sob even harder. They're on the hunt for tearful faces that will make everyone want to see more, make them want to read about the event of the year. I can already hear grannies gossiping about it at the hair salon during their perms, parents in the waiting room at the pediatrician's office, college students in line at the grocery store saddened by the cover of the TV guide at the checkout stand, saddened by my father's overly serious look, the one everyone associates with him.

Dozens of stars have turned out to pay their last respects to Édouard Bresson—or to afford themselves the opportunity to casually run into a particular reporter with a tissue in hand. Even the ones he couldn't stand, the ones who treated him like crap, have shown up. They're all here in this freezing, austere church, just to piss him off one last time, I guess. Ah, the beauty of human nature.

As I look around discreetly, I can't help but wonder if the mysterious Yoann is in the compact crowd of people dressed in black. I almost want to yell out his name, or call his number to see if a ringer will suddenly break the respectful silence, attracting looks of outrage.

The church is full to the rafters. People are even standing in the central aisle, waiting for the priest to begin before finding a more permanent spot. I'm sure he'll say that my father is with God now and that the angels have been laughing nonstop since his arrival. Then he'll invite us to join him in song, something about holy light and Jesus resurrected—everyone will know the words, except for me, so I'll have to pretend to sing along mournfully. Seeing the closed casket just a few yards away and knowing that everyone will soon walk past it, making the sign of the cross as a final goodbye, almost makes me want to laugh. *Come on, guys, my father didn't even believe in God.* The few times I went with him to a wedding or baptism, he always stayed outside on the church steps, smoking as he waited for the "religious baloney" to be over with. But his producer and manager insisted it was important we hold a religious ceremony, because "media-wise, it plays better." I don't know who agreed since I refused to have anything to do with organizing the funeral. I let his team take care of everything. They might not be family, but I'm sure they must have known him better. They are definitely better placed to say what Édouard would have wanted. In my humble opinion, he wouldn't have given a damn about the color of his coffin or whether his plot at Père Lachaise Cemetery is shady or not. He might have wanted to choose his eternal neighbors, to make sure he wasn't next to some loudmouth singer or unremarkable actor, but that's it. Maybe he'd have wanted to make sure someone would regularly polish the marble headstone since he could barely stand a drop of water on his kitchen floor. In fact, it's entirely possible he signed a contract with his cleaning lady. *Come visit me every Friday to polish my headstone, ensure it is unencumbered by rocks or dirt, and make the gold letters of my name shine bright, won't you?*

Jonathan is sitting in the front row, his wheelchair backed up against the pew. His wife and my two little cousins are with him. They look so much alike I would be hard-pressed to guess which one is Louisa and which one Marion. My uncle was always in the front row when he went to see his brother's shows. I know because you can see him on most of the DVDs. I've always wondered if he chose to attend the nights they made the recordings on purpose, as a way to have his own little slice of the limelight. Did he find it hard to be in his older brother's shadow, the way I found it hard to be his son? Maybe that's why he and my father never really seemed close. Maybe that's why Jonathan moved to Alsace.

Despite it all, Jonathan is now up near the nave while I hide several rows back with a thick scarf over my face and a beanie pulled down over my curly hair. If I had been able to put on my Ray-Bans too, I would have, but Manel suggested they would attract attention.

The priest climbs up onto the pulpit, assumes a humble posture, and begins speaking. I look down at the shiny leather shoes I probably won't ever wear again. Or maybe I will, for my wedding—who knows.

Around me I hear muffled sobs and sniffles of varying degrees of intensity. I see streams of tears and tissues crumpled in fists, cheeks roughly wiped. It suddenly hits me that this can't all be a masquerade. And if it's not, then it can only mean one thing: he's really dead. Dead and soon to be buried.

Disoriented, I focus on the imposing mahogany casket and its gold handles. I want to walk up the central aisle, right up to the box that supposedly contains my father. I want to lift it, to make sure it's heavy enough to contain a man's body, to make sure it's not empty. I want to open the sealed lid and yell at everyone present that I need to see his body, his face. I need to know that he's really inside. I need to touch him, to feel his cold, eternally still skin. I have to make sure—the casket could be full of bags of flour, cobblestones, dictionaries, who knows what else. Would that really be so unrealistic, after all?

I remember what my mom told me a few days ago. That Édouard's manager identified the body. Hervé Guyot, who's worked with my father for over fifteen years. The man who was always willing to follow his protégé, indulging even his craziest ideas—as long as it won over audiences and made mountains of money. The man who, I believe, organized the entire funeral down to the tiniest detail. Couldn't he be Édouard's accomplice in just one more tasteless prank?

I look around for Hervé and find him two rows ahead of me, on the other side of the aisle. His shoulders are hunched, and I notice he's wringing his hands. Then he sniffles and wipes his eyes. Seeming to feel my gaze, he turns toward me and smiles weakly, his face pale and ravaged by dark under-eye circles, apparently recognizing me despite my efforts to remain invisible. He looks so despondent that I suddenly feel sorry for him. Could he be that good at faking grief, could he be such a talented actor? Hard to believe, but anything is possible in showbiz.

I turn my attention to the single-file line of silhouettes moving toward the casket to say their final farewells. Could Édouard be somewhere in the church? Artfully disguised and made up, thrilled to attend his own funeral the same way he loved going into the audience incognito to chat up his fans before a show? Could he be that blond woman wearing huge, useless sunglasses? Or the old man with a graying beard staggering along with his cane?

"Are you looking for someone?" Manel whispers, confused.

"No, no. I was just thinking that . . ."

I'm suddenly conscious of how ridiculous my words will sound and stop myself. *I was just thinking my father might be here somewhere.* I shake my head, troubled by my own illusions.

And yet, when it's my turn to say goodbye, I feel compelled to stand in front of the casket for a few seconds, secretly hoping the lid will pop up to let out an explosion of multicolored confetti. I briefly imagine the scene and have to admit it would be one hell of a prank.

Behind me, someone clears their throat to let me know it's time to move on. Suddenly anxious at the idea that the funeral will be over soon and that we'll all go our separate ways, I place my hand on the casket, without knowing why. A little voice I hate rises up in me, like it always does when I'm anxious: *If the impatient person behind me is a woman, everything'll be OK.* Despite myself, I look over my shoulder and make eye contact with an irritated man who's so obese, he no longer has a neck. I reluctantly move away from the casket, tightly clutching Manel's hand, still securely in mine.

An hour later, they clumsily lower the casket into a hole with cement walls. Édouard still hasn't jumped out of it. Little by little dirt buries the gold handles, then fills the grave completely. And nothing happens. Nothing at all. People slowly withdraw. They leave the cemetery with measured steps, having finally given up hope of seeing Édouard again.

I stay there, frozen in place, stunned to see the funeral end like this. Even still, I imagine that a hand will burst out of the ground and reach out for me.

Manel leads me away gently.

"Come on, let's go home. It's over . . ."

It's over.

The next day, my bewilderment turns to anger. I feel furious and stupid at the same time. My father committed suicide, and when I think about it, I realize I could have predicted he would take the easy way out. It's the only thing he's ever done, really. He was never there for me or my mother. We were like a ball and chain he dragged around for a few years before finding the key and fleeing as fast and as far as he could, playing babysitter for a month in the summer and for a week here and there during school vacations, probably because he had no choice—my mother or guilt must have made him do it. Maybe he was even thinking about his image and reputation. It's totally possible. It wouldn't have been good publicity for people to say he didn't give a shit about his own son.

The truth is that my father never developed a real relationship with anyone, ever. The only thing that counted was his career. Being onstage, whatever the cost. And even that wasn't enough in the end, I guess. He had to go and throw himself off a balcony without thinking about anyone but himself—as usual.

My father's funeral is on the front page of every newspaper and magazine in the country. The *Libération* headline reads, "An Artist's Adieu." Very original. They probably pull it out every time a star passes away. *Paris Match* dares to pen the controversial "Édouard's Last Joke," which causes quite a stir. Copies are flying off the stands, the usual printing runs unable to meet demand. People have started collecting everything that even mentions Édouard Bresson. It helps those who were unable to attend the funeral feel like they're experiencing it vicariously. All his shows are part of the lineup on the major channels. My father is everywhere. Everywhere and nowhere at the same time.

The night of the funeral, there is a terrible school bus accident in northern France. Twenty children between the ages of six and eight lose their lives in an explosion caused by a fuel truck that barreled into them for no clear reason. Only the investigation will explain things. But the evening news opens with the ceremony at Saint-Ambroise Church. I see my face and Manel's behind the casket as it moves slowly forward. It's only afterward that the broadcaster mentions the accident. She affects a devastated expression, but it's hardly comparable with her wavering voice describing my father's funeral just minutes before. Even the president gives a statement, declaring that the world will be a little darker, a little sadder, a little duller without Édouard Bresson. What's next, the Nobel Prize for humor?

The world is a crazy place. Since when is the suicide of a nearly fifty-year-old man more appalling than the brutal death of twenty kids who didn't ask for any of it, not even for their field trip to the beach?

analYze

April 8, 2017

Before going back to Rouen, I decided to call the number my father left me, despite the bitter taste this treasure hunt has left in my mouth.

The worst part of it has been realizing that he took the time to prepare it all, that he meticulously organized his suicide several weeks or even months ahead of time. That he didn't jump off his balcony on a whim or in a moment of madness—far from it. What kind of person enjoys putting together a treasure hunt before ending their life? It is truly chilling.

The mysterious Yoann answered on the third ring and seemed to know who I was immediately. I'd barely had the time to falteringly say, "Hello. This is Arthur, Arthur Bresson . . ." before he exclaimed, "Oh! Arthur! I see."

As for me, I didn't see anything at all, but I let him take over, since he'd apparently been expecting my call. We planned to meet in a café near Place de la Nation. Before heading out, I packed all my things, ready to go home later that evening. I asked Manel to come with me to the café, but she wanted to do some shopping in the capital, she said. I think she feels like she would just be in the way since my father organized this little game for me, and me alone.

When I arrive at the café ten minutes early, I sit down at a little round table outside on the terrace where the previous customers' empty glasses have yet to be cleared. I raise my hand to signal the waiter, then order an espresso when I finally manage to attract the weary man's attention.

When a man around forty stops in front of the terrace and looks around for someone, I know right away that it's the famous Yoann. He's of average height and rather stout—the kind of guy who will end up with a double chin in a few years if he's not careful. But for now, it could still go either way. His chin-length brown hair is held back by a khaki headband that could seem effeminate, but it just puts the finishing touch on his bohemian look, along with his dark-green kurta with the sleeves rolled up and the black-and-white-checked kaffiyeh he has carelessly draped around his neck.

He identifies me quickly—I'm the only person who seems to be waiting for someone—then heads over, slaloming between the tables placed too close together and accidentally bumping an elegant woman's chair on the way, eliciting a heavy sigh. He mumbles an apology, but she returns to her glass of white wine, refusing to dignify him with a reply.

"Arthur?"

I nod and shake his hand. He sits down across from me.

"I'm Yoann. I'm really glad you called, even though I was surprised you did it so quickly."

His voice is calm, and though I generally keep my guard up with new people, I feel at ease right away.

"So my father told you I'd contact you?"

"Not exactly. We had lunch together last month. It'd been a while since we'd seen each other. He gave me a box for you and told me that maybe you'd call someday to get it. To be honest, he kept it all pretty vague and mysterious, and since I'm used to him being eccentric, I didn't ask too many questions."

Yoann hands over a brown paper bag he'd placed at his feet. I take a quick look inside and find an old plastic box, like the ones my father always kept around for possible reuse. "It could come in handy some-day," he would say as he stacked another one in his kitchen cabinet. I can't tell what's inside, though, since he's covered the sides with neon-blue gift wrap.

"Is this it? You don't have a special message for me or anything?"

Yoann shakes his head, an apologetic look on his face.

I'm confused. My father could have simply left a bunch of packages in his apartment. That way I wouldn't have to bother all these strangers.

"How did you know my father? Did you work with him on one of his shows?"

"No, not at all. We met through Hospital Clowns a long time ago. We worked as a team for almost ten years!"

I frown in confusion, and Yoann continues, just as surprised as me.

"Your father never told you about the organization or the time he devoted to it?"

"No."

He looks up, as if trying to retrieve his memories.

"We both volunteered in 2000. I remember because it was a nice round year. I wasn't even twenty-five at the time—gosh, I feel old! We hit it off right away. I guess we shared the same sense of humor. And both of us had just been dumped, so that probably brought us together too."

Yoann chuckles quietly to himself, and I think of how strange it is to hear someone talking about my parents' divorce like that. As if my mom had thrown my father out, when really he walked out on us to go live it up in Paris.

"His career as a comic had really started to take off, and I had recently been hired by a small theater company. I mostly did shows in day-care centers and schools, making barely enough to pay for my rent and food. We made our rounds at the hospital together every Monday night. We met in the lobby of the Gustave Roussy hospital, then changed into our costumes in the bathrooms on the pediatric floor. Ha! I still remember how the doctors looked at us when we came out of the john all dressed up and with our faces painted! Édouard wore these red capris with plaid suspenders—they always made me think of the singer from AC/DC—with a white button-down shirt and a polka-dot tie. Oh, and these awful fuzzy red slippers. Let me tell you, when he took them off after spending two hours with the kids, the smell overwhelmed the entire hospital! And let's not forget his huge burgundy satin nightcap, which hung almost all the way down to the floor. He looked ridiculous! But these old stories probably don't interest you . . ."

"They do, actually. Very much. My father never told me any of this. It's weird. What exactly did you do? Shows for hospitalized kids?"

"Not exactly. We went into every room to visit any kid feeling well enough to see us. Édouard's clown name was Shush—I'm not sure exactly why. Mine was Beanstalk, in contrast to my physique."

Yoann laughs again as he pats his ample belly beneath his taut shirt.

"Your father really enjoyed building relationships with the kids, week after week. Sometimes we saw them for a while, since some of them stayed in the same room for months, or would go home between rounds of chemo before coming back. I think he really liked it when we visited the nurses' desk and he realized he knew three-quarters of the kids on the list, that he was going to be able to pick up a joke he'd started the previous week. I always had a hard time remembering the kids from just their names, but Édouard seemed to keep it all in his head. With nothing but a name, he could tell you their age, what had brought them to the hospital, how they'd been over the past few weeks, and what we'd done in their room the previous week. Even the nurses were impressed. 'Goodness, we should hire you!' they'd say."

The waiter finally brings over my coffee and buses the empty glasses. Yoann distractedly orders a beer, impatient to get on with his story. His enthusiasm has piqued my interest, despite the fact that I feel like he's talking about someone entirely different from the father I knew.

"It's hard to explain, but Édouard and I experienced some extraordinary moments in those hospital rooms. Things that forged ties between us, things we could never really share with anyone else. Once we turned a fifteen-year-old girl's room into a nightclub! It was winter, so it got dark early, and I got out glowing bouncy balls and your dad turned off the light, and we started singing and beatboxing, dancing around until we were dripping with sweat. The girl, still in her bed, was doubled over with laughter. She had her hands in the air and was moving her head to the beat. Then her parents came in. I think they must have gone downstairs to smoke or get some food. I can still remember their faces as they stood in the doorway, their arms hanging limply at their sides, wondering if they should call security. Then the mom saw her daughter's face—I don't think she'd seen her so happy for a long time— and your dad closed the door behind them to make it dark again. He shouted that in this club everybody had to dance, then pushed a light saber into the dad's hands and told him to get his groove on. Édouard wasn't afraid of anything. The really amazing thing was that everything he did was so nuts that he got away with it. I can still see all five of us bouncing around the room until the girl told us she was getting too tired. I don't know if that family remembers Shush and Beanstalk, but we never forgot."

Yoann is pensive for a moment, then takes a sip of the amber beer the waiter has just placed hastily on the table.

"We also had some devastating moments in those rooms. A few times we went into the nurses' station and Édouard would ask why a particular child wasn't there that night. One of the nurses would offer a sad smile and say, 'He's gone,' and we instantly knew that it didn't mean he had gone home. We were supposed to maintain our boundaries—after all, we were working in pediatric oncology; you didn't have to be a genius to know some of the kids will never get better. But I don't think your father was ever really able to steel himself, though he was good at pretending—the organization's psychologist never realized how hard Édouard took it every time he found out a kid he'd been seeing for months had lost the fight. A few times Édouard fell apart when we left the hospital. He would start sobbing hysterically, unable to speak. I would stay with him, patting him on the shoulder without a word, because there was nothing to say. But even that pain didn't take away from the magical moments we had in those rooms."

I keep quiet, afraid that any reaction might jolt Yoann back to reality and put an end to his account of this part of my father's life.

"I think what marked both of us the most profoundly was a ten-minute visit with a ten-year-old boy named Ethan, if I'm remembering right. A kid we'd been seeing for two or three months. Every week we noticed his health was deteriorating, that he was getting progressively weaker. The nurses had told us he was there for palliative care from the beginning, but we couldn't believe it because he seemed so full of life. Then, one Monday, we turn up and the nurse tells us that he doesn't have much longer, that he's no longer talking, that we need to take it easy in his room—if he even lets us in. So we knock gently on his door, and let me tell you, it's hard to feel confident in a situation like that. When we crack open the door, we see Ethan lying on his bed looking tiny, almost wilted. His complexion has turned a waxy yellow. His mother is sitting next to him, in an armchair by the window.

She waves us in with a pitiful, heart-wrenching smile. Édouard walks over to the boy first, and I follow, taking his lead because I'm at a loss for words watching this little boy waste away as his mother holds his hand. 'Hello, friends, we've come to sing you a little song. I have to warn you that Beanstalk is always terribly out of tune, but it comes from the heart, so please pretend not to notice, OK?' Édouard whispers instinctively, and the mother nods gently in encouragement. Ethan's eyes smile, and we know he's there with us, even if he doesn't answer. Your father gets out his music box, holds it against the bathroom door to amplify the sound, and gently turns the crank. Brahms's Lullaby starts playing, and I clear my voice to sing. Édouard accompanies me, whereas he'd usually have let me sing alone so he could make fun of my mistakes with the children, who always thought it was hilarious. During a pause in the lyrics, I blow a few bubbles—it's our trademark. We called them dream bubbles, and the kids loved them. The youngest ones would giggle as they popped them, and we would tell the older ones that the bubbles would bring them sweet dreams for the night ahead. It sounds corny now, but it really wasn't. So we sing the song to the metallic accompaniment of the music box, and somehow it sounds perfect—I don't know how to explain it, but it was perfect. It was like both of us were doing exactly what we were supposed to. We keep our eyes on Ethan, who's staring right back at us. But out of the corner of my eye I see his mom start crying. Her son can't see her because he's turned toward us, so she lets her tears flow in silence, without making a single sound, and Édouard and I can both tell she's finally releasing emotions she's never allowed herself to feel. Her tears are filled with the grief of a mother who has to say goodbye to her child, and we're just there, watching her mute distress. We know that we just have to keep singing as if we haven't noticed, so that Ethan doesn't turn around, to keep him smiling dreamily at us, as if our voices alone are enough to carry him to a better place."

Yoann takes a deep breath. I can feel the intense emotions washing over him as he shares the story.

"And then we leave the room. Ethan's eyes are closed, and I don't know if he's sleeping or if it's just too hard for him to lift his eyelids. We usually jovially said, 'See you next week!' to his mother, but this time Édouard just says goodbye. 'Thank you for everything you did,' she replies hoarsely, and we all know what those words mean. It means that next Monday, a new child will be in the same room, in a bed that's too big for her. Another child we'll get to know, another child we'll help to fall asleep as we try not to get too attached."

There are tears in his eyes, and I feel bad for bringing something so painful to the surface.

"Your father and I never talked about that again. It was just too much, too hard to put into words. We never talked about it with the Hospital Clowns psychologist either. But even now, ten years later, I still think often about that kid. Every time I feel like quitting the organization, I think of Ethan and what happened in that room that night. And I keep going back to the hospital, every Monday night."

"Did my father keep going?"

"No. He left in 2009 or 2010, I think. He did it reluctantly— I know because whenever we saw each other afterward he would eagerly listen to my anecdotes from the hospital. I think it was really hard for him to leave Hospital Clowns, but he couldn't keep coming with the journalists and paparazzi hanging around outside the hospital, following him for a story about his volunteer work. Édouard hated it. I think the last straw was when a reporter from *Voici* came up to the floor and interviewed the families. That's when he decided it would be better for everyone if he stopped coming to the hospital. Maybe it was also getting too hard for him. He never said so, but maybe seeing the disease ravage children just became too much. I don't know."

Yoann and I talk for another hour. On the way back to my father's apartment, I feel totally lost. Torn between a desire to get to know this whole new side of my father—a generous, altruistic, sensitive side—and frustration at my inability to reconcile that kind of devotion with the way he neglected his own son. Manel would probably tell me not to make everything about me, but it's hard not to feel jealous of the little cancer patients my father tenderly cared for—no matter how messed up that is.

doubT

April 8, 2017

Back at the loft, I serve myself a glass of whiskey on the rocks, and sit in one of the club armchairs in the living room to open the box Yoann gave me. Manel will be back soon, and selfishly, I want to be alone when I see what Édouard has left me this time.

I rip off the metallic gift wrap to find two objects. A bottle of bubbles that's three-quarters empty and a small, round music box with a crank, painted navy blue with silver stars. Without thinking, I start turning the crank and hear the tinny melody of Brahms's Lullaby fill the room. It's like he knew exactly what Yoann would tell me today. If I were more cynical, I might even think he *asked* Yoann to tell me those stories, but the sincerity of the man I met was palpable. I open the bottle and lean back in the chair to blow a few bubbles. When I was little, I always tried to make the biggest bubble possible, blowing super slowly to keep it from popping in my face. I could spend an entire hour playing with bubbles in my mom's yard or on the balcony here. Now there's nobody to complain about the marks the soap might leave, but I can still hear Édouard exclaim, "What did I say, Arthur? If you want to blow bubbles, go out on the balcony!"

The bubbles float up into the air, then fall back to the white tile on the living room floor or onto the leather sofa. Before long, the bottle is empty, and I can't help but think that my father could have at least left me a new bottle. Since Manel is apparently in no hurry to get home, I rummage through the cabinet under the sink to find some dish soap to make more.

When I turn over the bottle of lemon-scented Dawn, to pour the chick-yellow liquid into the bubble container, I notice a tiny piece of paper taped to the bottom. I carefully remove it and find another name, along with an address this time: *Rita. 12 Allée des Capucines, Le Havre.* My father was apparently pretty sure I wouldn't be able to stop myself from refilling the bottle, like when I was little. I was always sneaking dish soap out of this very same kitchen, padding silently across the floor like a wolf. I smile sadly as I replace the soap under the sink.

I put the note in my back pocket and pack the bubble container and music box in my bag, then slide the key to my father's apartment onto my own key ring. Something tells me I'll be back soon.

The two-hour drive to Rouen is mostly silent. I'm lost in my thoughts, and Manel is focused on the road. Maybe she's purposefully leaving me time to digest what I learned from my father's friend, or maybe she's waiting for me to speak first, rather than trying to coax me into talking. With my head resting on the window, I gaze out at the opaque darkness dotted with glowing orange lights.

The fatigue that's built up over the course of the week crashes down on me without warning when I throw our suitcase on the floor in the entryway. I suddenly want only one thing: sleep. My father has been dead for a week. I feel like time has sped up, leaving me behind, lost and confused on the side of the road.

Manel finally asks me about my afternoon with Yoann, once we're in bed and I've turned off the lamp, right as I lean over to kiss her. I can't help but grumble that I don't want to talk about it yet. Then I roll away from her, my knees drawn up to my chest. She doesn't push it. She just strokes my hair, then curls up into her own little ball on her side of the bed.

A few minutes later, I hear her breathing slow and become regular. As for me, despite my eyelids feeling heavy as lead, I can't manage to fall asleep. Yoann's words ricochet through my confused brain. The hours file by on the neon-green alarm clock display, and I'm still awake. My tossing and turning finally wakes Manel, who is a very light sleeper.

"Are you OK?"

"Yeah, fine. It's just a little insomnia. Probably normal given the circumstances."

"Do you want to talk now?"

"I don't have anything interesting to say."

"You spent the whole afternoon with this Yoann person, but he said nothing at all? He just gave you the package and you stared at each other in silence?"

"I didn't learn anything new. My father was a stranger to me. I just got more confirmation of that fact."

Manel sighs and props her pillow against the headboard, then sits up.

"Stop it. The way you talk makes it sound like your father was the devil! Why don't you try to remember something positive about him instead of always rehashing everything he did wrong? You must have at least a few good memories that you can hold on to, right?"

"Honestly, I can't think of any."

"Oh, come on! Everyone has at least one happy memory of their parents. You just choose to tell yourself he wasn't good enough."

I'm getting angry. I adore Manel, but sometimes I wish I could tell her to shut up. I wish I could tell her that not everyone is lucky enough to have two wonderful, doting parents.

"Fine, give me a second . . . Oh, have I ever told you about the time I broke my arm climbing a tree? It hurt so bad I passed out, and the EMTs had to take me to the hospital. I was eight years old. It was July 14, Bastille Day. I remember because I missed the fireworks that night. The upside was that I got an awesome cast that everyone signed: my mom, my grandparents, my classmates. Even my uncle Jonathan and my aunt, who were on vacation nearby for a week, stayed a few extra days in Le Havre to make sure I was all right. Everyone left their mark on my cast, drew a little something—everyone but my father, of course, who couldn't even manage to get away for an afternoon to come see me. I guess he must have been too busy signing autographs elsewhere . . ."

A snide little voice in my head suggests that maybe Édouard was too busy strolling the halls of another hospital consoling children who were much worse off than me. I know it's horrible to think like that—or maybe it's just human, after all.

Manel rolls her eyes, probably thinking I won't notice in the darkness, but I'm no idiot. I can almost hear her eyebrows flick skyward.

"Oh wait, I just thought of something else! He'd promised to come to Le Havre for my high school graduation, so we could all celebrate together, even though he'd never liked my stepfather, Christian. My mom had reserved an amazing restaurant. Guess who didn't show? Guess who didn't even call?"

"All right, fine. I get it," Manel murmurs sadly.

But, strangely, I don't feel like stopping the flood of memories— I'm on a roll.

"There was also the time when I was being bullied, in eighth grade. I almost forgot! A gang of punks from the projects would shake me down every day when I left school and make me bring them money every Monday to avoid getting beaten up. One of them, with terrible buckteeth, was always playing with a nunchaku, twirling it around inches from my face. Sometimes he lost control, leaving huge bruises on my cheekbones or temples. I didn't dare tell anyone, so I made up excuses for my injuries. Every Sunday night I would take money from my mom's or Christian's wallets to keep the jerks off my back. My mom finally figured it out one day when she caught me stealing from her. I don't remember what she did about it, especially since I begged her not to call the principal, but those kids never bothered me again. The whole thing lasted three months, and my father had no idea. He never protected me from anything. But you're right, if I look hard enough in the dark corners of my memory, I should be able to find a game of Guess Who? that he played with me for a whole five minutes, all the while thinking about the next sketch he would write. Maybe he even let me win."

"OK, I get it; you can stop now. Your father was a horrible jerk. Period. Go ahead, be mad at him, but please don't take it out on me. It's not my fault. Good night."

Manel ferociously fluffs her pillow and goes back to her side of the bed.

"A horrible jerk. I think that's the most accurate description I've ever heard."

"Great," she mutters.

I'm still too upset to apologize, even though at least part of me realizes that she's done nothing to deserve my wrath. My father has always had a gift for bringing out the worst, meanest version of me. Too furious to sleep, I give up and leave the bedroom.

I turn on the TV in the living room, hoping to zone out, while simultaneously surfing the Internet. I disinterestedly check my latest notifications on Facebook, where I find an invitation to like a new page. Intrigued, I click the link and find myself face-to-face with a close-up of my father with the caption *Édouard Bresson Is Alive!*

The page description is clear: *This page aims to unite all Édouard Bresson fans who believe that his death was nothing but a spectacular prank. Édouard is alive! Édouard is immortal!*

I don't know who founded the recently published page, but it's already attracted more than a million people—1,004,521 fans to be exact. That's 1,004,521 people who refuse to believe my father committed suicide and who have been posting "proof" he's alive since April 1.

They all mention the huge prank he pulled three years ago, when he made everyone believe he'd been brutally attacked by a man who hated him, Basile Rossi. The news channels went all-in, rushing to broadcast the story that my father had been attacked on his way home from one of his shows. They interviewed him with his swollen purple lip and bloody face, and he swore he'd find the coward who'd beaten him up. The next day, the media reported that the so-called attacker had been arrested, interrogated, and released. Édouard explained that after thinking it over and speaking with Rossi, he had decided not to press charges. The pair even went on an evening talk show together. Basile Rossi, a confident man with bushy eyebrows and impeccably slicked-back hair, was thrilled to have the opportunity to say just what he thought about Édouard for the prime-time cameras. In his gravelly voice, he claimed that the comic was a common thief, an imposter who had stolen Rossi's sketches and shamelessly plagiarized his work for years, leaving him to flounder in suburban café-theaters. Seated across from him, Édouard remained impassive. The corners of his lips even turned up in a smirk. Things quickly got out of hand, and the presenter seemed overwhelmed by the vehemence of the two men, who looked close to settling things with their fists. "You should be ashamed of yourself, Mr. Bresson! You're a scumbag, a first-rate prick! You wouldn't look so proud if I gouged out your eyes and kicked in your teeth!" Two security officers finally dragged Basile Rossi away in front of Édouard, who was back to his usual stoic self. As soon as it was broadcast, the video went viral.

Right up until Rossi cheerily admitted to a captivated TV presenter that it was all just a joke. In fact, he and Édouard Bresson were one and the same. He took off his brown wig and thick eyebrows and went back to using his normal voice—the transformation was astounding. It was almost chilling to see how talented Édouard was, how he could become someone else so entirely. All he'd needed was a little help from the first talk show crew, who put the images together to make everyone think Édouard and Basile were really face-to-face.

The video is obviously at the top of the Édouard Bresson Is Alive! page. Everyone posts that it's proof my father is capable of faking his own death, capable of putting together a prank of ever-larger proportions to show off his abilities. And I agree—he definitely had what it took to plan such a huge scheme. But would he really have gone that far? Making people believe he's dead and holding a sham funeral without any thought as to the pain it would cause his loved ones, his friends, me?

The second video on the page is an excerpt from an interview he gave just before going onstage two years ago. One of the rare interviews where Édouard didn't take on one of his personas to answer.

The journalist holds out her mic and asks in a wispy voice, "Your shows have been sold out for months. How does it feel to enjoy such fame, fame that almost seems to have befallen you by accident?"

Édouard frowns, then replies, "I don't know if it was an 'accident,' but becoming a star isn't all it's cut out to be. Sometimes I wish I could go back to having a normal life!"

The journalist clears her throat, conscious she's upset my father, then continues cheerfully, "I understand, of course. But given your popularity, I doubt your fans will ever turn their backs on you!"

"Maybe I'll turn mine on them. Who knows! People choose to disappear all the time."

This last sentence flashes across the screen as my father says it, to highlight this clue he dropped for oblivious audiences.

People choose to disappear all the time. Is he talking about a prank he was considering even back then, or about his growing desire to end it all? Could he have faked his death to finally escape a public life he had come to hate? To run far away from it all, far from the stress and the pressure, far from everyone?

In which case, couldn't this treasure hunt really be a way to find him, like I thought in the first place? Could it be leading me to him?

It seems completely crazy. Completely surreal. And yet so completely *him*.

My eyes stare into space, unable to focus. Then I snap back to reality, suddenly completely exhausted.

Before turning off my phone, my thumb hesitates, floating over the screen.

Then I click the "Like" button.

Make that 1,004,522 fans.

Hear

I take advantage of my visit home to Le Havre for Easter weekend to go see Rita. My father only left me an address, so I have no choice but to show up and hope she's home.

Allée des Capucines is a small, quiet street lined with flowering Japanese cherry trees that are shedding their pale-pink petals all over the sidewalk. I stop in front of number 12—a townhouse identical to the others in the neighborhood, all with the same little yard, the same slate roof, and the same dormer window over the dark-gray garage door.

The doorbell doesn't work, so I knock half-heartedly. I immediately hear the high-pitched yapping of a dog. A voice cries, "Quiet, Filou!" and I hear steps coming closer. The door opens a crack, with the chain still on. A wary eye looks me over, waiting for me to explain myself. As the silent elderly woman studies me, I notice her skin is as wrinkled as an overripe apple forgotten at the bottom of a bag. A golden poodle growls protectively at her feet.

"I'm sorry to bother you. I'm Arthur . . . Bresson . . ."

I stop, unsure how to continue, hoping my father's surname will be my ticket in. But the woman doesn't move a muscle. She holds tight to the door, impassive, as if expecting me to begin lauding the virtues of a miraculous anti-wrinkle cream or offer to sharpen her knives.

"My father gave me your address. He may have left something for me with you."

The dog starts scratching at the door, increasingly riled. She pushes him back with her foot. I lose hope, wonder if maybe I'm at the wrong number, or maybe on the wrong street.

"Édouard Bresson—does that name mean anything to you?" I attempt again, playing my last card for this cranky old biddy.

Her face lights up instantly. She closes the door for a second to take off the chain, then invites me in with a warm smile. Night and day. Even the poodle seems to be wondering what's gotten into her.

"Why didn't you mention him sooner, my boy? There have been so many burglaries in the neighborhood lately that I've become suspicious, you see. Come in, I'll go get some juice and cookies!"

She points to the little mat where I'm to leave my shoes, then accompanies me to the dining room, where she invites me to sit at the table with its bright-yellow oilcloth before disappearing into the kitchen. She comes back a few moments later, carrying a tray with two glasses of orange juice and a package of rolled wafer cookies. She hands me one of the glasses, her hand trembling so hard I'm afraid she'll spill half of its contents, but not a drop goes overboard. Leaning all her weight on the table, she struggles down to a seated position and lets out a sigh of relief when she's finally settled in the chair across from me.

"It's unbelievable how much you look like Édouard. People must tell you that all the time, I guess?"

"Not really, no."

"You have the same eyes. The same mischievous look to you, mixed with a touch of stubbornness. Oh, and that weak chin is just like his. Much less that curly mop! The way you let out an awkward laugh after saying something. You must not even realize it, but you have his same tic."

I take a sip of juice, unsure how to reply.

"Did you know my father well?"

"I did indeed! Since before he was born! I was his parents' building manager in Gonfreville. I still remember Madame Bresson's enormous belly when she was pregnant with Édouard. Or maybe it was Jonathan—I'm not sure. My memory plays tricks on me these days . . . She would carry her groceries up the stairs all by herself, even when she was eight months pregnant. Of course, it's not like she could count on her husband to help out, no sirree. Your grandfather was a difficult man. You must not remember him, but he was a real piece of work. He was always yelling about something. I used to tell myself he died from being angry all the time. I'm sure his heart just gave out from being awash in so much rage."

I nibble at a cookie, surprised to hear this elderly woman tell me about a grandfather I never knew, a man who died before I could have any memory of him at all. And she seems so willing to tell me everything she remembers without me even having to ask.

"What was my father like as a child?"

Despite everything, I'm curious, since I know next to nothing about his childhood. Neither he nor my mother ever really talked about it—maybe because I didn't really ask any questions.

"Oh, he was a good boy. That's for sure. It wasn't easy for him, though. He stuttered so badly that nobody could understand what he was saying. Mr. Bresson was too impatient to wait for his son to spit out his jumbled words, so he stopped asking him questions altogether. Every morning, Édouard walked past my office without saying hello, so his father would give him a good smack and bark, 'Would it kill you to be polite?' But the boy still wouldn't open his mouth. At best, he'd wave to me to appease his father. I knew he kept quiet because he was afraid the 'Good morning' would get stuck on the tip of his tongue, that the *G* would refuse to come out. 'It's all right, he's just a kid! They're all like that at his age,' I'd say to Mr. Bresson, but the poor boy still got walloped on the side of the head. He was a difficult man."

"I had no idea my father had a stutter. Are you sure you're not confusing him with someone else?" I ask with a frown, wondering if Rita might have lost a few marbles. I think I would have noticed if my father had a stutter. As would his millions of fans.

"Sure as can be, son. It lasted a few years, and then—I'm not sure exactly how—it slowly disappeared. Good thing too, since his parents had plenty of other problems after Jonathan's accident."

I hold my breath. The subject has always been taboo. My mother told me once that my uncle fell through the floor of an abandoned house, but she didn't seem to know any more. She made me promise not to broach the subject with my father, so I kept quiet, afraid of hurting him or bringing back a sad memory. I was plenty curious, but I never dared bring it up with my uncle either—it seemed so indiscreet, insensitive even.

"Do you remember Jonathan's accident? What happened exactly?"

Rita shakes her head, her lips pursed. With her pinky, she pushes the wafer crumbs scattered in front of her into a little beige pile.

"There was talk in Gonfreville at the time. When a child—barely five years old—falls through the floor of a dilapidated house and ends up in a wheelchair, people have a lot to say. The residents were so angry that children had been able to access an abandoned building that the mayor was even forced to resign. The house was demolished a few weeks later, but the damage had been done. Nothing was ever the same again for the family. Jonathan spent a year in a rehabilitation center, and Édouard spent all his time wandering the halls of the building alone, unsure what to do with himself. Before that, I always saw the brothers playing together in the street, especially since their father couldn't stand any noise, so he sent them outside regularly. Lucien Bresson was really a difficult man . . ."

She shakes her head as she remembers my grandfather.

"They spent hours riding their bikes together. Édouard held Jonathan's seat to help him learn how to ride without training wheels. They were always chirping away in the street. Obviously, after the accident, there were no more bikes. For a whole year, there wasn't a shout or laugh to be heard in front of the building. Édouard played marbles alone. Once I even found him hiding behind a plant in the lobby, and when I asked him what he was doing, he told me he was playing hide-and-seek. 'All by yourself?' I asked. 'Yeah,' he murmured, 'I pretend Jonathan's looking for me.'"

Rita sighs heavily, and I can't help but feel sorry for my father when I imagine him stuck playing all alone.

"They were endearing kids, both of them—like most kids, I guess. When Jonathan finally came home, Édouard seemed to get his smile back, even though I could tell, when I saw them with their mother, that she had refocused all her love and affection on her younger son. Even before the accident it was obvious that he was her favorite, but it was much worse after. She was always sweet as pie with him, and when she stopped to get her mail, she only ever talked to me about Jonathan and the progress he was making—it was like she only had one son."

The former building manager gets up with difficulty and slowly walks toward the kitchen. Her Provençal floral-print dress makes me think of the ones I've seen in old catalogues and at markets—I always wondered who actually bought such old-fashioned clothing.

When she comes back, she quickly wipes down the table with a sponge to get rid of the crumbs. It's like she can't bear to wait—it's urgent. She continues her story, unperturbed, and I start to wonder if she's really talking to me.

"Luckily, it didn't seem to damage the relationship between the two brothers. When it rained, they would sit in a corner of the lobby, concentrating on their sticker books. They never fought. I remember because it was remarkable to see two boys who never even bickered. Especially since they quarreled often enough before the accident. And then Édouard started coming up with all sorts of silly things to distract his brother—I suppose because there weren't as many options to keep them occupied with one of them in a wheelchair. He would imitate passersby, walking behind them as he mimicked them. The neighbors weren't always pleased! Myself included, of course. Édouard would drape a scarf over his head and imitate me as I cleaned the lobby, poking fun at my perfectionism, as if housework were my passion! I just wanted my work to be irreproachable! But it did make Jonathan double over in laughter, so I tried not to take offense. I ignored them mostly. When they really got on my nerves, I told them to go play somewhere else."

I nod, but Rita looks at me suspiciously.

"You think I can't see you want to smile, son? There's no fooling me. I know exactly what you're thinking. Your father didn't have to do too much to come up with Zita the obsessive cleaner. Oh, don't look so shocked. I've always known Édouard was inspired by me and my little compulsions!"

She stands up once again, holding her lower back, then walks over to a closet, where she pulls out a dust buster. She turns on the machine to suck up an invisible crumb on the oilcloth that escaped the sponge. I struggle to repress my desire to laugh at this endearing woman who is so very like the character my father created—except that she hasn't started singing and playing air guitar on her broom yet.

When the table finally seems sufficiently clean to her, she opens her fold-out couch. I hear a terrible cracking sound that makes me wonder if it's the springs in her sofa or her back suffering from being in constant motion.

"Here. This is what your father left for you. I was really touched when I realized he came to see me the same day he . . ."

Rita stops short, the words stuck in her throat. She automatically brings her hand to her chest and grabs hold of the cross around her neck, as if the gesture might protect her from tragedy. I nod to show I understand, and her shoulders seem to relax slightly.

She places a closed wine crate in front of me. I run my fingers over the inscription, *Chasse-Spleen*, engraved in the wood and painted a dark brown.

"Thank you very much."

"You're welcome, my boy. It's the least I could do after what happened. So much misfortune . . ."

I don't know if Rita is talking about my father, Jonathan, or me, but I have no intention of asking. Maybe she means our whole family.

"There were good times too, you know."

Rita smiles nostalgically.

"Oh, I know there were, son. There was Magda, who infused the whole family with light! I still remember how awkward your father was when he decided to ask her out. One morning while I was watering the plants in the lobby, he came over, and I asked how things were going with the girl from the seventh floor. He blushed to the tip of his ears, then tried to deny his interest before finally admitting that girls were incredibly complicated. I remember telling him that all he needed was a little romance and kindness, that it was hardly rocket science!"

I want to laugh as I imagine my father asking the building manager for dating tips, but I do my best to remain impassive. Rita smiles.

"The next day, Édouard put an envelope in Magda's parents' mailbox, and she picked it up not long after. Their little game lasted nearly a week: he would put a letter in the box, and she would open it in the lobby, a big smile on her face."

I'm intrigued. "Do you know what he wrote to her?"

"No idea. I'm not the type to read people's mail! I guessed it was poems or love notes. In any case, it worked, because ten days later I saw them walk past my office, holding hands. When they reached the elevator, your father turned and gave me a victorious thumbs-up!"

There's something strange about imagining my parents at the very beginning of their story, something almost melancholy. Rita suddenly seems to feel the same way—her eyes dim, and her expression turns solemn.

"What a waste . . ."

This time I know exactly what she means, and can only manage to nod in agreement.

dIsmiss

April 17, 2017

If I close my eyes hard and try to envision my parents together, I invariably run into a black hole. It's like we were never a family—there was my mother on one side and Édouard on the other, with me being carted from one to the other every school vacation.

As I explore the deep recesses of my memory, only one scene stands out. I'm sitting at the bottom of the stairs, crouched in the shadows. My parents tucked me in bed and think I'm already fast asleep. I come down the stairs as quietly as possible, carefully placing my feet on each step to avoid any creaking. Even now, I can almost feel the hard wood beneath my feet and the cold banister against my cheek. My parents have closed themselves in the kitchen, and I can smell the faint scent of cigarettes emanating from the room, even though neither of them ever smokes in front of me. I'm four years old, maybe five. The scene happened so many times afterward that it seems like a daily occurrence to me, although I know my father was away more than he was home. First, cool discussion, hushed reproaches, the fitful rhythm of restrained anger. Then the voices grow louder, each one demanding to be heard, listened to, understood. Finally, after a while, when I start to feel cold in my lightweight pajamas, the yelling begins in earnest. My mother shushes him. *You'll wake Arthur.* Then fists bang on the table, cabinets slam shut, there's more yelling. *I can't take it anymore, Édouard. We can't go on like this,* her voice jagged from sobbing. *You don't love us enough to change.* Then my father sighing and saying, *It's always the same story, Magda. Why don't you understand I'm doing everything I can?* Crying, comforting embraces, wet kisses, sniffling, promises, *I love you; I love you too,* then silence. Silence, and I cover my ears to avoid hearing any more. I regret coming downstairs again, but know I'll do it again the next day, just to hear them, to try to understand, to feel close to them despite the closed door.

But that's all there is, my only memory of my parents together. Invisible in the kitchen, the muffled sounds of their biting words, their disillusioned promises they still pretend to believe. But to be fair, there must be other moments that just aren't burned into my memory like this one. Certain things unfortunately take up so much room in our minds that they overshadow all else, making impartiality impossible.

Alone in our apartment in Rouen, with the open wine crate in front of me and its objects spread out over the bed, I think of my father stuttering as a child, about what his life must have been like with a "difficult" father, a mother who doted on her youngest, and a brother who was the focus of everyone's attention. I wonder if the solitude I experienced as a child was anything like his, if maybe our childhoods had more in common than our out-of-sync, out-of-tune adult selves would have led you to believe.

Our lives intertwine sadly in the objects he placed in the wooden box. Faded Polaroids show Jonathan growing up and my grandparents slowly aging. Édouard isn't in any of the pictures, probably because he preferred to be invisible behind the lens. A bag of marbles, all scratched and dented from hitting the walls. A little harmonica with the faintest touch of rust, a Lee Oskar my father never wanted to lend me when I was younger—*You'll drool all over it; it's not a toy.*

Now I'm apparently allowed to play with it. But I don't feel like it anymore. Maybe because I'm older, or maybe just because Édouard isn't here to keep me from spitting in it.

I run my fingers over each object, picking them up, stroking them, then putting them back in the box one by one. I imagine my father placing them inside for me. I imagine his fingers holding these same objects, and I suddenly want to cry. The urge comes out of nowhere, swells up in my throat like a volcanic eruption, and I hate myself for being overwhelmed by a bunch of knickknacks.

A tiny pastel-blue anklet. *Arthur Bresson, August 13, 1993.* I can barely fit two fingers through it—my newborn leg must have been ridiculously small. I'm surprised this artifact isn't with the baby trinkets that my mother religiously hoards, alongside my umbilical clamp and my tiny first hat.

Also in the box: my first letter to Santa. *Dear Santa, I'd like a trampoline for Christmas.* My mother had said, "But there's no room in the yard for a trampoline, Arthur!" So I added, *And a bigger yard.* I didn't get either of them, obviously. That said, Santa Claus never got my letter.

A few clumsy drawings, and my first attempts at writing with big capital letters. *ARTHUR,* with the *R*'s backward, crossed out, then conscientiously rewritten properly.

Six black-and-white photo booth strips, one for each of the six years we were more or less a family. One of the pictures is missing from each of the shiny sheets of paper—cut out, I suppose, for my mother. My parents look so young. Our smiling faces barely fit in the frame. Only mine is always whole, in the middle. At the center of their world, as if I were the only thing bringing them together. Through the six strips of photos, I watch myself grow from a newborn into a little boy with missing front teeth. My father wears the same big smile every year—the picture of a happy father and husband. My mother's expression seems to dim over time, to lose some of its radiance and light. On the last sheet, her smile is a mask that her eyes belie. Six moments from our life captured by a click, and then it all imploded.

Why did my father keep all these things he couldn't have cared less about? How can he have collected all these memories and still jumped out the window without thinking of us, without reaching out for help? He called me that night. Three times. I didn't pick up. I wanted to unplug after a long week of reviewing for exams. The last thing I wanted was to get in yet another fight with him, to hear him tell me how I was wasting my talent by spending my time sitting in a university amphitheater, or that he didn't understand why I tried so hard to reject him. Or worse, I didn't want to realize he was only calling to talk to me about his show at the Stade de France, to hear him tell me how amazing and unforgettable it was, how it was the best day of his life. I should have picked up. If I had, I wouldn't be sitting here dwelling on it like an idiot. Manel would tell me not to be upset with myself, that my father wouldn't want that—or would he? My mother would sigh mournfully and tell me that it's not my fault, but maybe an insidious little voice would whisper that her son could have changed everything if he hadn't been too busy drinking beer after beer at a stupid college party.

If I had answered, could things really have been different? I hate this question, which has been forcing its way into my head at increasingly regular intervals, because I'm not responsible for any of it, damn it. Why did he call me that night? Was he looking for a sign, for proof that I still needed him? Was he going to ask me for help? Try to reconcile? Or was it just to tell me goodbye and hear my voice one last time? I'll never know now. Maybe I'm completely crazy to hope that he might be waiting for me at the end of this treasure hunt. Am I allowed to keep the illusion alive in my mind, without mentioning it to anyone else?

I add the bottle of bubbles and the music box to the crate. Everything Édouard has left me fits in this small pine container.

I pick up the stack of photos, look at them one last time before putting them away. I run my thumb over the faded dates written in blue ink on the back of the pictures. My father is only in one of them—a close-up of him and my mother smiling. Half of his face is cut off, but my mom's is whole. They're both blurry. I imagine my father holding his arm out, doing his best to frame the picture, my mother placing her head against his. They're so young, so in love, oblivious to what the future has in store for them. She's wearing a polka-dot headband. It must be windy because her brown curls cascade across Édouard's face. They look happy. I think they really were happy then, but with the knowledge of the shouting and crying that would separate them not so long after, I find their happiness here all the more devastating. I turn the picture over to check the date and calculate their ages, to count the years left before they mess everything up for good. *Summer 1989.* Four years before I was born. A little over ten years before chaos erupts.

My father's writing, in black ink, added recently. A note meant for me.

Isn't your mom beautiful?

postpoNe

"Do you miss your father?" my mom asks gently, without turning to look at me, her eyes focused on my half sister, Aurélie, who's playing in the backyard with a friend from school. The sound of their preteen chatter is muffled and faint, as is their frequent giggling. The glider we're sitting on moves back and forth. I start to feel nauseous and put down my foot to stop it.

Édouard has been dead for a little over six weeks now. I say "dead," because I have to say something, but I admit I still partially buy into the rumor that the suicide was fake, a rumor that's spreading like wildfire online. "Serious" news outlets obviously don't lend any credence to the claims, but things are complicated for me. My certainty that he's no longer of this world wavers with my mood, doubts, and even hopes. Rationale peremptorily shouts, "He's obviously dead. How could anyone—no matter how extravagant and rich—organize a fake suicide?" while another part of me dares to whisper, "But you never know. And come on, you're hardly the only one with doubts. Lots of people think he could have pulled it off . . ." I wobble like a Weeble, unable to turn the page, yet afraid that if I confide in anyone, I'll only earn their pity. Dead or alive, Édouard is gone, and either way, it hasn't changed my daily routine. After all, we hadn't seen each other for almost a year. He could have been on the other side of the globe, or holed up at his place—I never would have known. The only difference is knowing that if I suddenly wanted to see him, or talk to him, I couldn't. My reality is the same, but the possibilities have changed. I'm doing this treasure hunt because I am convinced it's the only way to put an end to all this, to make my way out of this uncomfortable place of uncertainty. When I'm done, I'll have the answers to my questions—I have to. And then I'll finally be at peace.

Mom turns toward me and affectionately repeats, "Do you miss him?"

I feel her gaze on my face and realize I haven't answered her question.

"Not really, no. I guess I'm just sad that the possibility of me ever having a father worth the name has evaporated."

My mother sighs sadly and gently places her head on my shoulder. Christian, my stepfather, raised me like his own son, but we never shared the type of bond he immediately had with Aurélie.

"It's such a shame you didn't reconcile before . . ."

She doesn't finish her thought. Perhaps because it's too painful to put into words.

"If it had been important to him, he would have tried to make up with me. He would have tried harder to keep us from having stupid fights. We were never really on the same wavelength."

I sound bitter, despite myself. The words pour out, unbidden.

"Don't say that. Somewhere deep down you know your father loved you. He didn't show it very well, but believe me, he loved you more than anything."

"Stop it, Mom. Let's not get all sappy. You know just as well as I do that he didn't give a shit about me, or anyone else—the only thing that interested him was his career. That's why he left us, isn't it?"

"Nothing is ever so clear-cut, Arthur. The situation was much more complicated than that. Your father always had a hard time forming relationships. I think he felt that putting up a wall between himself and the rest of the world was the best way to protect himself from emotions, failure, and disappointment. He came from a reserved family, where no one ever talked about their feelings, except for anger and resentment. That's how he was raised. Being funny and cracking jokes was his way of taming people who got too close, of forging ties without leaving himself vulnerable. I know you're angry at your father, for a lot of things, but someday you'll understand that he was only human, like everyone else. Neither better nor worse."

Under the weeping willow, where they've set up camp, the girls burst into laughter. They're probably talking about boys at their middle school. The sound is so pure, I can almost see it floating gracefully through the air. I suddenly want to be thirteen years old again too, to have nothing on my mind but pretty girls and my next math test.

"'Neither better nor worse.' You're talking about the guy who didn't even care when I broke my arm, who didn't bother to visit his kid in the hospital?"

I don't understand why she's defending the man who abandoned her when I was barely six. Maybe because you shouldn't speak ill of the dead?

My mother delicately takes my hand in hers, as if she's afraid I'll tear it away. Her singsong voice with its faint Italian accent is comforting, like being rocked.

"He was right in the middle of a tour. I know it's not an excuse, but there was no way he could make it to Le Havre. But he called every day to see how you were. He sent your X-rays to the most respected doctors in Paris to make sure you were receiving the best possible treatment and that your arm would heal properly. I even told him that it was just a broken arm, that things like this happen all the time, but he wouldn't relent—he had all the top orthopedists take a look at your file. So, sure, he wasn't there with you, but that doesn't mean you weren't important to him—far from it."

On the patio, Christian is setting up the barbecue. He proudly wears the apron Aurélie gave him for Christmas, which says *Best Dad Ever* in big red letters. The perfect family.

"Uh-huh. And when I was being bullied in middle school? How he never even knew about it? How's that for a stellar father-son relationship?"

I'm starting to feel like I've been dredging up the same memories, over and over, for the past month and a half, and I'm tired of having to always be on the defensive. Tired of having to prove that my father could not have cared less about me. I don't understand why it's so hard for them to admit it once and for all.

"I think there's a lot you don't know, Arthur. It might be my fault, actually. I probably should have talked to you about it at the time, but you were so ashamed and humiliated by those lousy kids that you made me promise not to tell anyone the day I found you stealing from my purse. I had no idea what to do, so I called Édouard and told him the whole story, because I didn't know how to make it stop. Especially since I was afraid I might make things worse by talking to the principal or even the police."

I look up at her, surprised. My mom sits up straight and looks me in the eyes, then earnestly continues.

"Your father is the one who took care of it. I thought he was going to lose it when I told him those little punks were harassing you. I don't know what it stirred in him, but I could tell he was fuming on the other end of the line. He said, 'Let me handle it,' and I knew that he would. I don't know what he did, but I do know that he came all the way up here just to make sure nobody would ever bother you again. He never told me who he talked to, but after that, it stopped. The principal became incredibly friendly toward me, more respectful than he had ever been before. Your father called me every night for months to make sure things were OK and that no one had threatened or hit you again. Édouard never told you about it because I swore to you I wouldn't tell anyone, and then broke my promise. He didn't want to start a fight between us. Don't you see, Arthur?"

I nod doubtfully.

"You're so convinced that your father never did anything for you, you'd rather believe that than accept the possibility that maybe he wasn't as bad as you make him out to be. I know losing a parent is painful, Arthur, but staying angry won't protect you. It'll only postpone things, like the lid on a pot—eventually, it will boil over. You know, our memories are always partial, in both senses of the word."

"Hmm."

My mother sighs at length, clearly annoyed by my obvious skepticism.

"Sometimes you have to try to put yourself in other people's shoes, to imagine how they felt about things. Your father and I split up, and just a few months later, I met Christian, at a time when I hadn't planned to get into another serious relationship. But everything felt so natural with him. And whether you believe it or not, I'm convinced that it was hard for Édouard that life went on without him. Hard for him to accept that, in some ways, Christian had replaced him as a father. Just because you give something up doesn't mean you're not devastated to see someone else enjoying the happiness that wasn't enough for you."

I frown, a little confused by my mother's philosophical musings. She rolls her eyes, exasperated.

"I remember once, for example, when your father called to see how you were doing. He called every weekend to check in on you. I answered and we made small talk, then he asked if you were here. I told him you were in the backyard kicking a ball around with Christian, and that I'd go get you. I still remember how hurt he sounded when he said, 'I can call back later if Arthur's busy.' Obviously, I called you in and you talked to him. You told him a few stories about school, friends, that sort of thing. You were so winded from playing outside that you had a hard time finishing your sentences. Then, less than five minutes later, you told him you had to go because Christian was waiting for you, and you handed me the phone. Your father didn't react. He just said he was glad everything was going well for you, and hung up. But his voice told a different story."

The smoke from the barbecue engulfs the yard as Christian fans the charcoal with a piece of cardboard to encourage the flames. The girls go inside, conspicuously pinching their noses shut as they walk past my stepfather. The Best Dad Ever better watch out. I clear my throat, choosing my words carefully.

"I don't understand why you're so bent on defending him. Maybe I do see everything in black and white, but you can't deny that he walked out on us, that he chose his career over his family. It's easy to run away and then feel sad that the people left behind get over you. Becoming a star was more important to him than living a boring little life with his wife and son!"

"You should have had this discussion with him. I can't answer for him. Back then, I couldn't take him being away all the time anymore, or his constant, contagious stress when he was home, but in retrospect, I'm not sure he really chose his passion over us. Everyone was always on his back, asking for more—his producers, his manager. They never left him alone, and I think he lost his way because he was so afraid of disappointing anyone, because he always tried so hard to be the best. I think most artists require more praise and affection than the average person—they have an innate need to be liked, to be *loved*. Your father's actions were always determined by that need. Everything about him screamed, 'Love me!' And I think it caused him more pain than happiness."

With his brand-new barbecue tongs, Christian carefully places an assortment of sausages on the hot grill. He turns to give us a triumphant thumbs-up. I guess we'll be sitting down to lunch soon. Behind him, in the distance, I notice black clouds massing, growing increasingly menacing. The weather was supposed to be sunny, but I guess you can't believe everything you hear.

"Do you think things could have been different if he had stayed with us?"

My mom gets up from the glider, probably to go set the table before the meat is done. She looks up at the dark sky, as if for answers.

"Probably. But your father never would have been happy as a real estate agent. That job drained him. Though it might seem strange to say this, I don't think his leaving had anything to do with us. If he had given up his passion to stay with us, he would have withered. He would have wasted away in a life that was too small for him."

When she looks back at me, I can't help but notice there are tears in her eyes. Christian mumbles his discontent as drops of rain fall on Le Havre.

"And maybe nothing would have been different at all," adds my mother. "Maybe it would have ended the exact same way."

Only the quiet creaking of the glider accompanies my mother's words. I try and think of something lighter to say, to keep things from getting too depressing.

"Oh, I've been meaning to tell you, I met Rita, the building manager from Gonfreville. She told me that Édouard left letters in your mailbox when you first met."

My mom smiles dreamily. "He did, that's right."

"So what did he write?"

"Oh, nothing particularly romantic! Every day he put in a picture of a handsome actor, and on the back, he wrote *Taken.* I got Tom Cruise, Alain Delon, Richard Gere. James Dean too, but on that one he wrote *Dead.* And on the last one, a picture of Kevin Bacon, he wrote, *In short, they're all taken, so maybe it's worth giving me a chance?*

I shake my head in disbelief.

"Seriously, that's what won you over?"

"It made me laugh, Arthur. Your father always made me laugh. Is that really so surprising?"

Before she walks away to help my stepfather, I gently grab her wrist. I bite my lip, trying to figure out how best to put into words the thought that's been haunting me despite my best efforts to quash it. My mom is waiting attentively for me to speak, so I forge ahead, without knowing exactly what will come out.

"I wanted to ask you . . . This might seem a little weird, but . . . did you see Édouard's body?"

She shudders, and I immediately regret having asked.

"No. Hervé told me there wasn't much to see, that his face was nearly unrecognizable after the fall. And I didn't want to see something I'd have a hard time forgetting afterward. I wanted to remember the face I knew. I didn't want to sully or pollute that image. Your uncle Jonathan felt the same way. Make sense?"

Without a word, I nod slowly. Given the fact that I didn't even want to think about the possibility of seeing my father in his casket—since I was sure nothing would be inside—I'm hardly one to throw stones. I'd like to ask her if she's ever imagined that Édouard might not *really* be dead, but I'm too afraid of her reaction. I bet she'd look at me with cloying compassion, convinced that I'm in full-blown denial. Or completely nuts.

aGonize

June 2017

At the end of last year, when I started looking for internships at Paris law firms, it didn't even occur to me to ask my father to put me up. I'd learned my lesson the last time I'd asked him for a favor. Not to mention that three months living with him would have seemed like an eternity, and I was sure that, even if he offered me a place to stay, neither one of us would have enjoyed it. I figured an old high school friend's beat-up fold-out couch in Montrouge, just outside the capital, would suit me much better.

And then Édouard jumped off the balcony, and the key to his apartment made its way onto my key ring, without anyone asking questions. There was never any police tape plastered across the front door, nor any lawyers demanding I hand over the keys until the estate had been settled.

So when the month of June finally rolled around, it seemed only natural for me to stay at his place. I hadn't set foot in the apartment since the couple of days I'd spent there for the funeral, and I must admit that it was harder this time, without Manel at my side to keep things light.

As soon as I walked through the door, I felt like a burglar. I jumped at the faintest sound, expecting to be arrested for breaking and entering.

I dropped my bags in my room, as Woody smiled and Buzz Lightyear looked on, eyebrows raised, then poured myself a whiskey in the glass Édouard had left on the coffee table and drank to his health. "Cheers, Édouard!" I said, and the two words echoed through the velvety silence.

The old Breton-stripe sweater my mom gave me has holes in the elbows, and one of the navy-blue buttons is missing from the shoulder. She cried when she gave it to me. "Your father got me again. When he gave me this package and told me you'd come looking for it, I thought he was planning a treasure hunt for your birthday this summer, like he used to. I was even happy for you! If I had known . . ." It's the sweater she gave him before his very first audition at Le Point Virgule, his lucky sweater—well, in a manner of speaking. It's mostly an important part of his identity for his fans, who only ever saw him wearing that one thing onstage. I could probably sell it for a small fortune. If I wanted to get rid of it, I mean. Apparently, some taxi driver managed to sell an autograph Édouard signed for him, dated April 1, for 5,000 euros.

Sitting on my childhood bed, I inspect the heavy wool sweater, looking for clues. Nothing on the tag. I hold it up to my face and breathe in deeply, eyes closed, as if the gesture might spark a series of memories.

Nothing happens. The only thing I smell is the rancid scent of mothballs.

In my father's closet, I find two piles of impeccably folded Breton-stripe sweaters. I gently fold the original like its six brothers, then place it on top of one of the unstable towers.

On my way out of the room, I'm seized with regret and suddenly change my mind. I slowly walk back to the closet. I take each of his cotton shirts off its hanger and sniff them, looking for a familiar scent. They smell like fresh dry cleaning. I fling them onto my father's king-size bed, then feverishly move on to a pile of T-shirts. There must be something in here that hasn't been washed, dried, and ironed. I throw things all over the room without thinking. Furious, I empty his drawers. Is this sterilized version of his life all he left behind? Did he really throw any and all potential memories into the washing machine before bowing out for good?

I finally return to the two piles of Saint James sweaters, which seem to be mocking me. My nose can't detect much anymore, numbed by the chemical scents of cleanliness. How is it possible that none of his clothes smell like anything personal anymore, or even *human*? It's like he never wore any of these sweaters or shirts, as if the person who lived here for years carefully erased all traces of life before extinguishing his own.

I hurl the last sweater across the room, where it thuds against the window and slides to the floor. I notice a piece of paper taped to the empty shelf. I climb onto a stool to decipher Édouard's handwriting.

An email address written in capital letters, to make sure I get it right: *LAURENCE.PEREZ@GMAIL.COM.*

I slouch to the floor, my back against the side of the armoire. I look around the messy room and suddenly want to burst into laughter at the thought of my father meticulously orchestrating this treasure hunt before throwing himself off a ninth-story balcony. It's so incredibly absurd.

Instead, I burst into tears. Nobody can see me with my runny nose, thank goodness, because I have no idea why I'm crying like a baby amid all these clothes I'll now have to refold and put away. I have no clue where the massive feeling of emptiness in my chest has come from, like a soap bubble growing inside me, ready to pop. My mother and Manel would probably say I'm finally realizing that my father is dead, that I'll never see him again. And maybe they would be right.

Maybe you don't have to miss someone for their death to be painful. Maybe you can feel suffocated and oppressed by everything you didn't have time to say, by the reproaches you didn't dare utter, by all the things that went unsaid over the years because neither party had the courage.

It's too late for my father to be proud of me one day, too late for me to see in his eyes that he believes in me, too late for him to hug me like a father is supposed to hug his son. Too late for him to explain himself to me, for him to apologize. Too late for him to stop distancing himself from me, and me from him.

It's too late for it all, so I'm stuck wandering through other people's memories, stuck trying to make sense of fragments from people who knew him better than I did, or at least differently.

It's too late, and I've only just realized it. I can try all I want to hold on to hope, I can try to keep my absurd theory alive, but deep down I know perfectly well that the chances of him coming back or of me finding out he's made a new life for himself are slim. Not nonexistent, but terribly slim.

The first day of my internship at Duval & Fichet is memorable, because when I arrive, the receptionist informs me that my mentor is on vacation that week. Nobody thought to let me know ahead of time, apparently, and nobody lost any sleep over what would happen to the new intern. I finally end up in an office with two junior associates, whose exasperated looks as I enter tell me just how eager they are to get to know me. They give me a few files to keep me busy. I finish reading them in two hours, but keep it to myself—I've realized it will be best to keep a low profile. I decide to go get a cup of coffee, and when I come back, my officemates, who are probably only a few years older than I am, both with perfectly groomed beards, are in the middle of an animated conversation.

"Can you believe the guy has managed to write and publish a biography in just three months? It's crazy!" exclaims the lawyer named Damien.

"I'm not all that surprised. People will do anything for money," says the other.

I decide to join in—since I'm going to share an office with these suits for three months, I might as well try to make friends.

"What are you talking about?" I ask.

They look at me guardedly, and I gather they see so many interns come and go that they're not really interested in forging a relationship with me. Nevertheless, Damien deigns to reply.

"Some guy just published a book about Édouard Bresson. Haven't you heard?"

I nod, suddenly regretting my decision to enter the conversation. Wherever I go, everything is still always about my father.

Laurent, the second guy, stares at me intently.

"Hey, isn't your name Bresson? Are you related to him?"

I wasn't able to use my mother's name on my internship form because it was an official document. I try to look surprised, then reply, "No, not as far as I know! Bresson is a pretty common name."

Damien and Laurent go back to their discussion, wondering if the biography could have been written before my father's suicide. As for me, I quickly pull out my headphones, plug them into my computer, and turn the music up loud enough to drown them out.

Manel is coming to visit me in Paris for the weekend. I think she's noticed I haven't been doing all that well lately, that I've been in my head a little too much. She must realize being alone in Édouard's apartment isn't exactly helping me to take a step back.

She shows up with her huge neon-pink suitcase—it's big enough for a three-week vacation. As soon as I see her at the front door, a weight lifts off my chest. With a mysterious look on her face, she heads straight to the computer in the living room. I can tell she's impatient to show me something.

"Look! Have you ever heard of the Hero Course?"

"Is it a cartoon?"

She shakes her head, her enthusiasm intact.

"No, it's an obstacle course. A real one, where you have to climb over huge walls, crawl through the mud, jump into barrels of freezing water, and climb trees and stuff."

I'm wary of what's coming next.

"There's one in Paris in November. Cool, right?"

Not so cool.

"Let's sign up!" she suggests.

I rub my chin, carefully choosing my words. "Um, how can I put this? Why in the world would we do something like that?"

She looks at me like I'm the dumbest guy on earth.

"Because it's awesome, obviously! It'd give us a reason to push our limits, to do something extraordinary, to test our physical abilities! I'm sure it'll do you a lot of good to train for this—you'll see."

I have to "train"? Manel is typing feverishly on the keyboard, signing us up. As usual, her contagious enthusiasm takes hold of me, and I watch videos of previous races with her.

"Did you bring your sneakers?"

She nods.

"Well, let's go lift some weights at the gym, then. Don't think I'll give you a boost when you get stuck on one of those walls!"

She gently slaps the back of my head, and I go get my workout clothes, feeling light at the idea of having a little fun with her—anything to distract myself from thoughts of my father.

gLimpse

With the exception of that first day, my internship has been intense. I barely have time to grab lunch between reviewing files, taking depositions, and going to court. It's a huge change from my last summer internship at the local government legal office in Rouen, where the only thing they wanted me to do was make passable coffee and two-sided copies, to save the rain forest.

As a result, the month of June went by in a flash—I hardly even realized that summer was here, and definitely had no time to enjoy it. After exchanging a few emails with Laurence Pérez, who lives in Toulouse—not exactly next door—I managed to set aside the first weekend in July to visit her. When I told Manel on the phone, she didn't complain, but I could tell from her cold tone that she was annoyed I was "wasting" one of the rare weekends we could have spent together by going to meet some stranger on the other side of the country. Before hanging up, I asked her if she really thought I was going to enjoy my twelve-hour round-trip train ride to pick up another package from Édouard, when I had a mountain of litigation files waiting for me on my desk in Paris. She apologized half-heartedly and told me she understood. I felt bad for not telling her the whole truth, that I just wanted and needed to get to the end of this treasure hunt, that it was the only thing tying me to Édouard anymore, that I couldn't help but hope for a grand finale. I would have felt stupid admitting all that, especially since I've spent the past three months insulting my father and pretending his death hasn't affected me. All of which would make Manel think that my resentment toward him is resolved, which is far from the truth. Can you be angry with someone and still want to get closer to them? I guess you can.

When I arrive in Toulouse, I'm delighted that Laurence Pérez lives just a few blocks from the train station. A fifty-year-old woman with skin to match opens the door. Her salt-and-pepper hair is cut short and impeccably styled, with just the right amount of volume—she must have spent quite a while in front of the mirror this morning.

She welcomes me in with a warm smile, the kind you save for loved ones after a long time apart.

"Arthur! I've heard so much about you that I feel like I know you. Come in, please. Make yourself at home!"

She moves aside to let me in, and as I walk past her, she gives me a hug, despite my instinctive step back. She places her hands on both my cheeks, then kisses them audibly. When she sees my shocked face, she realizes she's gone a little too far and apologizes.

"I'm sorry. I don't know what's come over me. I'll blame it on emotion."

Over a platter of sushi she'd been kind enough to get, Laurence tells me how she met my father after his first show at Le Point Virgule, how she loved his sense of humor, and how she followed his career. Using ample hand gestures, she explains how they became friends. She remarks on how surprised she was that my father remained so approachable over the years, despite his growing fame. "Approachable"—that's got to be the last word that comes to mind when describing my father.

"I would stay after each of his shows to chat with him. He was like an old friend, though I really didn't know much about his private life. I talked to him about his sketches, about my favorite parts of his shows. I told him about my life too, because that's just the kind of person I am. People are always saying that I overshare!"

I'm confused.

"So . . . you only ever saw him for a few minutes here and there?"

Laurence shakes her head, a nostalgic smile on her lips.

"No, we gradually became friends. In fact, I think the precise moment when I stopped being an ordinary fan and became a friend to him was Christmas 1999. I had seen his most recent show in Montpellier a few months earlier, and had told him, without thinking, really, that my husband had left me. That one morning he'd just packed his bags, kissed me on the forehead, and walked out on me and our twin daughters, explaining that it had nothing to do with me. I thought he'd come back, of course, that it was just a whim, that he'd quickly realize he'd made a mistake. But he didn't. That coward never came back. He disappeared, and my girls don't have any memory of him. The only things he left behind were a few smelly, sweat-stained shirts. Anyway, I told Édouard about it that night, without knowing why. I guess I felt like I knew him from seeing him onstage, like I could confide in him. It's strange, isn't it?"

I nod so she'll continue. She's not the first person to mention my father's innate charisma.

"After that, we started emailing periodically, sharing news. Well, to be honest, I was the one doing most of the emotional unloading. He would tell me to hold on, to keep going, that my two girls needed their mother . . . I'm a little ashamed to say it now, but at the time I felt so alone, so lost, like I would never be able to get back on my feet after my husband dropped me like a hot brick."

I've almost finished my sushi—the trip left me starving. Laurence is so talkative that she hasn't touched a single piece of her salmon roll.

"So, on Christmas Eve 1999, my first Christmas without my husband, I had just turned on a cartoon movie to watch with Perrine and Rose, with a bottle of champagne just for me. I was heavyhearted, but I was pretending to be overjoyed for the girls, who were so excited for Santa Claus to come. That's when your dad turned up. He rang the doorbell, and the girls shouted, 'It's Santa! It's Santa!' as they ran to open it. And, in some ways, it was Santa. There he was on the doorstep, arms dangling at his sides. 'I know this is your first Christmas alone with your girls, and it's my first without my son, so I thought I'd come keep you company,' he offered."

Laurence smiles, lost in her thoughts.

"What's funny is that he never seemed to realize that he came as much for himself as he did for me. Because he was clearly heartbroken not to be with you at Christmas."

I remember that Christmas perfectly, spent with my mom and grandparents. The empty chair at the table where Édouard should have been. At the time, I imagined that he was at some big party, with lots of famous guests who were much more interesting than us. He had left a gift for me under the tree, but I refused to open it when my mother told me who it was from. The package sat on my desk for months afterward without ever sparking my curiosity. I finally threw it away, and no one ever mentioned it again.

As Laurence continues talking, I realize what an important role she played in my father's life, even though they only saw each other once or twice a year, usually only for a few minutes after his shows. I never would have imagined that, even at the height of his fame, Édouard managed to forge meaningful relationships with fans. But Laurence is living proof.

"You know, I met your father at the very beginning of his career, when no one really knew who he was. At the time, you could feel his ambition, his burning desire to *be someone*. When fame finally came knocking at his door, when producers and journalists became interested in him, he was thrilled. It was what he wanted more than anything, to be recognized for his talent. When audience members asked for his autograph, he loved that too, of course. But then, over the years, people became more and more demanding, even aggressive, without realizing it, and I'm sure that in the end it was too much for your father. Things went south when he started to feel like he couldn't control it anymore. People took photos of him without asking his permission, they would interrupt his conversations to talk to him . . . I know he found it intrusive and nerve-racking. I think any person in his shoes would have had a hard time handling the constant pressure. Nothing would have convinced me to trade my anonymous life for his . . ."

I realize that it's strangely never occurred to me that Édouard's fame might have been as much of a burden for him in his adulthood as it was for me throughout my childhood and teenage years. Yoann's story made me realize that my father's popularity forced him to give up certain things, like being a clown at the hospital, but Laurence's words finally make me understand that his daily life must not have been a walk in the park. I've always imagined champagne fountains and mountains of money, his ego flattered every time he saw a poster with his face on it or a recording of an interview or show he'd done. I'd never thought about the flip side.

"You know, your father did everything in his power to keep you out of the media. It would have made him sick to know paparazzi were invading his personal life, bothering you or your mother, waiting for you outside your school with telephoto lenses. I know that was one of his greatest fears. He even told me that the one good thing about his divorce was that it kept journalists away from you. He really wanted you to have the most normal life possible. He wanted to protect you from the storm."

Laurence sighs and fiddles with her chopsticks.

"I find it so hard to believe that he decided to end it all like that. I mean, it's not that it's so far-fetched. I knew he always felt like an imposter, from the way he refused compliments, minimized his talents, and acted like he didn't deserve his success. I often watched him with his fans. When they sang his praises and told him how much they loved him, Édouard always looked over his shoulder, to make sure they were really talking to him, as if he had taken someone else's place. I know his exciting life was only the visible part of the iceberg. I know he hid so much. But it's still hard to imagine he felt that desperate . . ."

She laughs without looking up at me.

"It's probably stupid, but I sometimes hope that he just packed his bags and left, like my husband, that he's out there somewhere far away, on a secluded beach or at the North Pole. And that he's happy now. It's possible, isn't it?"

Laurence's maple eyes meet mine, and I'm surprised to read a glimmer of sincere hope there. She makes me think of the fans who still believe that Elvis will come back and shake his hips in his bell-bottoms again, the ones who are willing to entertain the wildest theories to avoid believing their idol is dead. I don't know if Laurence is pathetic or just endearing, but right now I don't have the strength to comfort anyone other than myself. I'm too busy with my own demons and doubts.

"Do you remember all the practical jokes he pulled over the years? The time he made the audience believe two police officers had come to arrest him? I was there that night, and everyone really believed it— my throat tightened as they put the cuffs on him! And every time he managed to take the place of his statue at the Grévin Wax Museum, just to enjoy scaring people who came to inspect the lines on his face? After a while, visitors couldn't tell if it was him or the wax replica anymore—and they started hoping they were being fooled. Your father always loved taking people for a ride, didn't he?"

Laurence looks at me insistently, her eyes fixed on my lips, as if expecting me to share some incredible revelation. As if she thought that obviously, if Édouard had an accomplice, it would be his son. I wish I didn't have to disappoint her and watch her shoulders slump forward when I tell her I don't know any more than she does. So I force a smile and agree.

"It's true. He always loved tricking people . . ."

My evasive reply seems satisfactory—soothing, even—and I can't help but think how I would give anything for someone to do the same for me, for someone to put an end to my grief.

I take the train back to Paris in the afternoon, still shaken by all her anecdotes about my father. At the train station, there are posters and billboards everywhere advertising the release of the DVD recording of Édouard's show at the Stade de France three months ago. "The Last Show by the Greatest Comic of the Decade," claim the huge signs every ten yards. In front of the Relay bookstore, a cardboard cutout of Édouard, his eyebrows raised—I suddenly realize his best-known expression is an exact replica of Buzz Lightyear's—seems to be staring me in the eyes.

I wonder how I'm ever going to forget my father if he's constantly popping up in my daily life. I move closer and decide it must be a life-size cutout since he's only slightly taller than me. I stare at the mint-green glossy paper eyes as they look back mockingly, like De Niro gruffly asking his reflection, "You talkin' to me?"

A disembodied voice overhead announces that my train will be leaving from platform 3, and I reluctantly turn away from Édouard. I drag my feet as I join the crowd of Paris-bound passengers.

Once the train is moving, I put my backpack on the empty seat next to me and take out the envelope Laurence gave me before I left. I open it carefully and pull out a small Moleskine notebook, its cover worn. My father wrote his name and drew a box around it on the first page, then surrounded it with all sorts of abstract drawings and floral arabesques, right up to the edges of the page. I randomly flip through the notebook and quickly realize that my father used it to jot down ideas for sketches and turns of phrase he liked. Almost every page features an inkblot or two, and I imagine Édouard slipping into his thoughts in search of inspiration, bent over his notebook, pen on paper.

I try to decipher his writing and find lengthy excerpts from the sketches that made him famous. Several pages are devoted to the obsessive-compulsive Zita. He even tried, more or less successfully, to draw her as he imagined her. He captured her grave expression, her palpable anxiety at the idea a speck of dust might escape her. One hand is poised on her hip, while the other holds a broom as if it were a precious scepter.

Other pages feature Alphonse, the despicable real estate agent probably inspired by his former boss and his years selling houses to naive clients. Édouard has drawn him too—I recognize his slightly hunched back, his hands rubbing greedily together as he sings the praises of a hovel to his imaginary clients.

It's all here. Maybe it's only a collection of his most famous sketches, because I have a hard time imagining his twenty-plus-year career would fit in a single volume, no matter how thick.

In the middle of the notebook, I find a page entitled *Arthur's Funniest Moments*, where Édouard has made a compendium of all the silly things I ever said or did as a child. For the most part, I don't even remember them, and my father's terse notes aren't enough to trigger my memory. Apparently, I once put diaper cream all over my face, then claimed, even with greasy white cheeks, that I had no idea where the tube had gone. Another time, I was bitten at day care, and my parents had indignantly exclaimed, "This is unacceptable! What kind of brute would do such a thing!" The next week, it appears I sank my teeth into a little girl, and my parents' position shifted: "It's true, Arthur bit her, but we all know that biting is normal for children his age, who are going through a crucial stage in their emotional, psychological, and motor development." I recognize the sentences, which I've heard my father deliver onstage, in his show called, *A Kid? Thanks, but No Thanks!* All at once I realize that most of the sketches from that show were directly inspired by me. I can't decide if I should be touched or upset. I can't decide much of anything at the moment.

As I flip through the pages, I find memories of my parents' first years as a couple, more anecdotes from my childhood and teenage years. It's not a diary, since it only contains stories that could be turned into sketches, only the funny moments from our life as a family of three, but there's something private about these pages.

When the train pulls into Gare Montparnasse, I look up and massage my neck, tight from spending six hours bent over Édouard's Moleskine. I'm starting to feel closer to my father. Maybe this treasure hunt is working after all. Maybe I'm finally getting to know him through all these stories and objects. And yet, when the game is over, when I reach the end, when there are no more hidden messages or packages to receive, no more strangers to meet, I'll be alone again.

Alone like an idiot who got to know his father too late.

I haven't been to Édouard's grave since his funeral. Hundreds of tourists walk through Père Lachaise every day after carefully deciding which stars' final resting places they want to visit or photograph, but I have yet to set foot in the bucolic cemetery. It's not that I don't care, or that I'm afraid—it's more that I don't feel the need. There are plenty of people to place flowers on Édouard's grave, but not me. I wouldn't even know what to do if I went. I can already see myself, arms hanging clumsily at my sides, my expression awkward. Should I stand still in front of the headstone, looking serious? Sit on the grave to silently commune? Talk it out with him, as if monologuing might bring me some answers and stop the dizzying questions? Stare at his name in gold letters and wonder once again if his body is really buried under the marble slab? None of it's for me.

On the way to his apartment, my phone rings. A blocked number. An unknown voice speaks when I answer.

"Hello, I'm trying to reach Arthur Bresson."

"Speaking," I answer suspiciously, without bothering to correct the caller about my last name.

"I'm sorry to bother you, but I'm a journalist at *Gala* and I'm writing an article about your father and his, uh, departure."

I can't tell if the slight hesitation is because he's uncomfortable with the euphemism or if he's emphasizing the double entendre.

"I don't want to be interviewed. How did you even get this number?"

I'm surprised a journalist is calling me at nearly ten o'clock on a Saturday night. Does he think he's got the scoop of the century or something?

The man clears his throat and evades my question. He refuses to give up.

"The story I'm finishing up focuses on the rumor that's been circulating since April 1, the possibility that Édouard Bresson may have faked his suicide to disappear and be free of the spotlight."

Astounded by his nerve, I stop short in the street, where I'm bumped and pushed, other pedestrians giving me dirty looks because I dared slow down their dash through the city.

"You've got to be kidding! Is this what journalists do these days? Peddle ridiculous rumors and lies?"

"I understand your reaction, but there's a Facebook page whose numbers are still growing, and they all believe he's alive."

"I don't see what that has to do with me. Why don't you go interview them?"

The man continues unabated. He's probably afraid I'll hang up on him.

"There are people who say they've seen him in the United States. Several say they ran into him in Florida, and one of them even posted a photo this morning, so I wanted to get your opinion. Knowing your father, do you think he could have fooled everyone like this?"

"Knowing your father." The expression makes me smile sadly. I am probably one of the last people this journalist should talk to. I move the phone away from my ear and press the red icon to hang up. The man will probably assume he's upset or angered me, when, really, I just don't know how to answer. If he's right, it would mean my father didn't commit suicide, but also that he was willing to cause me pain to gain his freedom, willing, I guess, to never have any contact with me again in order to protect his secret.

I want to ignore the journalist's suggestion, but I feel compelled to visit the *Édouard Bresson Is Alive* Facebook page. Compelled to see the picture he mentioned. I scroll through the feed for a few seconds until I find a blurry photo taken on a packed bus. A man's face is circled in red. Blond hair in a crew cut, short beard, sunglasses with thick red plastic frames. A nose and a mouth that, I'll admit, resemble my father's. But that's where it ends.

On the right side of the page, the counter reads *2,758,451 fans*.

Almost three million people refuse to accept the truth, refuse to give up hope.

They still believe in my father.

So why can't I? The constant uncertainty is killing me, making me feel schizophrenic. How can I get this idea out of my head?

After making a quick dinner back at my father's apartment, I suddenly realize I don't have a new clue to continue the hunt. Did I really read the entire Moleskine notebook? I must have missed something. I open it up again and eagerly study the pages.

After a few minutes, I smile in satisfaction. This time Édouard didn't go to any great lengths, but I was so absorbed in what I was reading that I didn't pay attention to the little dots he placed under certain letters—it was a code we used when I was little. Together the letters provide contact information for someone new: *Jean Spitzer, 15 Route des Embruns, Gonfreville-l'Orcher.*

Another trip back to where it all started, then.

ruffLe

July 14, 2017

I take advantage of the long Bastille Day weekend to go home to Rouen, where Manel happily jumps into my arms. Though she keeps a respectful distance from Édouard's treasure hunt, I always tell her about each meeting in detail afterward, to involve her in the whole thing. Despite her palpable disappointment, she agrees to let me make a round-trip to Gonfreville-l'Orcher on Saturday afternoon to see the mysterious Jean, whose telephone number I've been unable to find.

I park in front of number 15 Route des Embruns, which turns out to be a sad-looking pale-gray rectangle barely distinguishable from the gloomy Norman sky. I run through the names on the apartment building's intercom until I reach the letter *S*. I buzz the name and wait, ready to introduce myself through the unfriendly metal receiver. Nothing happens.

I buzz a few more times, then wait in front of the graffitied door to the building for about ten minutes, unsure how to proceed. *If someone finally answers, everything'll be OK.* It's hard to quiet that annoying internal voice or even ignore it. I think about leaving a note in Jean's mailbox, but it's inaccessible, inside the lobby.

Just as I finally decide to give up, the door suddenly opens. I find myself face-to-face with a man around fifty and at least a head taller than me, with a thick brown beard. He looks me over suspiciously, as if I might be a burglar scouting for my next job.

"You live here?" he barks rudely.

"No, I was hoping to see someone, but he must not be home. I guess I'll come back. Would you mind if I left a note in his mailbox?"

The man stares at me silently.

"It'll only take a minute, then I'll come right back out, don't worry," I add more hesitantly than I intend.

"Who's it for?"

It doesn't even sound like a question—more like an order. I try to remain calm, but the guy is built like a bouncer and is so intimidating I have to force myself not to take a step back.

"It's . . . it's for Jean Spitzer."

For a second I'm afraid he's about to grab me by the collar and throw me to the curb. And, though it's really beside the point right now, I'm sure he has bad breath. He looks like a guy who has bad breath.

"What do you want with him?"

"Just to leave him my number so he can call me. That's it . . ."

The man pulls a pack of gum out of his pocket, and though I'd like to ignore him, I find myself waiting for his approval to go leave my note.

"Don't hold your breath for that call."

"Why not?" I ask with feigned indifference. This guy is really starting to piss me off. I have better things to do than stand around trying to get him to talk.

"Because he's been in the hospital for a week. Broken hip. Bad luck. That said, maybe climbing a ladder to paint his ceiling at the age of seventy-five is asking for it . . ."

The man sucks three pieces of menthol gum into his mouth at once, seemingly satisfied with his remark.

"Oh," I mumble, unable to think of anything clever to say. Probably for the best.

"Why did you want to see my father?" he finally asks, delivering the final verbal punch that threatens to send me into the ropes of our imaginary ring. So this is Jean Spitzer's prodigal son.

"I think he has a package for me. Something my father gave him. I guess they knew each other somehow. I don't know any more than that."

I instinctively stick out my chest and act casual.

"So who's your daddy, then?"

He smirks at me as "daddy" echoes in my ears, the *a* sound short and nasal in the working-class accent he makes no attempt to mask.

"Édouard Bresson."

I expect those two words to have their usual effect and wait for the guy's eyes to light up—if it's even possible for this blockhead's eyes to light up. Strangely, he seems to retreat into himself slightly, as if I've just threatened him. I have a hard time believing he's never heard of my father, particularly in the town that's always proudly broadcast its claim to fame as the birthplace of the comedian of the century.

"Édouard Bresson . . . ," he repeats, lips pursed. Then he puffs up again and looks at me menacingly.

"I start work in twenty minutes. Come with me and we'll talk on the way. You can see where your grandfather slaved away his whole life. The biggest refinery in Normandy. I'm sure the magnificent Édouard never brought you to see it."

He heads toward his car, parked in front of the building, seeming sure I'll follow. And I do, even though I'm annoyed that his offer once again sounded more like an order.

His car is full of trash: Twix wrappers, used tissues, other candy wrappers. I push a pile off the passenger seat and onto the floor before sitting down, disgusted.

"So you're Édouard's son. My father never told me he received anything for you . . ."

"Do you know how my father knew yours? Your father was a friend of my grandfather's, right?" I ask, biting my lip.

"Yep. He and Lucien Bresson were thick as thieves at the plant, and after hours too. My old man spent more time in the bar near the refinery or at Lucien's place than he did at home, that's for sure. I never knew why, but my father was fond of Édouard. He talked about him all the time, as if he didn't have a son. I'm his son," he adds with a meaningful glance, to make sure I'm following.

I nod. He looks back at the road and continues.

"I think he felt bad for Édouard. It's the only thing that makes sense. That wimp could barely string three words together without stuttering . . . I always wondered how he went on to climb onstage and talk in front of an audience for hours. Back in the day he couldn't even say his name!"

"I'm sorry, but . . . So, you knew my father too? You're about the same age, right?"

The guy snorts, and I can almost hear the phlegm gathering at the back of his throat. I cross my fingers in hopes he won't spit out the window.

"Yeah. We were in the same class in elementary school. Let's say your father and I didn't get along so well, if you catch my drift. I made fun of him often enough."

I keep quiet. I'm not surprised for a second that he was a bully. His huge paws tighten their grip on the steering wheel. I feel like he could crush it without too much effort.

"My name's Ludo," he announces, as if expecting me to recognize it, but I've never heard of him before.

"I was with them the day . . . the day of the accident."

Seeing my confused expression, Ludovic continues, annoyed to have to explain.

"His little brother's accident. I was with them when we went to check out that old abandoned house. Actually, it was my idea."

I can tell I shouldn't pepper him with questions, even though I feel like my family's great secret is about to be revealed. I have a thousand questions, but I force myself to remain calm, as if what Ludovic is about to tell me is of no importance.

"The statute of limitations is up now, so doesn't matter if I talk about it . . . I dared Édouard to follow us into that house because I was sure he didn't have the balls to do it. But he did. We were all scared shitless inside, though. The tiniest draft nearly made us all piss our pants and run out the door, but our pride made us stay. His little brother, Jonathan, just kept complaining, whining that he wanted to go home, that he was cold, that he was scared, that he was going to tell his mom, blah, blah, blah . . . We would have been better off without him. When we went upstairs, I dared Édouard to go into a bathroom, where people said some psycho had locked up and raped kids, then left their bodies in the bathtub for weeks. He walked along the bedroom walls to get there, because the floor was clearly rotten. He made it to the little bathroom and opened the door as we all held our breath. At that exact moment, his whiny little brother started pulling on my hand, squealing that he needed to pee, that he couldn't hold it, that his mom would kill him if he wet his pants. He'd been so annoying the whole time that I had to hold myself back from smacking him. Instead,

I pushed him into the room and said, 'If you have to piss, there's a toilet in there. Go on!' I can still see him running across the middle of the room, both hands pressed against his crotch. I mean, really, nobody can blame me. The kid wasn't my responsibility, after all."

Ludovic parks his car in the refinery lot, seemingly waiting for me to agree with his last statement. I raise my shoulders, unsure what to say.

"He fell right through the floor. I still remember the creaking noise it made and can still see his arms raised above his head as he disappeared."

"What happened next?"

"No idea. My buddies and I got the hell out of there. We didn't want to be caught. We were sure the kid was dead, that he'd broken his neck on impact. I always said that house was cursed, and it turns out I was right."

We get out of the car in front of the imposing refinery. Its monumental chimneys suddenly make me feel tiny. Ludovic heads toward the entrance, but I don't move. He turns around and looks at me doubtfully.

"You don't want a tour?"

"No thanks, I'll pass. I hope your father recovers quickly. If you ever find a package for me, could you please send it to me, or call so I can come pick it up?"

I quickly jot down my name and phone number. This guy gives me the creeps; I want to get away from him as quickly as possible.

"Here you go. Please call, OK? It's important."

Ludovic shoves the paper in his pocket without so much as a glance. Before I leave, he grabs my arm. The few seconds it takes him to speak seem to go on for an eternity. I can see he's looking for the right words, weighing them carefully.

"You know, kids are cruel. My daughter is always bugging her friends at school—pulling their hair and telling them their clothes are ugly. There's nothing unusual about it."

He rubs his beard as he speaks, and he looks a little less cocky. He's clearly waiting for me to agree with him. A little voice tells me he's actually hoping I'll *forgive* him, despite knowing hardly anything about what he did to my father. The only thing I know for sure is that he's a coward.

I hold out my hand. His grip is firm, almost insistent.

"I hope you find the package," I repeat one last time. "It's all that matters to me now."

Bewilder

August 2017

I don't hear from Ludovic or his father for over a month, but time flies at the firm, where I have to pick up the slack for all the partners and associates who are away on vacation. Manel came to stay with me in Paris at the end of July, after finishing her internship at an advertising agency. She's been enjoying a month off before beginning the last year of her degree program in Rouen, while I work nonstop in an effort to prove myself and handle all the tasks piling up on the tiny desk I've been assigned.

I'm making my father's apartment my own, little by little. I'm finally starting to feel at home there—well, almost. When Jean Spitzer calls me one night, I hold my breath, relieved that the "game" my father planned won't be cut short after all. On the other end of the line, my grandfather's friend's voice is weak, so I have to focus to understand.

"Ludovic gave me your number. Édouard did leave a package for you with me. I'm so sorry we weren't able to meet when you came to Gonfreville."

"Oh please, don't worry about that. What's important is your recovery. Your son must have been worried . . ."

I doubt Ludovic has ever worried about anyone but himself, but it's the only suitable piece of small talk that comes to mind to comfort the elderly man.

"I always had a soft spot for your father, you know. Even though we rarely saw each other anymore . . . He was a good kid, despite all the obstacles life put in his way. I'll send you the package he left with me. It'll be easier that way. I don't want you to have to waste any more time."

I thank the elderly man, who seems out of breath from our short conversation. I give him the address of Édouard's apartment and hang up.

I receive a tiny package a few days later. Manel sits down next to me on the couch to watch me open it. Inside the box, I find eight carefully arranged packs of Tic Tacs. She moves to grab one, but I stop her.

"Wait, we can't mix them up right away."

"Why? They're just half-empty Tic Tac boxes!"

The transparent plastic boxes are far from full, it's true. One has just a single piece of candy inside. All the tiny treats are green, and I smile.

"What's so funny? I don't understand. He could have sent one full one instead of eight mostly empty ones," Manel says, her brow furrowed in confusion.

"Édouard left only the green Tic Tacs because when I was little I hated the orange ones. He would open two boxes, empty them into a bowl, and we would sort them. Then we'd put the green ones back in one box and the orange ones in the other. He always said they tasted the same, that I was being silly, like someone who prefers blue M&M's— but he always left me the green ones anyway and ate all the orange ones himself."

"The lemon ones, you mean. The orange ones are orange flavored. Everyone knows that!" exclaims Manel.

"He thought they were all the same."

"OK, great, but that still doesn't explain why these boxes are almost empty."

"There has to be a reason. We just have to find it."

It takes me nearly an hour to figure out Édouard's riddle. Eight boxes. I count the number of Tic Tacs in each one. Ten, fifteen, fourteen, one, twenty, eight, one, fourteen. I had the same code once in another treasure hunt he planned for me, with grains of rice in little glass jars. Each number corresponds to a letter of the alphabet, and together they form a word or sentence.

The tenth letter of the alphabet is *J*, the fifteenth *O*. I work the rest of it out and come up with *JONATHAN*. I've been expecting my uncle to be one of the people to contact.

I have to wait until the beginning of September to go visit my uncle in Strasbourg, though, because his family has gone on a two-week vacation to Portugal.

Manel turns on the TV, eager to see the next episode of an English series whose title I can never remember. I head to Édouard's desk to look over a few files I brought home from the office. I have a meeting with the partners on Monday, so I need to be up to speed by then to avoid looking incompetent. As the hours pass, the loose pieces of paper end up scattered all over the place, so before heading to bed—Manel's been asleep on the couch for a while now, though the British actors drone on—I decide to see if I can find a stapler in the desk drawers, to keep things more organized.

In the bottom drawer, I find a framed old *Ouest-France* article: "Baccalaureate Results: Emotions Run High," reads the exuberant headline. There I am in the black-and-white—or rather yellow-and-gray now—photo, scanning the list for my name, hoping to find next to it

Passed or even *High Honors*, which I'd been working hard for all year long. My hand grips my collarbone—that's probably why the photographer chose to take the picture. I look anxious, though I know I wasn't particularly emotional. I was absolutely sure I'd be among the 80 percent of kids my age who pass. In fact, I'd say that if I was feeling anything at all, it was disappointment. Just five minutes before the photo was taken, Édouard had texted me that he was sorry, but he wouldn't be able to come to Le Havre to celebrate after all. I remember that day as if it were yesterday.

I don't know how he got the article—I doubt my mother sent it to him. Yet he'd framed it. This from the man who never congratulated me on school achievements and was entirely uninterested in my academic career after high school. All he ever said was "Don't waste your talent, Arthur." And yet he kept this article.

I place the frame back in the bottom of the drawer, exactly where I found it. I stand up and cover Manel with a fleece blanket. She groans gently in her sleep, then curls into an even tighter ball, her knees against her chest. I turn off the television and pad silently into my father's bedroom.

Trying not to make a sound, I close the door behind me and take my phone out of my pocket. Without thinking, I scroll through my contacts to the letter *E* and the only person whose name starts with that letter. It doesn't ring—his voice mail picks up immediately. I instinctively close my eyes to concentrate on his brief message. "Hi, this is Édouard. Looks like I can't pick up right now, so call me back later if it's important!" His tone is cheerful, overly so, maybe. I hang up, then tap his name to hear his voice again. After the beep, I almost want to leave a message I know he'll never get, but when I open my mouth, I don't know what words to use or how to express the regret I feel for not answering when he called that night. I don't know how to tell him how mad I am at him for taking his own life without warning. I suddenly feel ridiculous and a little ashamed at the idea of leaving a message for a soulless voice mail. So I give up. There's a lump in my throat as I put my phone away.

The next morning, as soon as Manel opens her eyes, I grab the present I've been keeping under the bed. She looks at me, confused, and asks, "What's this for? It's not my birthday." I answer playfully that I don't need a special reason to give my girlfriend a present, then urge her to open it.

What she finds inside sends her jumping for joy. I'm relieved to get the reaction I was hoping for. She gleefully unfolds the athletic wear and tries on the shoes.

"The top and pants are water-resistant." I use the sales pitch I heard in the store. "I hear they're perfect for the obstacle course we're doing."

Manel nods, tries them on, and looks herself over in the mirror. I show her a pair of gloves tucked in the bottom of the box.

"These are to protect your hands when you have to climb a rope or go across monkey bars." She kisses me fiercely, and I can tell she can hardly wait for November. I put on my own outfit, and we head to the Bois de Vincennes for a run and to try out the fitness circuit. We have exactly three months to train for this obstacle course. Three months of intense running, sit-ups, pull-ups, planks, and push-ups.

Perfect for clearing my head—at least, I hope so.

recEive

September 2017

Louisa and Marion welcome Manel and me with squeals of joy as they hurl themselves at me for hugs. The little girls—who aren't so little anymore—gesture in excitement, and I once again remind myself that I should visit more often.

"How's first grade so far? Not too tough?"

Louisa, who's always quick to laugh, giggles and rolls her eyes. Her annoyed look is a preview of her preteen years, which are just around the corner. I recognize the obvious signs from having a half sister just a few years older than my cousin. Pretty soon she'll start saying everything is "so stupid" and spend most of her time locked in her room with the music on, sure that no one could ever possibly understand her.

My uncle rolls up behind her, and I lean over to greet him. He hugs me awkwardly, a little longer than necessary, and I realize I haven't seen him since my father's funeral. Manel leans down to embrace him. He smiles warmly at her.

My aunt is in the backyard, pruning her rosebushes, but as soon as she sees us she hurries inside to say hello.

"We're so pleased you could come visit this weekend! You've brought nice weather with you too. It rained all week here."

We spend Saturday leisurely strolling through downtown Strasbourg. My cousins are thrilled to do a little window-shopping and devour huge cones of gelato at the end of the afternoon—probably the last ice creams of the season.

My uncle and I don't really have time to talk until after dinner, when the women and girls sit down to a game of Monopoly on the covered patio. I start by mentioning the treasure hunt, and he nods pensively.

"Yes . . . the night of his show at the Stade de France, I went to see your father in his dressing room. In fact, that's the last time I saw him. It still makes me uncomfortable to know that Édouard knew we would never see each other again. He gave me this package for you. I put it into my backpack without giving it a second thought, then left, just like that. Without noticing anything amiss, without imagining for a second that my brother had just told me goodbye forever."

He rolls over to the sideboard in the living room, opens one of its doors, and takes out a rectangular box. The loud thud it makes when it hits the table in front of me tells me it's pretty heavy. I'm not ready to pick up the package yet, so Jonathan suggests I tell him about the treasure hunt so far.

"If you don't mind sharing, of course," he adds, picking at his fingernails.

As I watch my uncle fiddle nervously with his cuticles, I suddenly realize that Édouard's death has affected people other than me. Of course, I always knew my mother had lost the father of her child, that Jonathan had lost his big brother, that others had lost a friend or a colleague. I clearly understood that other people were grieving, were still processing my father's sudden death. But this is the first time I've really felt it in my heart, the first time I've felt sorry for their loss, the first time I've experienced empathy for all the other people my father left behind when he jumped from his balcony nearly six months ago.

I tell my uncle all the details of my various adventures, from Paris to Toulouse and Normandy. I describe the packages and objects Édouard left for me. I describe each meeting. He makes fun of me as he imagines the scene with Buzz Lightyear at Disneyland Paris, laughs heartily when I mention Madame Rita, and seems moved when I tell him about the friendship my father cultivated with one of his first fans. He's not at all surprised when I mention Yoann and Édouard's ten years playing clowns at the hospital.

"Your father was always very generous with his time, but he never liked talking about his volunteer work. He didn't want to be praised for his generosity—it would have made him uncomfortable. He did so many shows pro bono to benefit various charities, like the Red Cross and local soup kitchens. He even performed in prisons to give the inmates a good laugh. I remember he often ended his shows by saying, 'All of the laughter collected this evening will be donated to the person in the third row who frowned all night!' It was a joke, like all the rest, but there was some truth to it. He always donated a part of his profits to charity—and made the beneficiaries sign a confidentiality agreement. As if his generosity could come back to haunt him, as if he were afraid someone might use it to accuse him of opportunism. I never really understood . . ."

I finally realize why my father's supposed fortune is relatively modest—besides his Parisian loft and a few investments, my inheritance isn't likely to make many people green with envy, regardless of what the tabloids say. It turns out he gave away his money little by little, here and there, his whole life. Given everything I've learned about him over the past six months, it makes sense. He never felt like he deserved his success, so he shared it with others, people he may have seen as more worthy.

When I finally tell Jonathan about my most recent meeting with Ludovic Spitzer, his expression turns serious. I relay what the gruff man told me, particularly about the accident in the abandoned house.

With a pensive look on his face, my uncle nods in agreement as I tell the story—*his* story.

"To tell you the truth, Arthur, I hardly remember that day. I was barely five years old, and my memory didn't record the scene like Ludovic's and Édouard's did . . . I remember falling, the cloud of dust, and shouting. That's about it. What has really stuck with me, however, is what happened after. The year spent in a rehabilitation center far from home, far from my mother and brother, especially. I missed being with him so much, missed watching him climb up to the top bunk before I fell asleep and following him around when our father threw us out of the apartment. He sent me letters, and I had to beg a nurse to read them to me. Most of the time he just relayed the trouble he got into at home and at school. It sounds silly, but it felt like his letters were the only thing that tied me to our lives from before, the only thing that proved that someone was still thinking of me—*waiting* for me—outside that horrible place that stank of bleach and medicine."

I can hardly imagine how hard it must have been for such a young kid to spend a year away from home, fighting to survive and adapting to no longer having the use of his legs. And at the same time, I catch a glimpse of the guilt that must have overwhelmed my father, until it finally ate him alive.

"But the other kids, they never had to explain themselves? It was Ludovic's idea to go into that house. They're the ones that ran off and left you two there . . ."

My uncle smiles sadly.

"No one ever knew they were with us. Édouard told everyone he was the one who came up with the idea of exploring the house, that he had taken me inside not knowing it was dangerous. I was little, so I confirmed what he said once he explained it would be better that way, that it wouldn't do any good to tell on the others. Much later, I realized that it was mostly a way for him to accept all the responsibility for my accident, a way for him to punish himself. But it was too late, and it wouldn't have changed much anyway. The few times I tried to talk to him about it, he clammed up and told me there was no point in reliving the past . . ."

Ludovic Spitzer's face suddenly pops into my head, and I instinctively clench my fists in anger—and frustration at my inability to do anything about it.

When I finally start to unwrap the box in front of me, Jonathan backs up his wheelchair to leave, but I signal him to stay. I don't mind having someone with me when I open it.

Inside, I find a jelly jar full of small, colorful objects. I unscrew the blue-and-white-checkered lid and pour a few pieces of pastel sea glass into my palm. White, green, orange—all worn by the waves.

I look at my uncle in bewilderment. Jonathan picks a few out of my hand and rolls them between his fingers, a nostalgic smile on his face. He explains that my father collected them as a child, that they spent hours together on the beach in Le Havre digging through the sand to find the colorful pieces of glass, that Édouard would spend entire afternoons hunting for the treasures left behind by the receding tide.

One of the translucent pieces of sea glass has a small piece of paper carefully taped to it. I pull off the tape and unroll Édouard's message: *This one is for Jonathan.* I hesitantly hand the pale-green triangle to my uncle, who lifts it above his head to better study it in the light of the setting sun.

"Well, how about that. I haven't seen this thing in years! It was your father's favorite piece of sea glass, his good luck charm. He was so convinced it was magic that he never let it out of his sight. He would only put it away when he slept. Kids imagine all sorts of crazy things, don't they . . . Can I keep it?"

"Of course. Apparently, he wanted you to have it."

Jonathan runs his thumb over the piece of frosted glass, his thoughts distant. I don't want to disturb him, especially since I see a tiny envelope, the sides barely one and a half inches, at the bottom of the jar. I pick it up with the tips of my fingers and realize that it's a sheet of paper folded into an origami rectangle. On one of the sides, Édouard wrote: *LAST ONE. OPEN ON THE STAGE OF THE OLYMPIA.* So this is his last letter—when I've read it, the treasure hunt will be over.

A strange melancholy takes hold of me. My uncle puts the piece of sea glass Édouard left him in a drawer of the sideboard. His meager inheritance seems to be of great value to him. The muffled sound of the women laughing as they fleece each other at Monopoly reaches us from the patio. I try my best to put on a happy face before going to join them.

acknOwledge

October 2017

"So you're just quitting? You're going to keep the letter on your night-stand and stare at it every morning when you wake up and every night when you turn out the light, and that's it?"

Manel is furious, and I want to hurl a spiteful "How is it any of your business?" in return, but I hold myself back. I don't want to spend the evening fighting with her. She forges ahead.

"I mean, really, Arthur, it's been sitting there for over a month, and you still haven't opened it. Aren't you dying to solve the mystery? Haven't you ever wondered if maybe it's actually blank inside? Given what you've told me about your father, that'd be his style, wouldn't it? A final prank to pull on his son, an empty envelope!"

I continue ironing my shirt for tomorrow, concentrating on not creasing the sleeve or looking at Manel, who's clearly itching for a fight. That said, she's not far off base: it wouldn't be totally out of character for Édouard to leave me a blank sheet of paper. I'm annoyed I didn't think of that myself.

"He says you have to read it on the stage of the Olympia, so what are you waiting for, exactly? For someone to call and ask you to do a show Saturday night?"

I finally lose my temper as a cloud of steam suddenly puffs out of the iron, briefly blinding me.

"Easy for you to say! Do you think I can just turn up and tell them I need to borrow the stage for a few minutes? Want to know why that goddamn letter is still lying there, why I haven't done anything with it? It's because I know exactly what my father wants to tell me! The same thing he tried to tell me my whole life: that I was born to follow in his footsteps, to be Édouard Junior! All of these months spent meeting people and gathering packages to finally realize, yet again, that he never bothered to figure out what *I* wanted or who I *am*! Months spent trying to get to know him, trying to get closer to him, to realize in the end that he never really changed, that he still thought he knew best!"

Manel sits down on the bed, caught off guard by the storm she's unleashed.

"What did he think would happen? That I would suddenly drop out of school to begin a career in entertainment with my puppets? That I'd make the rounds of all the small stages until the A-list venues opened their doors to me and the Olympia added me to their lineup? He must have been completely insane to think I'd suddenly have an epiphany and change my whole life to be just like him! Even if I was talented and wanted a career in that crazy world, what would have been the point? Simply to follow in his footsteps? What would I have gotten out of it, except a constant comparison to him? As if living in his shadow was a desirable goal! I went blue in the face trying to tell him that I didn't have his talent or his passion. I told him over and over again—for nothing!"

Manel's expression turns to sadness, and I can tell she feels sorry for me. I don't need anyone's pity. When she speaks, her voice is gentle, as if she were trying to calm a child having a temper tantrum.

"I understand, Arthur. Why don't you just open the letter here, then? Your father can't make you do anything you don't want to anymore. You don't have to go to the Olympia to read it."

I cross my arms over my chest and frown.

"That would be cheating."

"He's not here to see, you know."

Manel bites her lip as soon as she's spoken, probably asking herself if she's gone too far, if she's been too harsh.

"But I'm here, and I would know I cheated."

"In that case, since your father was apparently a huge disappointment to you, why don't you throw the envelope in the trash?"

I don't answer.

"You can't. Because you need to know what's inside. Am I right?"

I nod, my jaw clenched. Manel stands up from the bed and moves toward me slowly, seeming afraid I might run off like a frightened cat.

"To summarize, then, you have a letter you don't want to open here, but that you also can't forget about. There aren't a thousand different possibilities. Find a way to get up on the stage at the Olympia. You have to read what he wrote and finally move on. Do it for yourself."

At the end of the weekend, Manel returns to Rouen, her heart heavier than she wants me to know. I'm glad we'll soon be done with this long-distance thing, since she's coming to live with me for her final internship. I tell myself everything will be better between us when she's back here for good, even though I know all too well that I won't be able to live my life to the fullest until I've finished this treasure hunt.

Throwing myself into reviewing for the bar exam isn't enough. I spend a good part of Monday going through Édouard's things in this loft that now belongs to me. In fact, it's always been mine, it turns out, since my father transferred the title to me just after buying it.

He's been gone for six months. It's time to figure out what I want to keep and what can go. Maybe I'll feel lighter when his things leave the apartment.

The doorbell rings. I can't believe it must already be six o'clock. I find Hervé, Édouard's manager, standing in the hallway. He seems to feel just as awkward as I do.

"Come in, please," I say as I shake his hand and move aside to let him in. He stays in the hallway, arms dangling at his sides, then runs his hands through his hair to smooth a rebellious strand. I head toward the living room and invite him to follow.

"It's all here, in this box."

Hervé looks around wistfully. He seems awash in memories, probably of times he spent here with my father. His eyes settle on the grocery bags full of Édouard's clothes, which I'm about to give to charity. I completely emptied out his closet today, taking every last shirt off its hanger, carefully folding each pair of jeans and each T-shirt. I kept only his first Breton-stripe sweater, the one my mom gave me a few months ago. Part of me is devastated and feels like by getting rid of his things, I'm throwing away a part of him. The other part knows it's important to let go. That the things Édouard wanted me to keep were the things he included in the treasure hunt. The rest is all just fabric and paper.

Hervé slowly walks over to the box I've pointed out and touches the wool of the striped sweater on top.

"How many are there?"

"Six."

He nods almost imperceptibly, and his fingers tighten around the limp fabric. I haven't seen him in several years, except for a glimpse at Édouard's funeral, and I notice he hasn't aged well. He appears even shorter than I remembered, shrunken and hunched over, and I wonder if it's due to the passage of time or the shock of my father's suicide.

"Do you really think people will want to buy them?" I ask.

"You can't imagine how much fans are willing to pay for a relic of their idol," Hervé replies sadly.

I smile as I imagine the homeless men who will soon be wearing Édouard's boxers and merino wool socks, without even knowing it. I'm the one who came up with the idea of auctioning off the sweaters my father wore onstage to benefit Hospital Clowns. Hervé agreed to take care of everything.

He picks up the box, clearly in a hurry to leave.

"It was nice to see you again, Arthur. You seem like you're doing well. I can't stay too long; I have a meeting on the other side of Paris in an hour, and . . ."

"No worries. Thank you for taking care of all of this, for coming by to pick up the sweaters. I'm sure Édouard would have been grateful."

We face each other, both of us as awkward and hesitant as a recent graduate at a job interview. I accompany Hervé to the front door and turn the landing light on.

"I'll let you know how the sale goes, OK? If you'd like, I can send you the check, so you can give it to the association yourself."

"No," I say, shaking my head. "You give it to them. Thanks, though."

Hervé puts the box down at his feet to shake my hand again, and when I feel his fingers against my palm I decide to ask my burning question, the one I've wanted to ask for so long—even though I'm afraid he'll look at me as if I've suddenly lost my mind.

"Before you go, I wanted to ask . . . You'll probably think it's stupid, but . . ."

He looks at me, confused, waiting. I take a deep breath.

"You really saw my father's body, right?"

"What do you mean?"

"You're the one who identified him that night . . . Are you sure it was really him?"

Hervé stops moving, and I feel like time has paused. His expression fills with commiseration so intense I want to look away to avoid seeing his compassion, his *pity*.

"Without a doubt, Arthur. It was definitely him. Have you really thought I might have made a mistake all this time?"

His tone is so sweet I can't help but clench my jaw.

"No, I didn't think you made a mistake. It's just . . . I thought . . ."

Despite all my efforts to remain stoic, my throat fills with sobs. Hervé sighs deeply, then hoarsely finishes my thought.

"You imagined your father might have put together a monumental practical joke to make everyone think he was dead."

I nod in agreement, but hearing Hervé say it out loud suddenly makes my theory seem so grotesque that I regret asking the question.

"It would have been right up his alley, I agree. But I saw him with my own eyes, Arthur. He's dead. Édouard is dead."

I look Hervé straight in the eyes and see he's trying his hardest not to start crying. The timer on the light runs out, and the landing suddenly goes dark. He bends over to pick up the box of sweaters again, and I manage to articulate, "OK. Thank you, Hervé. Have a good night," before hurrying inside and shutting the door.

With my back against the wall in the hallway, I hear him start down the stairs, clearly so eager to leave he'd rather take the nine flights than wait for the elevator.

I stand there—stock-still, empty, holding my breath.

And then the second hand of the big clock hanging on the wall across from me starts moving again.

I have one last room to go through. My own.

I gaze a final time at the room I stayed in for so many summers, then pick up the *Toy Story* toys and stuffed figurines and put them in a box that will probably make some child very happy. I strip the bed, fold the Disney duvet cover, and add it to the rest.

Finally, I climb onto the bed to carefully take down and roll up the large Woody poster, to avoid damaging it.

The thumbtacks have left a myriad of unattractive little holes in the pearl-gray wall—at least my father will never have to see them.

The evening wears on, and the apartment is growing increasingly dark, but I don't turn on the lights. For the first time, I do something I haven't yet dared to do. I head toward the balcony, open the French doors, and step barefoot onto the cold tile. The cool air does me good. I move closer to the edge and place my hands on the freezing metal railing. Maybe in exactly the same spot my father placed his, over six months ago.

I look out into the distance, then down at the nearly deserted street below and at the lighted windows across the way. I wonder if maybe a neighbor saw him jump, fall, hit the concrete.

What was he thinking when he stepped over the railing? Did he have any doubts? Did he hesitate? Or was he sure of himself? Did he take a deep breath, filling his lungs as if diving into water? Did he let himself fall like a deadweight, desperate to escape the inescapable loneliness that none of us knew tortured him? Did he jump, thinking himself a superhero for a split second, ready to fly into the night sky? Did he just let go? Did he close his eyes or keep them open right up until he hit the ground? Did he change his mind? Did he decide to step back over the railing to go inside and forget all about it, then slip or lose his balance at the last minute? How long was his fall? One second, five?

What was he thinking?

Was I there, in some corner of his mind, or was I the least of his worries? Was he mad at me for not picking up when he called? Was he upset that I wasn't there to save him?

Could I have saved him? Would I have been able to keep it all from happening, to keep him from reaching the end of his rope? If I hadn't done my utmost to hide our relationship from the world, if I had been nicer when I asked him to help me out for that charity evening, if I had tried to patch things up between us instead of letting resentment settle in, if I had reached out first, if I had listened to Manel, who told me to let it go and keep my criticisms to myself, if I had gone to the Stade de France on March 31 rather than burying the tickets he sent me in the bottom of a drawer, if I had taken a few minutes to call him after his show, just to see how it had gone.

If I had at least picked up the phone.

If, if, if.

maKe peace

The house lights have been on for a few minutes now. The last audience members are leaving the Olympia, taking their satisfied din with them. When I climb onto the stage, I instinctively hunch down, convinced that a deep voice will soon be shouting at me to get off. *Who do you think you are, kid?!*

But no one hassles me, because Manel got the venue director to let me use the stage for a few minutes after some new comedian's show. I was so busy wringing Édouard's envelope in my hands that I can't even remember the guy's name. He must have been good, though. People were laughing hysterically all around me. Even Manel was captivated by the energy radiating off the comic with a shaved head and bulging biceps.

She didn't have a hard time convincing the venue director. She told me the guy really seemed to miss my father, that he smiled sadly, shoulders slumped forward as he sighed and said, "What a tragedy . . ." I'm no dupe—I figured that my father had once again meticulously organized everything for this final stage of the treasure hunt. It's easy to imagine the scene between the two men. *I want to surprise my son. I can't tell you any more than that, but I need your help . . . If all goes to plan,*

he should contact you soon and ask to go up onstage for a few minutes . . .
I can hear his enthusiasm, his childish excitement. Then the director
nods. *Of course, no problem, Édouard! You can count on me!* Nobody in
the milieu could say no to Édouard—there was no need for bribes or
even for him to insist.

Was my father really crazy enough to think that when I found
myself on the stage I'd have a revelation and suddenly realize my place
was in the spotlight too?

I'm uneasy in the heavy silence. There's nobody here, but I feel like
I have to prove myself, like I'm about to discover something profound,
something *crucial*. I just hope the stage crew won't tell everyone about
this—there's no way I'm going to let some second-rate journalist turn
this into a tear-jerking melodrama. *Before committing suicide, Édouard
Bresson organized an amazing treasure hunt for his son.* I can already
imagine the nauseating headlines.

I brush off my pants, to have something to do with my hands, and
notice there's not a single piece of dust on the immaculate stage. I look
out at nearly two thousand red velvet seats, seemingly waiting for me
to tell some hilarious joke, and I suddenly feel very small. And totally
ridiculous.

My knees start to wobble, knocking into each other in the empty
space. A wave of vertigo suddenly rushes over me—the seats sneak up
on me and the balcony ripples mockingly. I don't know what my father
felt when he went onstage, but I hope it wasn't anything like this sense
of uncontrollable anxiety.

I pull the envelope out of my back pocket with trembling hands.
Whenever I used to get stuck during treasure hunts as a kid and feel
like I'd never crack his coded messages, Édouard would remind me
that the important part was the journey, not the prize at the end. Deep

down I know that no matter what he says in this letter, it won't resolve anything, that the people I've met and the stories they've told me over the past six months are what really counts.

But that doesn't help with my nerves. It doesn't change my conviction that this is it, that it's irreversible.

Anxious, almost feverish, and probably deathly pale, I slip my index finger under a corner of the carefully folded paper and open it to full letter size. I'm afraid of being disappointed yet again and tired of being angry. I can't bear to add to my solitary grief.

Suddenly, music fills the large room, breaking the silence, bouncing off the mute walls and seats. I immediately recognize the fiery beat, the repeated muffled note of the electric guitar, the energetic, rage-filled cymbal clashes. The melody filters through my pores to some deep place inside of me, and suddenly a mental video of my father and me breaks through to the surface. It's like watching an old home video on VHS, but in my head.

I'm jumping around my room in our apartment in Le Havre, where we lived the first few years of my life. I must be four or five years old. Across from me, my father's shuffling back and forth, his fists in a boxing stance at his chin, elbows tight against his chest. The lead singer of Survivor belts out the lyrics to "Eye of the Tiger," and Édouard pretends to box with me. We're both raring to go, determined though on the verge of laughter. To reach my father's height, I climb onto my bed, still jumping. My little feet don't make a sound on the comforter—the music drowns out the creaking box springs as the bed threatens to collapse with each impact. I pretend to take a jab at my father, who dodges the hit in slow motion, then lowers his head and dives into me. He wraps his arms around my thighs and lifts me into the air like a sack of potatoes. I fall over his shoulder upside down, unable to stop him as he runs around the apartment, pumping his fist in time to the halting rhythm of the heady guitar melody. In the kitchen, Mom is making breakfast. She sighs that we'll be late for school, but Édouard wraps his arms around her waist and lifts her up too, spurred on by my squeals of joy.

Onstage at the Olympia, the music gently fades, the decibels gradually decreasing until the silence returns as quickly as it fled. My heart is pounding with emotion. This is the first time I've ever managed to conjure up a memory of us as a family of three, the happy family I had come to believe was just a myth. I feel like I've brushed up against something intense, something *real*, where the music and sensations, the feeling of my father's arms around me, the joy that filled the apartment, were all palpable despite the dulling effects of time. One perfect, happy memory—like new, protected from wear and tear since I hadn't ever revisited it. I feel weak and sit down on the stage to avoid toppling over. If Édouard or my mother had told me the story, I probably wouldn't have believed it. I would have been sure they were making it up, or at least exaggerating, embellishing the past.

But everything I remembered was real. All of it.

So the three of us really did have happy times together. It was a long time ago, but it was real.

I think back on what Manel said after Édouard's death: "You must have at least a few good memories that you can hold on to, right? Everyone has at least one happy memory of their parents."

I guess this is the one I'll cherish for the rest of my life, the one that I'll keep safe in a corner of my mind for when the anger or bitterness well up again. This is the one I'll have to conjure from the depths of my memory, to make sure I don't forget it, neglect it, or belittle it again.

Did Édouard know what memory this song would call up for me? Once again, I have to admit that he was a master of performance—somewhere behind the curtains, a member of the stage crew was waiting to play the famous song from *Rocky III* as soon as Édouard Bresson's son got onstage. I have to say it: my father's last treasure hunt was a masterpiece.

I look down again at the piece of paper I've been fiddling with for so many minutes now.

I start to read my father's handwriting for the last time—I'm painfully aware of the finality.

> *Contrary to what you might think, I know you had absolutely no desire to climb up on this stage. It took me way too long to figure that out.*
>
> *I just wanted you to put yourself in my shoes for once, on a stage where I stood so many times over the years. I wanted you to contemplate the seats in front of you and imagine what it's like to have thousands of people hanging on your every word, to have thousands of people come just to see you—to have thousands of people you can't bear to disappoint.*
>
> *In the end, I really only ever had one goal: not to disappoint anyone. Unfortunately, we don't always realize our goals.*
>
> *One last thing before I go. I'm not sure how to avoid getting all weepy as I write this, but I'm proud of you. I should have told you that more often, I know. Always get it in writing, as the expression goes, so here it is:*
>
> *I'm proud of you.*

I carefully fold Édouard's letter back into the rectangular origami shape he crafted. The first letter he sent me, which I've read at least a dozen times, comes to mind. A single sentence from it echoes through my brain: *I did the best I could.*

I finally understand what he meant. I finally understand that it wasn't just a lame excuse to cover up his mistakes or shortcomings. *My risotto is terrible, but I did the best I could. I got a D– in math, but I did the best I could. I cheated on you with your best friend, but I did the best I could. I abandoned you as a child, but I did the best I could.*

That's not what he meant.

Dad did do the best he could. He *really* did the best he could. Like most parents, who are just children determined not to be afraid, determined to pretend they've got it all figured out. Like most adults, who suddenly find themselves grown up one day.

He did the best he could.

And, in the end, his best wasn't so bad. It was good enough.

A few days later, it's finally time for us to run the Hero Course—time to prove that our runs, push-ups, endurance exercises, and weight training were worth it. As we wait to get into the staging area, Manel draws black stripes onto my cheeks, so I look like a real "warrior," she says. The course should take about three hours, and I can't help but wonder if we haven't overestimated ourselves. The group of really built guys in front of us, who are hyping each other up and slapping each other on the back, isn't making me feel any more confident.

"I'll go put our things in a locker while you get our bibs, OK?"

Without waiting for an answer, Manel disappears into the crowd with our coats and bags. After ten minutes or so, it's finally my turn at registration, where a volunteer offers an enthusiastic, "Welcome to the Hero Course!" in the exact same tone Buzz Lightyear uses when he says, "To infinity and beyond!" I hold out our IDs, and he goes through a pile of bibs until he finds ours.

"Here you go. Good luck!"

Manel's bib reads *8456—SAADI.* Behind it, mine says *8457–PAZZOLI.*

I contemplate the rectangle of plasticized paper for a moment, as the guy with the shaved head behind me in line loudly demonstrates his impatience. He's apparently in a hurry to get his bib and go let off some steam.

I look back toward the bespectacled volunteer who helped me, but he's in the middle of a discussion. I lean toward the table and grab a black marker just as Manel joins me. She's put her hair up in a high ponytail, with a barrette on each side to make sure not a single rebellious strand slows her down during the race.

"Ready?" she asks, eager to take her place at the starting line.

I hold up my finger to ask for a minute.

Heart racing, I look back at my bib. I take the cap off the marker, cross out *PAZZOLI,* and write *BRESSON.*

My name.

Manel sneaks a glance and bites her lip in confusion.

"I guess you've forgiven your father, then?" she asks with a shy smile.

I study what I've just written. I want to explain to Manel that things are far—very far—from that simple. That a treasure hunt, even a great one, isn't enough to make it start raining bubblegum-pink confetti and make everything OK.

Everything is not OK. I've discovered my father wasn't the jerk I thought he was, that he was just a guy like everyone else, who did his best not to disappoint anyone, who valiantly fought his anxiety. But that doesn't make it all better. It doesn't erase the years of missing him, of loneliness, of resentment. And it certainly doesn't erase the overwhelming regret I feel at how things ended between us, the bitterness of all the things I never said to him.

But it is what it is. Édouard is dead, and I'm alone now. And the only choice I have is to roll with it—to push back the anger and grief so they won't keep me from moving forward anymore. There's no point rehashing it forever. Édouard is dead, and it's too late for things that could have been, for things that will never be.

Manel is standing next to me, waiting for an answer. Have I reconciled with my father? Not entirely. I guess I'll drag my grief around with me for a while longer, taking two steps forward, then one step back. I'll still be angry with him for not being a good father, then realize he did his best. I'll hate him for not letting me get to know him before he died, for not fighting hard enough to get to know me, and for leaving us all behind, then forgive him for not being able to go on. I'll remember his selfishness and all the times he wasn't there, then tell myself it's all my fault, that I was the selfish one, really, and that if I had acted differently he might still be alive. I'll tell myself that though he wasn't the best of fathers, I probably wasn't the best of sons.

Does forgiveness go hand in hand with guilt?

Do you have to miss someone for their absence to feel like an all-consuming abyss? Why is my father's death so painful, despite the fact that it changes nothing about my daily life? Despite the undeniable proof that he loved me? Despite the fact that I can now finally admit to myself that I loved him too?

Manel is staring at me, and I have absolutely no idea how to explain everything running through my mind, so I grab her by the waist, hug her tightly, and whisper in her ear, "Yes, I have." It's just easier that way.

She pulls away and gestures toward the hordes of people in athletic gear walking past us. "Come on, it's about to start. They're lining people up."

She heads off, half running. "First one to the starting line wins! Come on!"

I watch as the distance between us grows, my eyes focused on the shrinking *8456* on her bib.

And a little voice whispers, *If she turns back one more time, everything'll be OK.*

ABOUT THE AUTHOR

Amélie Antoine's bestselling debut novel, *Interference*, was an immediate success when it was released in France, winning the first Prix Amazon de l'auto-édition (Amazon France Self-Publishing Prize) for best self-published e-book. She is also the author of *One Night in November*, written as "a call to remember," and a memoir, *Combien de temps*. *The Last Laugh of Édouard Bresson* is her third novel. Antoine lives in northern France with her husband and two children. Visit her at www.amelie-antoine.com.

ABOUT THE TRANSLATOR

Maren Baudet-Lackner grew up in New Mexico. After earning a bachelor's degree from Tulane University in New Orleans, a master's in French literature from the Sorbonne, and a master of philosophy degree in the same subject from Yale, she moved to Paris, where she lives with her husband and children. She has translated several works from the French, including Amélie Antoine's novels *Interference* and *One Night in November*, the novel *It's Never Too Late* by Chris Costantini, and the nineteenth-century memoir *The Chronicles of the Forest of Sauvagnac* by the Count of Saint-Aulaire.